THE NATION'S HOPE

THE NATION'S HOPE
Copyright © 2016 Kenneth T. Zemsky

This is a work of fiction. Any references to historical events, real people, organizations or real places are used fictitiously. Other names, characters, places and events are products of the author's imagination or are used fictitiously and any resemblance to actual events, places, organizations or persons living or dead, is coincidental.

All rights reserved. No part of this book may be reproduced in any form or by any means without permission in writing from the author at GraceNotesPublishing@gmail.com. The views expressed herein are the responsibility of the author and do not necessarily represent the position of the publisher, Grace Notes Publishing.

Cataloguing-in-Publication Data

Zemsky, Kenneth T., author.

The Nation's Hope/Kenneth T. Zemsky

Pages cm

ISBN 1530268265

1. American politics. 2. New York City Mayoralty 3. Buckley-Lindsay-Beame-Dickerson-Fiction. Title: The Nation's Hope.

Designed by Grace Anthony

Summary: Fifty years ago, beneath the gleaming structures of the World's Fair, New York is a city in decay. A beautiful pioneering journalist is assigned to cover the city's response to the crisis in one of the most pivotal elections in its history. As 1965 beckons, two candidates are poised to do battle: the long-serving Democratic incumbent mayor, and the handsome young congressman running as a fusion candidate. The latter is an erstwhile Republican, whose party has calculated that the only way to survive the previous year's Goldwater debacle is to pivot far to the left of the political spectrum. The campaign is upended by a crippling newspaper strike…and the emergence of a brilliant contrarian, who believes the way forward is not to the left, but sharply to the right, as he strives to give birth to modern conservatism.

*To Grace, Richard,
Marisa, Christine and Caroline*

THE NATION'S HOPE

A NOVEL BY
KENNETH T. ZEMSKY

CHAPTER 1

GET ME NICKERSON!

"GET ME NICKERSON!"

No sooner had the new temp, Betty, seen the bureau chief shoot out of his office and hear his roar than her heart muscles tightened and her sphincter muscles relaxed—dangerously so. It was not yet eleven o'clock on her first day on the job, and already Betty felt near a nervous breakdown. She was only a temp—the chief's regular secretary had taken ill—and Betty desperately needed to impress the temp agency. Jobs in Washington, D.C. were hard to come by.

If only President Johnson paid more attention to job creation. Instead, that damn fool LBJ was running around the White House turning out the lights, his attempt at economizing. Another part of Johnson's economy moves involved budget cuts at several federal agencies. This included the Department of Commerce, from which Betty had been laid off.

Betty could not afford the luxury of looking long-term for a permanent position. She had a child at home to raise, alone. While in desperate need of steady cash flow, Betty rarely bemoaned her economic situation. Death had a way of putting things in perspective, especially when the person who had died was your husband, the one great love of your life. Everything paled in comparison to the day the uniformed Army officer notified Betty that her Bill, a military advisor detached to a unit in Da Nang, South Vietnam, had been the unfortunate victim of an errant rocket grenade.

After the funeral and then the burial at Arlington National Cemetery, the Pentagon notified Betty that she did not qualify for full widow's benefits. Bill had not been stationed in a war zone. Timing is everything in death, as in life. Bill's demise occurred months before Congress passed the Gulf of Tonkin resolution, naming Vietnam an official combat zone.

Despite Betty's appeals and his impressive seniority, Congressman Joel T. Broyhill could not do anything for her, chiefly due to a lack of desire. "Where the hell is this Vietnam place, anyway?" he had asked his receptionist while Betty was sitting right there, waiting to see him.

Many Americans at that time thought the oddly named country was somewhere in the Caribbean. Others opined it was an island in the Pacific. Still others claimed it was somewhere in Asia, "sort of between Russia and China." Such levels of geographic acumen were not atypical in the innocent days of mid-1960s America.

In any event, Betty needed this job to work out. She quickly calmed herself and reached for the office directory to contact this Nickerson person before the bureau chief erupted once again. Betty reasoned that rapid response was the only way to keep the chief at bay—and defer her nervous breakdown. For the bureau chief was the proximate cause of her anxiety attack.

In the two hours since she had reported for work, Betty had become painfully aware that the chief was a touchy-feely fellow. Touchy as in the slightest disturbance set him off, and feely as in every time the chief contrived to get Betty alone in his office, he tried to feel her up. Betty was proud of her figure, but she resolved after today to wear the baggiest, most matronly outfits possible. For today, however, she would have to rely on her adept skill at fending him off.

As soon as the bureau chief retreated back into his office, Betty quickly thumbed through the newsroom directory to locate "Bob Nickerson." She called him, informing the reporter that "Mr. Hayes wants to see you immediately." Betty was rewarded with an expletive. The reporter's sphincter muscles undoubtedly also suffered from bureau chief mania, for in a flash he was at Betty's desk. "Go on in," she informed him. The reporter took a deep breath before he knocked on and then opened the chief's office door.

"What the hell are you doing here?" the chief barked.

"You wanted to see me," reporter Bob Nickerson said.

"No. I didn't. What the hell would I want with *you?*" Storming past Nickerson to glare at Betty, the chief yelled, "I told you to get me Nickerson!"

Betty's mouth opened as she pointed a finger at the retreating reporter. "But...but that's...."

"Never mind!" The chief grabbed Betty's phone. "I'll call myself!" He punched in the numbers, barked out his order and stormed back to his lair, but not before muttering, "Stupid girl!"

"Have I fallen into a rabbit hole?" Betty wondered. Confused, she busied herself with some filing. Her task was interrupted moments later by a voice asking, "Mr. Hayes wanted to see me?" From her position, head stuck in drawers below desk level, Betty thought it was one of the sweetest, clear-as-a-bell voices she had ever heard. Betty immediately straightened and again her mouth popped open. The tall, shapely woman before her was either a model or the reincarnation of the Blessed Mother awaiting Raphael, DaVinci or another master to paint her portrait.

"You...you're Nickerson?" Betty stammered.

The woman's eyes sparkled as she laughed. "That's what he calls me. Brad has his own rather unusual nicknames for us." The woman held out her hand. "I'm Nancy.

Nancy Dickerson. Get it? N—Dickerson. In his mind," Nancy motioned with her head toward the chief's office, "it gets shortened to Nickerson."

Betty gladly shook Nancy's hand.

"Don't let him get to you," Nancy said. "And if he acts inappropriately, *suggestively*, do what I do."

Betty cast a questioning look, prompting Nancy to explain.

"I told him if he ever touched me again, I would kick him in his balls until his nose bled."

Now it was Betty's turn to laugh.

"The other thing," Nancy added. "When he talks, pretend the voice you hear is Donald Duck in one of his rabid rants. Then he won't seem so threatening."

Nancy grinned at Betty, then walked into Hayes's office, closing the door behind her.

Bradley Hayes, Washington bureau chief of NBC News, looked up. "Oh, Nickerson. You're here at last."

"You only called thirty seconds ago."

"Siddown."

Nancy sat in a chair facing the chief, adjusting the pearls she wore over her blazer as she did so.

"You're always pestering to cover more politics," Hayes began. "That's why I gave you the opportunity to cover the Inauguration."

"Reporting on what the First Lady wore to the Ball hardly qualifies as a chance to cover the political beat," Nancy retorted smoothly.

"See? Always bustin' my chops," the chief muttered. He stared at Nancy. She stared back.

"No matter," Hayes finally said. "Let's talk politics. You follow the last election?"

Nancy fought the urge to curse. "Oh, honestly. You would have to be comatose not to have followed it." Lyndon Johnson, of course, had won in a landslide in one of the largest pluralities ever recorded. Johnson's coattails were such that a record number of Democratic senators, congressmen, governors and state legislators had been swept into office as well. The results were so overpowering that several pundits predicted the demise of the Republican Party.

"Why did LBJ win so convincingly?" Hayes asked.

Nancy unconsciously smoothed her skirt. "Several factors," she answered. "He was the beneficiary of the long national wake after Jack Kennedy's assassination. The country is enjoying peace and prosperity. There is a strong liberal consensus across the land. And…his opponent was inept."

"Very good," Hayes nodded enthusiastically as if awarding a point to a stellar student. "Yes. Mr. Goldwater was fairly incompetent as a campaigner. Kept putting his foot in his mouth. Did not have the fire in his belly to campaign all out. Worse, he was part of a fringe within a fringe within what was already a distinctly minority party.

"Goldwater thought he could remake the GOP into a conservative consensus," the bureau chief continued, "but the country is too far to the left of the political spectrum. You see how the Goldwaterites were characterized?"

Nancy knew this was a rhetorical question. She also knew the conservatives who'd wrested control of the nominating process in 1964 had been castigated as backward-looking racists, John Birchers, and fascists.

Hayes interrupted her reverie. "Johnson may not be the sharpest blade in the drawer, but he took the temperature of the country. Why, Ol' LBJ tried to block the Civil Rights Act of '57. No, no progressive instincts in them Texas bones. Yet it all changed when he got to the White House. Then he tacked to the left. His whole Great Society is just an effort to capitalize politically on the liberal majority view."

The chief paused and took a sip of his coffee, looking directly at Nancy the whole time. For her part, Nancy remained silent. Waited him out. And wondered where this was heading.

At last, Hayes put the cup back in its saucer. "You think the Republicans are dead?"

Nancy shrugged. "Rumors of their demise are somewhat exaggerated. I am not even sure conservatism is dead. Maybe the problem was with the messenger, not the message. With someone other than Goldwater...."

Hayes cut her off. "Like who?"

Nancy shrugged. "Well, what about that actor who delivered a televised speech on Goldwater's behalf? Raised a record amount of contributions."

The chief snorted. "Ronald Reagan?" he demanded, pronouncing the name as "Ree-gun."

"What?" Nancy retorted. "They say he may run for governor of California. If he wins that...."

"Interesting but naïve," Hayes said with a dismissive wave. "There's no way the people will elect a novice actor. Mark my words. After the California election, no one'll ever hear of this Ree-gun guy again."

"I think it is pronounced Ray-gun."

"No, it's Ree-gun. But no matter. He and the conservative movement are dead. I do agree with you, however, that the Republican Party is not. Know why?"

Nancy inclined her head, indicating that he go on. Which he proceeded to do.

"The smart money controlling the GOP realizes there is a liberal consensus in the land. They know the way to get back in the game is to out-liberal the liberals, in this case, the Democratic Party."

"You're thinking of people like Rockefeller in New York, Romney in Michigan and Scranton in Pennsylvania," Nancy inserted.

"And then some.... You ever hear of John Lindsay?"

"Congressman from New York. Represents the Silk Stocking district," Nancy said. "Won reelection with over seventy percent of the vote."

"And he's farther to the left than anyone you can think of in the Democratic Party," Hayes added. "I believe he's considering running for mayor of New York City."

"Republicans almost never win in New York City, absent extenuating circumstances," Nancy noted.

"True. But the polls show Lindsay has a chance. He pulls it off, it will have ramifications for the political cycle for at least a generation."

"I had not thought of that," Nancy conceded.

"That's why *I* am the bureau chief. Also 'cause you all," he made a sweeping gesture that was meant to refer to everyone in the newsroom outside his office, "are infected with Potomac fever. So tied to the Washington scene, you can't see what's happening anywhere else."

"Fortunately, we have you," Nancy said.

Hayes nodded, taking her tongue-in-cheek comment as a compliment.

From past history, Nancy could tell from the insipid look on Hayes's face that the chief was about to launch into a narrative about his intellectual prowess. Not wanting to waste the next thirty minutes of her life, she interceded.

"I still believe it may be premature to write off the conservative movement."

Hayes scoffed. "Write 'em off. As they say in Boston, they're deader than Kelsey's nuts. Lindsay, Rockefeller and the rest are going to refashion the GOP. Soon there will be a two-party liberal majority the likes of which we have never seen. You won't even be able to utter the 'c' word, conservatism will be so discredited.

"Regardless," the chief continued, "I want us to be on the cutting edge of this story, the election that will change a generation. I also want to break NBC News of this Potomac fever."

Finally, he got to his point. "Nickerson," he said, "I want you to go to New York and cover the mayoralty election."

Nancy perked up. "Yes! I can easily get to the City, interview the major players, have a piece ready to air in two days."

Hayes was waving his arms wildly. "NO! NO! NO! You don't understand. I'm not looking for a short piece to fill air time. I want you to move to New York for the duration of the campaign, the next eight months."

"Why me?" Nancy asked. "Why not Herb?" Herb Pennock was the bureau's chief political correspondent.

Hayes stood and crooked his finger. "Follow me," he said, leading Nancy to his office door, which he opened. "Herb!"

Four rows over, a balding head attached to an overweight body picked itself up from a desk with considerable effort. "Yesh?" Herb's eyes were beyond bloodshot. Even from some thirty feet away, Nancy could swear she smelled the alcohol.

Hayes closed his door. "That's why I can't send Herb. His brain is in a pickle jar."

"But surely…." Nancy began to protest but was abruptly cut off.

"Nickerson." Hayes lowered his voice and looked directly into her eyes. His look and tone gave off all the earmarks of sincerity, a trait so rare in the bureau chief that Nancy was momentarily taken aback. "Nance. You have terrific reporting instincts. I have to admit, no one has been more surprised by that than me. I mean, you being a girl and all."

Nancy inwardly bristled but once again held herself in check. She was used to this sort of treatment. Moreover, she was intrigued by what the chief had to say.

"It is so rare for a woman to move up in the organization, but I really think you have a legitimate shot. How does bureau chief sound?"

In spite of herself, Nancy grinned. "Wonderful. But where are you going?"

Hayes chuckled. "Nowhere. I'm not talking about my job. The spot in New York will open up next year when Arthur Haller retires. You move to New York, excel at covering the Lindsay campaign, bond with the boys in the newsroom and…who knows?" He paused to let Nancy savor the idea. "The New York bureau is prestigious. Lotta' news comes outta' New York. Plus there's the *Today* show. You put in a coupla' years as New York bureau chief, then if I get promoted and this spot opens up…. From there, who knows? You could end up taking over for Huntley or Brinkley. Imagine. The first female news anchor."

Nancy looked away, her mind racing. "I…don't know what to say."

"Just say you'll do it."

"But my family is settled in northern Virginia. I can't uproot my kids after all they have been through. It is hard enough with a working mother. Besides, Dick's business is here."

"The road to the top requires sacrifice, Nance."

She shook her head. "I can't, much as it breaks my heart."

Hayes shrugged. "Then don't relocate. Commute."

Nancy straightened.

Hayes noticed as he grabbed a cigar and lit it. "Get a place in Manhattan, stay there a few nights a week, come home for long weekends."

Nancy pondered the possibilities.

"Just one thing," Hayes growled through a cloud of smoke. "This bureau is on a tight budget. So no fancy hotel. Find cheap temporary lodging in New York. And no planes, either."

Nancy smiled. "You're worried for my safety, planes being so prone to mishap. That is so sweet, Brad."

"Nah. It's just that they cost too much."

"You're a regular Albert Schweitzer. I guess the trains are a good option."

Hayes shook his head. "Also too costly. Take a bus! Above all, be sure you scoop the rest of the New York press on this campaign."

Nancy took a deep breath. "That's not going to be easy. I do not have any contacts in New York political circles."

"So? Leverage your D.C. ties. And develop your own sources in the Lindsay campaign. He's a real good-lookin' fella. Maybe you and he...."

"Brad! I'm not sleeping with John Lindsay!"

"That's up to you. I say you do whatever you have to, to get the story. Heck, I remember one time I had to bed someone for a scoop."

Nancy feigned surprise. "A *woman?*"

"Of course a woman! What'd you think? A fish?" He paused, then got a horrified look. "Hey! You don't think I'm one of them fairy faggots, do you?"

"No, you're all man," Nancy deadpanned.

"So," Hayes growled, "what do you say?"

"I...still don't know."

Hayes pointed his cigar at her. "You turn this down and you know what they'll say? They'll say it just goes to show girls have too many issues to belong in the workplace."

Gritting her teeth, Nancy said, "You just made up my mind for me. Tell New York to get my office space ready."

"Good girl!"

As Nancy turned to leave Hayes added, "Let me know if you got any questions."

With a huge smile, Nancy opened the office door and said, "Just one. That woman you slept with for the story...was she alive at the time?" Then she quickly slipped out and closed the door behind her, locking in the string of curses her boss promptly let loose.

· · ·

A moment later, Hayes again shot out of his office. "You!" he yelled at his temp secretary, taking a moment to stare down at her cleavage. "Get me Bright!"

Betty giggled, hearing a duck's voice in her mind.

THE NATION'S HOPE

"What's so funny?" Hayes demanded.

"Uh, nothing, sir."

Now that she had the hang of it, Betty perused the office directory. When she saw "Barry White," she said, "B. White... Bright. Perfect!" and called the newsman to the chief's office.

In a flash, White appeared.

"What the hell you doin' here?" Hayes yelled as soon as the reporter opened his office door.

"You called for me."

The chief raised his voice further. "Not him! Tom Swift!"

"You said Bright, sir," Betty replied, refusing to raise her voice.

"Yes," Hayes yelled back, "Bright as in Tom Swift, who actually is not so Swift. That's why I call him Bright!" Hayes turned back to his office after he had told White, "You know how these girls are."

. . .

Nancy caught part of this exchange from her desk, where she was throwing a few things together for her suddenly pending trip to New York City. She was also screwing up enough courage to break the news about her new assignment to her husband and children. Before leaving the newsroom, she passed Herb Pennock's desk. Maybe he had some contacts in the Empire State.

She sat on the corner of his desk. "Herb," she said softly, "do you have any sources in New York that may be of use to me?"

Herb did not reply, so Nancy touched his shoulder.

Herb raised his head. "You the nursh?" he asked.

"Herb. It's me. Nancy."

"Oh," he laughed. "New York? Tom Dewey still the governor?"

"Not for eleven years."

"Oh. Say. When did you become a nurse, Nancy?"

"Forget it," she carefully guided his head back onto the desk. "Sleep tight, Herb."

"You a good nursh," he mumbled.

As she walked off, Nancy remembered one last stop she needed to make. The sports desk. While not a huge sports fan, Nancy did make it a point to curry favor with the sports beat reporters. Any tidbit they provided came in useful when she was trying to extract some nugget from a congressman. The male of the species seemed to have two major Pavlovian responses. Rats might run through a maze after food pellets, but most human males salivated over two things: sex and sports. Many were the days that Nancy bemoaned the fact there were hardly any women on Capitol Hill with whom she could bond over shared interests. Steering clear of any talk of the male fascination with sex, she relied on sports, especially any useful nuggets she could glean from the NBC sports desk, to buddy up with the male power structure.

"Hey, Dick," she called out, aiming two index fingers at the sportswriter. "Pitchers and catchers have reported."

Dick Schaap was on temporary assignment to Washington. "Very good," he said with a grin. "They have indeed reported and not a moment too soon. I was getting pretty sick of covering the off-season sports no one cares about. So how are you?"

"All the better for seeing you," Nancy replied, then asked, "How do the Senators look this year?"

Schaap shook his head. "You know what they say about Washington. 'First in war; first in peace; last in the American League.'"

"That bad?"

"Worse. They have one good pitcher, Camilo Pascual, and...and that would be it. Unfortunately, though they changed the rules and one player is not enough. You need nine players to make a team."

"How about in New York?"

He rolled his eyes skyward in thought. "Funny you should ask. The only team in all baseball worse than the Senators is in New York. The Mets. If the Senators played in the National League, they would at least be guaranteed not to come in last. The Mets are that bad."

"Eew!"

"You got that right."

"The beat writers must hate covering them."

"Au contraire. They love it. As awful as the team is, the City has taken a shine to the lovable losers. Plus they keep finding entertaining ways to lose. Finally, the manager. Casey Stengel is great copy. Says the most amusing things. He also leads the league in drinks with the writers."

Nancy explained she was heading to New York, and Schaap pulled out a business card and scribbled something on a piece of paper. Handed it to Nancy. "This will get you in to see Case."

"Thanks, Dick. But I'm not covering sports up there."

"Do it. I promise if nothing else, it will be worth the entertainment factor. And you'll get some valuable items that you can use with your political friends."

Nancy nodded with a "that makes sense" look on her face and thanked Schaap. Then she asked him for any other breaking trends on the New York sports scene.

"Two things," he said. "The Yanks are dead."

"Come on. I may not know a lot about sports, but even I know the Yankees always win."

"Uh-uh. Not anymore. They have aged overnight and have not grown a crop to replace the current stars. Mantle's legs are shot, and there is no new Mickey on the horizon."

Nancy's brow wrinkled. "Why does it matter if his legs are gone? You swing with your arms."

"Nancy. All the power comes from here." Schaap motioned to his hips and legs. "Trust me."

She decided that was an intriguing insight.

Schaap then told her the second thing he believed was about to shape New York sports for the next decade. "The football Jets have a new quarterback who will rewrite the rules. Guy's name is Joe Namath. He's so good and so colorful that he'll be at the center of forcing the two leagues, the NFL and the AFL, to merge."

Nancy decided to jot down some notes on this revelation.

Before she left Schaap, Nancy told her colleague she could not understand one thing. "If the Senators are so bad, why don't we petition to move the team into the National League?"

The sportswriter chuckled. "Baseball is so tradition-oriented that the teams and leagues are set up just the way they always will be. Mark my words. There will never be a realignment in Major League Baseball."

The only other advice Schaap imparted was to instruct Nancy to interview the new Mets player-coach, Yogi Berra, if she got a chance. "One of the smartest baseball minds around, though he hides it well."

With that, Nancy checked her watch and left the newsroom, making a beeline for home. Just a few hours later when Wyatt "Dick" Dickerson walked in the front door, he was greeted by three surprising sights. Nancy was home early. Usually, she did not get in until well after the evening news had aired. Second, she was wearing his favorite dress, one that he always found incredibly alluring. Third, the house smelled great!

"What did Estelle cook?"

"I had her make your favorite. Veal piccata. Then gave her the afternoon off."

Dick's mouth watered. His stomach rumbled. He'd been so busy he had skipped lunch.

Then he cocked his head. It was incredibly quiet. "Where are the children?"

Nancy told him which friends' homes they were each staying at. "Tonight is just us," she purred.

Dick washed, thanked his good fortune and tucked into dinner. It tasted every bit as good as it smelled. Not only the veal but the broccoli casserole and home-made biscuits as well. And the Prosecco Nancy had selected for the occasion went well with the food.

"Boy!" Dick patted his stomach after a while. "That was fantastic! I don't know if I could handle dessert."

Nancy grinned. "Dessert is something that is so special, it'll have to wait until a little later," she said. "First, how was your day?"

Dick offered a few items, none of which was out of the ordinary. Then he asked about her day.

"Mine *was* out of the ordinary," Nancy began. "Brad called me into his office."

"That creep! Did he try to grope you again?"

"Not this time. This time, he had something interesting to discuss. There is the possibility, just the chance, mind you, of a bureau chief position opening up."

"Why, Honey that's wonderful! You've worked so hard…!"

Nancy explained the position was in New York, and she would have to cover the Lindsay campaign there first as a possible precursor to the new job. She also noted that, down the line, she might then return to working in Washington when Hayes moved on from his position.

Dick wrinkled his forehead. "What did you tell him?"

"That our family was involved. That I had to talk to you first."

Dick looked at his wife. "What you have to do is tell him 'Yes!'"

"You realize this will take me away from you and the children for long periods of time?"

He kissed her forehead. "We'll make it work."

Nancy stared at her husband. "Are you sure?"

Dick nodded. "I know you want this and have worked hard to get recognized. I also realize how hard it is for a professional woman to be treated as a professional."

"The other mothers will think I am simply horrid to leave you all in the lurch."

Dick smiled. "Just tell those other mothers to fuck off."

Nancy laughed. Dick almost never used profanity.

They spent the next hour discussing ways to make the New York arrangement work. Dick suggested he could shave a few hours off his office time and work from his home office. Nancy said she could work the bus schedule between Greyhound and Trailways and extend her weekend stays. Both agreed to approach Estelle as to increasing her hours as housekeeper/governess. Dick also had an excellent suggestion: When Nancy was inundated and hard-pressed to make it home, he could bundle the children up and visit her in New York.

"They've never been," Nancy noted.

"Then it's time they experienced it. New York is an exciting place."

. . .

That was the part Dick and Nancy stressed to two of their children the next day as they broke the news to their children, Jane and John.

"Are you all right with this?" Nancy asked, "with Mother working for a while in a different city?"

Little John said, "It's what you do. A reporter's job is to go where the news is."

Young Jane said, "Only if I get to go up to the top of the Empire State Building. And shop at Macy's."

"Will the ape still be there?" John wondered aloud, the story of King Kong suddenly on top of his mind.

Dick said, "I think he's safely put away for good."

When Jane inquired about apes and John explained King Kong, she said, "Sounds like Sister Stephen." Sister Stephen had a habit of chiding the children with the refrain, "Monkey see; monkey do." That plus her abundance of facial hair led to the children christening her "The Big Ape."

As Dick laughed, Nancy quickly covered her grin and sternly cautioned Jane never to utter that in earshot of the good sister.

"I'm not stupid, Mother."

Dick pointed out to his daughter that she was about to have an opportunity to become even more educated. "Mother will leave for New York this week to find living quarters, and soon after we'll visit her and go to the World's Fair."

"Goody!" Jane clapped. "Julie Anderson at school is always bragging that she went there last year. She is sooo annoying!"

• • •

The next morning, Nancy perused the New York classifieds for available short-term leases. The pickings were exceedingly slim. She called the one person she knew in New York, a cub reporter by the name of Jim Lehrer, and explained her problem.

"Do what New Yorkers do," Lehrer advised. "Check the obituaries."

"Isn't that rather gruesome?"

"No, it's rather the only way you will find a place to live."

Sure enough, Nancy quickly found some leads through the obituaries and had no trouble getting the families' phone numbers through directory assistance, though she did feel awkward extending condolences to the next of kin and then immediately explaining why she was calling. Three phone calls led to agreements to see a few apartments. Nancy's next stop was to visit the city.

• • •

The first place was the priciest, a two-bedroom on the East Side near the United Nations on offer from a bereaved family member who insisted on what he called a "vig" of $25,000. Nancy gulped—and moved on.

Door number two was way up on the East Side in Harlem. Nancy's was the only white face for blocks, which would have been fine as far as she was concerned. The deal breaker, though, was the atmosphere of the neighborhood. Trash was all over the streets and sidewalks. Gangs of young men were openly ingesting harmful substances on street corners, several making suggestive comments loud enough for Nancy to hear as she passed. "I like a little white meat." "White ho' lookin' good." "C'mere, baby, an' let me ride you white ass."

Nancy never made it to the interview for that apartment and practically held her breath until safely off the subway stop at Times Square, an area that was more racially balanced, but no less dangerous. Signs all around her advertised XXX shows while whores and pimps openly solicited. "Why the heck do you want this job, Mr. Lindsay?" Nancy whispered to herself.

The third target was in the Hell's Kitchen area at Fifty-Second and Tenth.

The "realtor" was a greasy fellow named Mario. He wore a white tee with a pack of cigarettes rolled into one of his sleeves.

"Why do they call it Hell's Kitchen?" Nancy asked. "Is this the culinary center?"

Mario guffawed mightily. "Cutlery is more like it!"

"As in knives and forks?"

"As in switchblades."

"Is it safe here?"

"If you travel in pairs and carry a gun or at least some pepper spray." He explained that the Hell's Kitchen name came to be when a policeman patrolling the beat commented that the area was so hot (as in dangerous), it was like hell.

"More like Hell's Kitchen," his partner corrected, and the saying and the name stuck.

The apartment Mario showed Nancy was on the first floor. As he unlocked the door, another door across the hall opened and a mountain of a man appeared. He towered over Nancy and seemed to glare at her. "This is Tiny," Mario introduced. "He an' his, uh, associate, will be your neighbors."

Nancy extended her hand, which was dwarfed in Tiny's. "What do you do?" she asked.

Tiny replied that he and his apartment mate were actors.

Nancy brightened. "Oh! Where are you appearing?"

"Right now," the giant said, "we're waiting for a break. To make ends meet, we work at the diner over on Sixty-First."

Inside the apartment, Nancy asked Mario, "Will I be safe with those two across the way? I'm married, you know. I don't want to have to fight off unwanted advances on a regular basis."

Mario laughed. "Then you have nuthin' to worry 'bout. Like he tol' you, they're *actors*."

Nancy looked at him, befuddled.

"You know. They're queer."

"You mean unusual?"

"Hoo boy! No, I mean queer as in fags. Homos. Like to travel the Hershey highway."

Nancy held up her hand for him to stop. "Got it!"

Inside, the apartment wasn't bad. It was a little water stained here and there, and the rugs were threadbare, but this was just a pit stop after a long day's work for only a few days a week. The price was right, especially with the cheap budget NBC provided. Nancy and Mario shook.

"Are there some papers I need to sign or something?"

"Like what? We jes' shook. That not good enough for ya'?"

Nancy acknowledged that this was fine, and Mario gave her the key. She gave him twenty dollars back by way of deposit. As soon as he left, she slumped on the sofa, wincing at the squeak the springs made. Next stop: report to the NBC bureau at Rockefeller Center.

CHAPTER II

HE IS FRESH AND EVERYONE ELSE IS TIRED

"That was then. This is now."

Congressman John Lindsay rubbed his eyes as he looked out the window of the Cannon House Office Building at the Washington Monument, the White House on his mind. He turned toward his chief aide. "I don't know, Bob. We just announced that I was *not* a candidate for mayor. What was it? Two months ago?"

Bob Price nodded. "Yep. March 1. Voters have such short memories."

"Short," the congressman conceded, "but not bereft of immediate recall."

"Wanna bet?"

Lindsay shrugged as Bob Price went on. "Look. We got a problem here that we can convert into a golden opportunity."

"I'm looking at the big picture…," Lindsay insisted.

"So am I," Price said, cutting him off. "And the big picture is to put John Lindsay in the White House. Problem is, you're not gonna get there from the House of Representatives.

You've been there four terms. We need to find a stepping stone, somewhere between the lower House and the White House."

Lindsay shook his head. "We've been over this. The odds of winning the mayoralty are not good, that's why we decided to sit this one out." The congressman tugged at his ear. "As I recall, the intermediary slot we agreed upon was to go for the governorship."

Price let out a deep sigh. "That was when we thought Rockefeller wouldn't run. But he announced yesterday he would stand for a third term. You're both in the same party. Hell, both in the same *wing* of the same party. And to go against Rocky's billions.... No, that route is now closed.

"Same problem with the Senate," Price went on. "Jake Javits is every bit as liberal a Republican as you, an' he won last time out by over a million votes. Going against him in a primary would hurt your standing in the party irreparably. And be a totally uphill battle."

Lindsay noted that the other party held the junior senate seat.

"Pah!" Price snorted. "Remember your congressional campaign slogan? 'The District's Pride; The Nation's Hope'? Going against Bobby Kennedy hardly represents the sound political judgment one would expect from our nation's hope. Besides, he's not up for reelection 'til 1970. That's an eternity in politics. We have to strike while the iron's hot."

"What if Bobby is out of the state picture before then?"

"Where's he goin'? No way LBJ is letting him back in the cabinet or anywhere close to the White House. No, at his age, Bobby is going to be around for years and years, I'm afraid."

"That's what a lot of people said about his brother."

Price grimaced. "Who would'a thought someone'd take out President Kennedy? That's a once-in-a-century event. No way Bobby will suffer the same fate.

"Anyway, the governorship is now out, as are the two senate seats. The only viable spot in our fair state for you is as mayor of New York City. We can win this, Jay-viel." The nickname stood for the letters of the congressman's full name. John Vliet Lindsay.

Congressman Lindsay pondered the many imponderables related to making the race. Robert Wagner had won three impressive terms already and had the powerful benefit of incumbency. The Republican Party in the city of New York, if not in the country, was moribund, courtesy of Barry Goldwater's disastrous campaign. Democrats outnumbered Republicans twelve to one in terms of voter registration. Plus, Wagner had the solid support not only of the Democratic chieftains but of Liberal party powerhouse Alex Rose.

Price stood for a minute and stretched. Even standing, he looked like an unmade bed. About the same height as the sitting congressman and ten years younger, Price had already developed a paunch, wore rumpled suits and had a perennial five o'clock shadow. The contrast with the handsome, fortyish Lindsay was striking. The strategist resumed his seat, ticking off points in rebuttal to the congressman's concerns.

"One. Fuh-get about Wagner. The city is falling apart. Three poor terms do not deserve another. Plus, he's tired. People are sick of him. Want a fresh face. That's why Murray Kempton wrote what he did about you. 'He is fresh and everyone else is tired.' How true.

"Besides," Price added, "I'm not sure Wagner's gonna' run."

"Come on, Bob."

"Jay-viel, I'm serious as a heart attack. He knows his polls are down, especially in a race against you. You think he wants to mess up his legacy by going out a loser? I also hear he's tired of the job. You wait and see what four or eight years of that does to you, never mind twelve. Plus, his wife died, and he's close to re-marrying. I hear he's concerned about starting off a marriage with all his time consumed by public affairs."

Lindsay's eyes widened. "Where do you hear this stuff?"

Price grinned. "I got my sources.... The important thing is if he don't go, we need to be in position to inherit his liberal mantle. If he does go, we take him."

"How?"

"Simple. We out-liberal him. We'll be more democrat than the Democrats. That's the future for the Republicans and the country, anyway.

"As for your status as a Republican...." Price waved his hand dismissively. "We're not gonna run exclusively as Republican. We're gonna run *away* from the party."

Lindsay chuckled mirthlessly. "So we run without Republican, Democrat or Liberal affiliation. What's left?"

"We shall be above party. Remember your history."

Lindsay looked at him blankly.

"We're going to take a page from a recent famous mayor."

Still an empty stare.

"Had an airport named after him?" Price prompted.

The congressman blinked. "JFK? You're wrong, Bob. John Kennedy was never mayor of New York. He was from Massachusetts."

Price winced. "Wrong airport. I was thinking LaGuardia."

Lindsay knew the Little Flower had run, and won, as a Fusion candidate, but was still surprised when his strategist explained that was what they would do, run as part of a grand coalition that crossed party lines. Select running mates from different parties.

Price painted the picture in his mixed-metaphorical way of speaking. "The campaign would be a three-legged stool. Run as the brightest picture of liberalism. Present JVL as a fresh, Fusion candidate."

"That's two legs. What's number three?" Lindsay inquired.

"It's time for a change. The city is in desperate straits. Crime is up. Revenues down. The middle class is fleeing. The bosses have ruined the city."

Congressman Lindsay wondered aloud what specific policies Price had in mind that would save the city.

"That's the beauty of running against the status quo," Price said. "You don't need specific answers. Remember the old Groucho Marx song. 'I'm Against It.' Whatever is bad about the city is their fault, and you're against it."

"It is appealing," Lindsay agreed, "but still...."

Price, gratified his man had shifted from the "not running" column to "undecided," decided to go ahead with his plan to push Lindsay a little further. The two were scheduled to ride Amtrak's Northeast Flyer back to New York, this being a Friday and the close of congressional business for the week. Lindsay and Price would head back to press the flesh in the home district, where Price intended to impart another nudge to the unsuspecting congressman.

Back in the Empire State in the early evening, Price escorted his candidate to the swank 21 Club. There, Congressman Lindsay soon found himself surrounded by a quartet of scintillating dinner mates: A. M. Rosenthal of the august self-proclaimed "paper of record," *The New York Times*; industrialist and noted political donor Harold Vanderbilt; Governor Rockefeller's aide, George Hinman; and Democratic donor Henry Ford II. Rosenthal quickly set the table, metaphorically speaking.

"Notwithstanding your pledge to dedicate yourself to House business, Congressman," the famous editor said, "the fact of the matter is New York is a city in serious decline. It is indeed worthy of salvation. The needs of the many outweigh those of a single congressional district."

"Here! Here!" Vanderbilt seconded, raising his glass of Jack Daniels in a toast. The industrialist then added that if the congressman would consent to undertake the salvation of New York City, he was prepared to help bankroll his campaign...to the tune of $2.5 million! A staggering amount in 1965 dollars.

"What's more," Vanderbilt said, "I have commitments from four other financial titans, Mrs. Vincent Astor, Mrs. Nicholas Biddle, William Paley and Roger Blough, for an additional four million!"

Lindsay was thunderstruck; Price grinned wildly.

Rosenthal came back with the firm commitment that *The Times* would back Lindsay to the fullest extent possible.

"An endorsement?" Lindsay asked.

"Plus more," came the reply. "All the favorable coverage that's fit to print."

Ford joined the fray. "We're all tired of Bobby Wagner. There's a good reason for the two-term limit."

Lindsay reminded Ford that the two-term limit was applicable only to the president, not to the mayor of New York. No term limit existed for the mayor.

"Well, there ought to be," Ford argued. "I always believe in the 80-and-5 rule. Eighty percent of a person's best ideas and energy come in the first five years on the job. After that, the law of diminishing returns takes over. Wagner's well past that."

The discussion then turned to the problems of the city and how the Wagner administration appeared incapable of resolving them. Such problems ranged from the sluggish economy, deteriorating revenue base, high juvenile delinquency rates, and inadequacy of the public school system, to substandard housing, rising crime, drug abuse, labor unrest, and still more. Talk drifted to what an energized, liberal administration could do to rectify matters.

The conversation was going strong through the second course when a man came out of the kitchen and timidly approached Lindsay. From the man's embroidered shirt, it was apparent he was a 21 employee. He waited until there was a lull in the discussion.

"A-scuse me. You are Congressman Leendsay, no?" He spoke with an Eastern European accent.

The 100-watt Lindsay smile shone. "Indeed."

The man held out his hands and grasped Lindsay's in both of his. "My wife and me, we from Albania. We hope you run for mayor (it came out maj-or). You are the best thing since Pres-dent Can-a-dee (Kennedy). We have so leetle. We need you to help New York, sir." He averted his eyes, seemingly embarrassed.

Lindsay stood and gripped the man by the shoulders. He asked the immigrant's name. Upon hearing it, he said, "Juro, I thank you for what you have said. I shall consider it most carefully."

Juro grinned, revealing two prominently missing teeth. "Oh, thank you, sir! Thank you, Meester Leendsay! I must go back to work now. I had to tell you this."

As the man turned to walk away, Lindsay resumed his seat, accepting the warmly appraising glances of the group Price had assembled. Undetected, Price slipped a folded pair of bills into Juro's hand.

"That must tell you something, Congressman," Rosenthal opined.

"It does. It does," Lindsay intoned. "However, it does not provide a roadmap to defeat our incumbent mayor."

"We think we can see a path to victory." Hinman was emphatic. Looking to Price, he said, "Robert, you have the poll we commissioned?"

Price pulled a sheaf of papers out of the inner pocket of his suit jacket. "Wagner is only ahead by three points, 39-36. Twenty-five undecided. And that's before we've even begun to campaign. The congressman has a much higher unknown quotient, but in the course of the campaign, we will introduce him to the voters. In no time, his name recognition will match Wagner's. Bear in mind, even though the congressman is less well known, right now, at least, he has a huge favorable rating. Eighty-seven percent! Wagner, on the other hand, is viewed unfavorably by 57 percent of likely voters. Even many of those supporting him for now. These can be swayed."

The conversation then turned to how stellar the numbers were. When he filtered out the ego factor, even Lindsay had to admit the positives were surprisingly favorable.

Talk quickly turned to campaign strategy as the four political neophytes tossed out a number of ideas. Price had his own strategy, but he held his tongue. Right now, it was much more important to stroke these fat cats.

Dinner broke, but not before Lindsay promised to rethink his pledge of non-candidacy.

• • •

As Lindsay and his strategist stood on Fifty-Second Street watching the trio leave in their chauffeured limousines, the congressman remarked with a smile, "Why do I have the feeling this was an orchestrated affair, Bob?"

Price held up his hands, palms out in a "who, me?" gesture. "There is no denying the genuineness of their admiration for you, sir, and their enthusiasm."

"That is for sure." The congressman looked at his watch. It was late, but Price urged one last thing before they retired. "Dessert."

Lindsay patted his full, though enviably flat stomach, about to beg off, but Price intervened. "Just a brief stop. This is important."

• • •

While Congressman Lindsay and Bob Price had been at their dinner meeting, Nancy Dickerson had just gotten off the Greyhound bus at the station on Washington's seedy New York Avenue. As dismal as her immediate surroundings were, she was happy to stand and breathe in some fresh air after her first week on assignment. The squalor of New York Avenue had been more than matched by the tawdriness of her bus ride. For one, Nancy's seat was near the back, where the combined smells of the diesel and the clogged-up restroom were especially pungent. Second, her seatmate was an overweight person of glandular proportions who took up a seat-and-a-half. Unfortunately, that extra half seat was Nancy's. Yet that was not the worst of it. Third and most vile of all, somewhere around the Delaware Memorial Bridge, Nancy's seatmate, apparently in a deep slumber, allowed his hand to drift over and rest on Nancy's knee.

"Excuse me," she whispered. Then a little louder. No response. Sighing and with a face registering utmost distaste, Nancy gently lifted seatmate's hand and placed it on his own lap. Only to have it wander once again, back to Nancy's knee. This happened three times in all. The reason it did not occur a fourth was this. After the third, the somnolent gentleman's hand crept slowly from Nancy's knee up her thigh.

Nancy turned to the apparently sleeping man. "All right, Sleeping Beauty," she hissed. "Touch me once more and I shall break your hand into so many pieces, it will take the Army Corps of Engineers to reassemble it." The hand promptly retreated to its rightful spot, never again to encroach upon Nancy's zone of privacy.

The distasteful episode left Nancy fully awake. For the duration of the Greyhound ride, she reflected on her first week in New York. A mixed bag, but all in all, an auspicious start. She had found the bureau at Rockefeller Center no problem. The newsroom was a beehive of activity, people darting to and fro, much like Macy's in Herald Square as soon as the doors first opened.

She'd stopped one young man rushing self-importantly as if to cover the Lindbergh landing or the Kennedy assassination. "Excuse me," Nancy said, "Can you show me to Mr. Haller's office?"

The young man stopped long enough to look her up and down the way he would appraise a choice piece of livestock. "Oh," he said after a last, leering glance. "You must be the new girl." Nancy was about to correct him, but he was off with a "Follow me!"

While leading her past a desk covered with papers, he pointed and called back to Nancy, "These need to be filed!"

Nancy kept trying to tell him that she was not here to do filing work, but the whirlwind was off and she was forced to keep up in his wake. At last, he stopped...at the coffee station. "Before you start the filing, get me a cup of coffee. Black. And clean out the pot real good; it hasn't been cleaned since Thursday." Nancy glanced at the pot, which appeared to have organisms swimming in it. Forget about Thursday; she guessed it hadn't been cleaned since the Eisenhower Administration. And the coffee station was a mess with papers, grounds and discarded sugar packets all around.

"Listen!" Nancy said, finally raising her voice. "Do you know when the tax deadline is?"

The young man actually stood still for a moment, staring at her. "Uh, yeah. Fifteenth day of March for corporations. Fifteenth day of April for individuals."

Nancy smiled, but there was a noticeable frosty edge to her voice when she spoke. "You will get your coffee on the fifteenth day of forever! I am not the new...*girl*. I have been assigned here from the D.C. bureau. I...am...a...reporter. Ree-por-ter!"

The fellow scratched his head. "A *girl* reporter?"

Nancy sighed. "Oh, honestly. No. I'm the professional wrestler Gorgeous George, here in disguise. Yes, I'm a female reporter! Now where is Mr. Haller's office?"

He pointed to a partitioned office halfway down the hall. As Nancy headed in that direction, another man entered the coffee area.

"Who's she?" he asked.

The first man answered, "Some girl reporter from Washington. She must be on the rag or something."

Without breaking stride, Nancy called out, "I heard that! And I am not!"

At the indicated door, she knocked politely and then entered when she was instructed to do so. "Mr. Haller?"

Haller looked up, broke into a wide grin, then rose and offered both his hands. "Nancy? Nancy Dickerson? How are you?"

"All the better for seeing you, sir," she smiled in return, pleased that his manner was all warmth.

"When the front office told me you were coming, I made it a point to look you up. Of course, I have watched a few of your reports. You are a very good reporter. Welcome to New York. Come in. Come in. Have a seat."

"Thank you, sir."

Haller held out his hand. "I haven't been knighted yet. Please, no sir. Just Arthur."

"I'm pleased to meet you…Arthur."

Arthur Haller looked more like an academic than a newsman. He was a little stooped, balding, with a white fringe. He wore a blue wool sweater over corduroy slacks. Smoke whirled from a pipe in his ashtray.

Haller watched the smoke a moment, perhaps wistfully, then turned his gaze back to Nancy. "Putting you on Lindsay makes sense. I have my most experienced local political reporter covering the Wagner campaign. He has a little advantage as he's developed sources over the years here in New York. But I'm sure he will help you catch up. Plus, Lindsay is new. His people as well. There are no established ties on that side. And you're a capable reporter. You'll develop your own sources soon enough."

"Yes, sir. I mean, Arthur."

Haller reached for the phone and made a quick call. In a moment, the reporter on the Wagner beat arrived. The bureau chief introduced them. "Nancy Dickerson. Gabe Pressman." While Pressman was young, he was one of those people who looked as if he'd been born old. He also looked as if he'd been on the beat for decades. He was short, moon-faced, did not have smile lines, and had droopy bags of skin under his eyes.

Suddenly the scholarly Haller's voice turned iron. "Gabe, you *will* extend every courtesy to Nancy as she gets acclimated."

Pressman nodded and addressed Nancy. "It's going to be a good race." Whether he was referring to their own pending reporting competition or the Wagner-Lindsay race, Nancy could not tell.

When they were alone again, Haller looked up at the ceiling in remembrance. "I've worked the newsroom for some pretty amazing elections. Dewey Defeats Truman, for example," he said, chuckling. Nancy did as well at the famous mental image of the Chicago newspaper that incorrectly, along with most of the country's pundits, heralded the wrong victor in the 1948 presidential sweepstakes.

"The FDR campaigns. All of them," Haller continued. "Rocky's first win in '58. LaGuardia. But you know what?"

Nancy shook her head, inviting him to go on.

"This could well be the granddaddy of them all. Lindsay-Wagner is going to be a rip-roaring race that will shake this city up. You are lucky to be on the ground floor, M' lady."

"I do appreciate the opportunity," Nancy said. "And the chance to work for you."

Now it was Haller's turn to smile. *"For* me? We'll be working together. This is a good one for me to go out on as I hand the reigns over to the future." He motioned pointedly at Nancy.

"Uh, sir, I hardly expect...."

"You are the future, Nancy. Oh, maybe not you, per se, though I'd put my chips on you. I mean women in general. Look at the demographics. It's only a matter of time before women share in the running of our country, our businesses. You...you are the Moses."

Nancy looked a bit puzzled at the reference, and the bureau chief noticed. "No Jewish blood?" he quipped. Before she could respond, he added, "No matter. You are one of the few blazing the way.

"You know I'm scheduled to retire?" he continued.

Nancy nodded.

"They talk to you about the position?"

"Not directly."

Haller snorted. "Leave it to news executives to fail to be direct. A word of advice. Never...never trust 'em. They will say or do anything to get you to do their bidding. They may or may not be ready to put a woman in this chair. But do not rely on their implied assurances. And don't ever let them define your self-worth. Do the best you can. That's all you can do. And when all else fails, you will always have a body of work to fall back on, allowing you to hold your head high.

"At any rate," he added, "*I* will give you a fair shake."

"Thank you, Arthur," Nancy said. "That means a lot to me. I wish you were in charge of the network."

Another snort. "Saints preserve us! If I were, I'd fire every one of those empty suits." He reached for his pipe, then hefted it high in a toast. "To the future."

Nancy beamed her acquiescence.

"Well," said Haller as he produced a monogrammed handkerchief and dabbed at his forehead, "down to business. Get settled in. Start nurturing sources. See if you can get us a piece we can use with Lindsay or one of his top campaign aides."

"Arthur? What if Lindsay sticks by his pledge and does not run? You seem so certain he will."

"I *am* certain."

"How can you be?"

Another chuckle. "I have my sources."

"Care to share?" she said coyly.

"If I did the reporting, would I have any need of you or the other reporters? Go do your job." This was said with a wide grin. "Oh, and Nancy?"

"Yes?"

"Be sure you talk to Rose. Unless I miss my guess, that could be the key to this election. Also, you're going to need some help. Campaigns get rather hectic, and you can't be in two places at once. We have three interns. Select one as your private staff for the duration. Go see my assistant in charge of the interns. I'm too old to have anything in common with students, so that's one part of the job I've delegated. Gave it to a young kid I think has a future in this business. Plus he has a winning personality, so he's the right person to nurture the interns. His name is Chuck Scarborough. Actually, he's out this week. Touch of the flu bug. First thing next week, go see Chuck. He'll set you up with your own intern."

Haller rose, signaling the session was at an end. He extended his hand, which Nancy shook firmly. "Good luck, Nancy."

"Thank you, Arthur."

Back in the newsroom, Nancy was quickly approached by Gabe Pressman.

"He take your head off?"

She pulled at her cranium with both hands. "Seems to be still attached and in working order."

"Just wait. He give you any advice?"

"Some. Where do I find Rose? I'm not sure who she is."

Pressman smiled, quickly suppressing his grin as if in fear that someone would detect his display of mirth. He looked at Nancy dead on. "The 'Rose' he was referring to was *Alex* Rose. Head of the Liberal Party in New York."

Nancy barked a short laugh. "Well, that could have been embarrassing. Thank you."

"Now you owe me."

"You will be sure to collect?"

"I always do." And he was off.

And followed immediately by a short, plain woman in a beige dress that only accentuated her plainness. "Arthur asked me to get you settled in. I'm Alice. Alice Kammerlin. No, not Alice Kramden, like in *The Honeymooners*."

Not a habitual TV watcher, Nancy did not get the reference. Not that it mattered. Alice Kammerlin was friendly enough. Turned out, she was one of the secretaries from the typing pool.

Alice showed Nancy to her cubicle. Where to get supplies. Location of the restroom. Coffee station.

"I've seen this."

"They ask you to brew a pot?"

"Actually, yes."

"Will you?"

"When hell freezes over."

"Wow!" Alice was suddenly wide-eyed. "A rebel! I'm sticking with you!"

The rest of the tour was plain vanilla. Alice did impart two interesting tidbits. "If you ever get in real early, you might see some of the people from the *Today* show. They broadcast in the next room. You know, since they got that young newswoman, Barbara Walters, I just love the show. She has such a nice way about her, and she's the best interviewer.

"Over there," Alice said, pointing in the opposite direction, "is where the *Tonight* show broadcasts. Their new host, Johnny Carson, is so quick on his feet. I think he's the funniest man on television. The problem is, the show runs ninety minutes. When I stay up to the end, I'm pretty wrecked the next morning."

"It's a good thing television doesn't broadcast around the clock," Nancy observed.

"You're telling me," Alice replied. "After Carson is the *Late Show*, an old movie from the '30s or '40s, and then the national anthem signals the end of the broadcast day."

Nancy thanked Alice. Loaded up with supplies, a cup of bitter coffee (someone had cleaned the pot—hopefully) and a swirl of thoughts, Nancy perched herself in her cubicle. The first substantive task she undertook was to work the phones. Almost without fail, any GOP-connected person she called told her the same thing: "We take Congressman Lindsay at his word that he will not run. We are disappointed but have to honor his wishes."

It was a weird thing. The Republican Party in the city was moribund. Not only was it difficult to locate credible sources, but those Nancy did find were low on the pecking order. How low? Nancy caught one of the chieftains as he was hurrying off to work—driving his taxi.

The only person who broke the mold was the head of the Manhattan Republican Club, Vince Albano. From her brief discussion with him, Nancy realized Albano was the only Republican in the entire city to have even the semblance of an organization. "No wonder they never win," she muttered.

The strange aspect was that the farther Nancy got from the city, the more reliable and helpful her phone calls became. State officials had no knowledge of Lindsay's intentions. She did learn, however, that Governor Rockefeller had pledged $500,000 of his fortune to aid Lindsay's effort—if he ran. Nancy tucked this away for future reference.

Higher up the food chain was where Nancy struck pay dirt. At the national level. The gravelly-voiced Senate Minority Leader Everett Dirksen of Illinois kept Nancy on the phone for over a half hour. He did provide two useful sources on the House side. When Nancy called those, she got two numbers that she knew would be the coin of the realm. Shortly thereafter, Gabe Pressman nosed over, causing Nancy to bury the paper on which she'd just jotted down some notes. She did not know yet where Pressman stood. Moreover, these were now her contacts, the result of hours of effort. She found it amazing that yakking on the phone for hours on end could so drain one's energy.

Nancy knew she could ill afford decreased energy levels. Not only was Chuck Scarborough down for the count with the flu, but she learned that much of the newsroom had succumbed as well. So much so that Arthur soon asked if she could pinch hit and cover a non-political story just breaking. It was a garden-variety murder, except this one had sensationalist overtones. All the hallmarks of tabloid journalism.

A woman, estranged from her husband, was being arraigned on charges of murdering her two young children. By all accounts, the woman was a looker. A cocktail waitress by the name of Alice Crimmens. Nancy, of course, agreed to pitch in and cover the arraignment.

Due to the late nature of the request, Nancy was behind the rest of the press corps already gathered at the courthouse. To be sure she was on time for the hearing, Nancy raced out of her cab, forgetting to affix her press credentials around her neck.

Inside, a score of uniformly male reporters was abuzz over the cocktail waitress. Not a one of them had seen Mrs. Crimmens yet, which only heightened their interest. That, and their overactive libidos, for all had heard that the accused's attractiveness was out of this world.

As soon as Nancy entered the room, three of the pack journalists shouted, "There she is!" Transitioning quickly to a wolf pack, the herd raced toward Nancy. For her part, Nancy looked behind her, unable to understand the fuss.

"How did she break out?" one scribe shouted.

"She may be dangerous!" cried another, which slowed the intrepid male corps. It also got the attention of two on-duty police officers, who quickly rushed over, guns drawn. One grabbed Nancy by the shoulders and flung her around, nervously fumbling with his handcuffs.

Showing surprising strength, Nancy shrugged the much larger officer aside and then turned and yelled, "What in blazes are you doing?"

The other officer shouted, "We have to subdue you, Mrs. Crimmens!"

With a look of pure disgust, Nancy cried out, "I AM NOT ALICE CRIMMENS!" Taking a breath, she said, "My name is Nancy Dickerson. NBC News.... Here!"

When Nancy reached into her purse for her credentials, the entire assemblage fell back, expecting her to produce a weapon. One of the manly correspondents fainted; four others dove under a table.

When at last Nancy held her press pass aloft, the sigh of relief in the room was audible. "Excuse us, Ma'am," one of the officers said. "It was an honest mistake."

"Why?" Nancy growled. "Do we all look alike?"

A number of the journalists were nodding affirmatively to this statement.

"Oh, honestly!" Nancy exhorted. "Do I look like a cocktail waitress?"

Now every head in the room nodded.

"Oh, Lord," Nancy implored, looking upward as she counted to ten, her lips pursed.

In short order, the real Alice Crimmens was produced, setting off a flare of flashbulbs and inane questions.

"Mrs. Crimmens! How do you feel?"

"Did you kill them?"

"Have you seen your husband?"

"How will you plead?"

A phalanx of police ushered the woman to the front of the room. Eyes downcast the entire time, Crimmens did not make eye contact with a single person.

As Nancy observed her, she realized the defendant, while uncommonly attractive, looked nothing like her. Crimmens's hair was red to Nancy's brunette. Her figure was a little more, uh, buxom, and she was shorter. Nor was there a facial similarity. Yet throughout the twenty-minute proceeding, during which bail was set at a million dollars, the reporters and not a few of the cops kept craning their necks for looks at Alice, and then at Nancy. Nancy simply blew out some air as she dutifully took notes, determined to ignore them all.

In the evening editions, everyone referred to the ruckus at the arraignment that occurred upon the arrival of Mrs. Crimmens. Not a word was said about the earlier melee involving Nancy, despite the papers' supposed commitment to full and complete reporting. Not that Nancy minded. She had no desire to be part of the story.

The *Daily News* was acknowledged to have led the pack in its journalistic endeavor. Unlike the other tabloids, the *News* carried wall-to-wall pictures of Alice, featuring one revealing cleavage shot, one that showed a lot of cheesecake, and an old photo an enterprising journalist had snagged of Alice in her skimpy cocktail waitress uniform.

Back at Rockefeller Center, Nancy filed her report. She'd never thought she would see the day when other stories were more lurid than the political beat. Once off camera, she sighed. "I can't believe they confused us. To think they treat us all like we look alike."

Unobserved, a quiet voice next to her surprised Nancy with the comment, "I share your pain, sister." The speaker was Bob Teague, a young black reporter in his first months on the job.

The only other person who learned of the derangement at the arraignment was Nancy's husband. On the phone that night, Dick asked if anything unusual had happened that day.

"Well, I almost got arrested."

"What! Speeding again?"

"Dick, I don't have the car with me, remember?"

"So, what crime or near-crime were you responsible for?"

"Impersonating a cocktail waitress," came the deadpan reply.

This was greeted by an uncomfortable silence, which Nancy broke by asking Dick what he was thinking.

He cleared his throat. "I was envisioning you in our bedroom in a cocktail waitress uniform."

"Do you men really have only one thing on your minds?"

"Right now I do," he said, sharing a laugh with his wife.

• • •

As Nancy gulped in the fresh air in Washington that Friday, back in New York, Congressman Lindsay and Bob Price headed to a late "important" meeting, as Price had characterized it.

Lindsay was surprised to find them at a Lower East Side office. When they entered, there was but one dim light and a projector, over which an overweight, rumpled, thirtyish man with frizzy dark hair labored.

"This young man," Price introduced, "is one of the savviest of the new generation of media experts. Congressman, meet David Garth."

Lindsay towered over Garth as the media, uh, kid, beckoned his guests to sit at a small, pock-marked conference table.

"The floor is yours, Professor," Price urged, prompting Garth to break into a toothy grin.

Pointing to a box in the corner of the room, Garth said, "This is going to win the election for us."

"It looks like a television set," Lindsay said.

"Very good. TV is the wave of the political future."

"That may be somewhat of an overstatement," Lindsay noted. "This town is dominated by the newspapers. There are nine of them, six morning editions and three afternoon dailies." He looked at Price and chuckled. "Though that is a far cry from the old days when there were fifteen New York City-based newspapers."

"That is so 1950s," Garth replied. "This is the future. 1965. The day is coming—and indeed is now here—when people will rely on TV for all their news and entertainment. Newspapers will eventually die off."

"Much as no politician would mind, heaven forbid," Lindsay cracked.

"Listen," Garth continued. "How did JFK beat Nixon?"

Lindsay answered, "The debates."

"Right. The *televised* debates. Among radio listeners, Nixon was judged the winner. Over the tube, however, it was a much different story. Kennedy was handsome, glamorous, well-spoken and Nixon was...well, he looked like a used car salesman.

"And what about the Johnson-Goldwater election?" Garth continued.

"The image I remember," Lindsay said, "was the Daisy ad."

That was a reference to the infamous commercial of a pretty little blonde girl in a field counting off the petals on a daisy, only to be replaced by the voice of mission control, "Three, Two, One..." and the image of a detonating mushroom cloud. The simple message read, "Vote for President Johnson." The unmistakable impression was that the conservative Goldwater was a dangerous warmonger who would embroil the country in nuclear Armageddon. Goldwater would lose the election in one of the largest landslides in U.S. history.

"It all seems like selling so much soap, though," Lindsay observed. "Somewhat unseemly for a politician."

"What about politics isn't unseemly?" Garth shot back.

The congressman looked to Price, who inclined his head as if to say, "He's got a point."

Garth went on. "I do agree with you that every one of the old candidate ads looks like they are selling soap or aspirin or cigarettes. I have something else in mind. We will sell...*you!*" Garth was looking directly at Lindsay now, piquing the congressman's interest.

"You are young, good looking, athletic, the perfect person to highlight on camera," the portly pundit said. "I propose we run a clip of you talking about some issue with a city street in the background. That will fade to a shot of you in a moving car with the printed message 'Vote Lindsay!' The moving car shot will give the feel of moving into the future."

Garth hurried to the projector and flipped a switch to display an early, slightly crude prototype of what he had just described. Lindsay was instantly mesmerized. Garth was as well, but his eyes were glued on Lindsay, not on the images of the congressman. "Mirror, mirror on the wall," the pundit thought to himself, "what politician watching himself can avoid the spell?"

When the clip ended, Garth added that they would saturate the airwaves. "We will make you a rock star, Congressman, like those singers from England who came over last year. What was their name? Some sort'a bug."

"The Beatles," Price inserted helpfully, smiling at the media geek's lack of familiarity with pop culture.

Lindsay asked what such a saturation campaign would cost.

"I'm guessin' five hundred thousand."

Lindsay whistled. "That is unheard of!"

Garth shrugged, explaining this was the wave of the future.

"The world according to Garth," Price threw in.

Congressman Lindsay looked at his aide. "Actually, that's sort of catchy. Someone should write a book with that title."

Price ignored the comment, wholly absorbed in the campaign aspect of the discussion. "We will budget three hundred thousand."

"Bob?" Lindsay exhorted.

Price held his hand up. "Money will not be a problem, I assure you. Remember how much those guys at 21 pledged? And that was just four of them."

Garth said, "I can devise a respectable campaign for three hundred thousand. But with five hundred, you will win by a lot more."

Lindsay laughed. "Remember what old Joe Kennedy told his son before the Wisconsin primary? 'Don't spend one penny more than is necessary. I'll be damned if I'm going to pay for a landslide!'"

The group enjoyed the mirth, though it was accompanied by a vague pang brought on by the image of the youthful president slain well before his time. The country had yet to recover from this unimaginably violent event. Lindsay had been among those who'd questioned whether the Kennedy assassination had presaged a growing violence in the country's culture and had pledged his efforts to bring a halt to all this craziness. It was this innate idealism, as much as his good looks, that placed him as preeminent among politicians to whom the people were looking for future leadership.

The congressman looked at the image of himself frozen on Garth's projection screen. Then he looked at Price. "All right, Bob," he said, "if we go, we can do the television strategy. However, I do not want to neglect the newspapers. I still believe they control the city and are the key to public opinion."

Garth was about to protest, but Price held up a quieting hand. While he might be the candidate of tomorrow, Lindsay was not omniscient regarding the future.

Price told the congressman not to worry, that this was the reason he was scaling back the TV budget by two hundred thousand dollars, leaving ample funds for print ads.

Lindsay nodded, his brow knit in thought. "That, of course, presupposes that I am a candidate."

Garth's mouth opened in surprise. He looked to Price. "You told me he was gonna' run!"

Price looked momentarily, uncharacteristically, worried. "Ah…ah…," he stammered with a helpless shrug, "we're working on it."

Lindsay looked from one to the other and then told Garth, "I am actively re-assessing my position."

Garth's whole body sagged in relief. After wondering silently why only politicians say things like "actively re-assessing my position," he pondered the fact that when a politician says he's "re-assessing" anything, a promise was about to be broken.

The congressman and Price took their leave, shutting down for the evening. Garth planned to sleep in late the next morning, a Saturday, the only day he could catch up on the rest his eighteen-hour weekdays deprived him of. It was also his preferred way of observing the Sabbath.

Not everyone had the energy level of David Garth, who was ambitious to make his mark. Yet even Garth would have marveled at and admired the energy level of Lindsay and Price. For as long as their week had been and as late as their business with Garth extended Friday night, Lindsay and Price were up and ready to go just six hours later. Lindsay fervently believed that walking the district strengthened his appeal to voters. It also turbo-charged the congressman's convictions.

Lindsay's district was the Seventeenth, the so-called Silk Stocking District because of its inherent wealth. On this particular day, Price planned to widen Lindsay's reach by bringing the congressman into lower Harlem, about as far from Silk Stocking neighborhoods as black was from white in 1965.

In the white neighborhoods, Lindsay was greeted as the conquering hero. The residents of the Seventeenth District went out of their way to shake Lindsay's hand as enthusiastically as he shook theirs, his jacket off, shirt sleeves rolled up, his smile at mega wattage.

"Good to see you, Congressman!"

"Glad you're on our side!"

"Please run for mayor…we need you!"

Through it all, Lindsay was jovial but noncommittal. It all turned when the walking tour hit Harlem, however. There, most people looked at the congressman blankly. Even when he offered his hand, most shook it reluctantly, if at all. They did not know what to make of this crisply dressed young white man exuding enthusiasm and optimism. Others made it clear by glaring at the congressman or simply turning away from him that they did not trust Lindsay...or any white person, for that matter.

One spry elderly black woman seemed almost amused by the congressman's foray. She was more voluble than the rest and took to following alongside Lindsay and Price. This had two unintended side effects. The woman was an authoritative source on the community, a tour guide if you will. Secondly, Lindsay was instantly more accessible with the woman by his side. People began approaching him, albeit hesitantly. But approach they did. "We are making some progress," the congressman whispered out of the side of his mouth to Price. He then thanked the woman, who had introduced herself as Viola, for her "Negro presence."

"Progress is a white leader comin' here," Viola said. "Never happened in my memory. An' I be sixty-eight years old!"

As they crossed their third block, Lindsay commented on "the Negro problem." He noted the garbage strewn all about. He asked Viola if the Sanitation Department ever came to pick up the refuse.

Viola harrumphed. "Damn garbage men come here once a week."

"Only once a week!" Lindsay was horrified.

"Yeah, but it don't matter none. Even when's they come, as soon as they leave, the trash gets tossed all about."

"Why?" Lindsay asked.

"You ever seen the insides a these 'partments?" she challenged.

The congressman shook his head.

"When the inside's as shitty as the outside, what 'centives there to try to keep the neighborhood lookin' nice?"

"But surely you have pride," Lindsay countered.

"Hah! Thass a good one! No pride here. We live in shit; we die in shit. There be no 'scape. Is jest the way it is."

Price noticed his patron's look and wisely held his counsel.

Further along, they came to an abandoned lot. Debris, broken glass, an old sofa with the stuffing hanging out, some weeds. And two little boys tossing pebbles at the sofa, a game that was desultory at best.

Lindsay mused aloud that it would be more constructive and healthy if the children played at the playground.

"This is the playground!" Viola hissed. Then she cackled loudly.

Lindsay approached the children. Knelt on one knee. Told them he was a United States congressman and he would make sure they would have a better life. Then he hugged each. The two brightened, giggled and ran off, but not before the adults heard one of the boys ask the other, "Who that white guy say he is?"

"Dunno. I think maybe he from the Army."

"Didn' look like no soldier."

"Som'a them are tricky."

Lindsay asked Viola why people in this area voted for Wagner if all they got in return was such squalor.

She informed him they did not vote.

"Why?"

"Oh, prolly they too busy pickin' up their degrees from Harvard an' getting' their fat paycheck to build pools an' such!"

"This will change, Viola," Lindsay said in all seriousness.

"Oh, you some kinda' knight on a white horse?" she mocked.

"No," Congressman Lindsay responded. "This is one knight who has just gotten off his high horse."

He turned to Price. "Bob, I'm doing it. I'm going to run."

Price clenched his fist and pulled it downward and toward him. "Yes!" For the strategist, all the surrounding blight was shut out. All he saw were unicorns and rainbows. Ideas swirled as the campaign he had long dreamed of beckoned.

Lindsay and Price returned to the congressman's district office to make a few preliminary plans, setting things in motion. For one thing, there were reporters Price had to call with the "exclusive" tip.

There was no one else in the office this late on a weekend. Yet before Lindsay and Price closed up shop, the perennially disheveled David Garth came huffing and puffing in.

"Glad I caught you guys!" Garth said. "These two messages came in for you last night. I forgot to give 'em to you."

Price was thunderstruck. "How in the hell did she know we'd be at Garth's? And how did she find us? And who in creation is...," he glanced at the notepad again, "...Nancy Dickerson?" Price looked up. "What does it mean?"

Congressman Lindsay smiled as he, too, looked up, fully aware of who Nancy Dickerson was. "It means we have arrived!"

CHAPTER III

HAIL! HAIL! THE GANG'S ALL HERE!

At the beginning of every campaign he had run in his life, Robert F. Wagner, the 102nd mayor of New York, felt unbridled enthusiasm. Even when he was unsure of the outcome, gearing up for battle was the most exhilarating, intoxicating brew he knew. Better than sex. That particular thought struck Wagner because he had recently read the early accounts of the Alice Crimmens case. Most particularly the accounts in the *Daily News*, which had plastered its pages with images of the lady. No, Wagner corrected himself. Crimmens was a woman, but she was certainly no lady.

She was pretty, Hizzoner thought, in a trashy way. Not his type. Besides, he believed looks were overrated. Wagner much preferred a wholesome girl. One who got up in the morning to make breakfast for her man before he set off to earn the bacon. Who cared for the children. Ran the household. The sort who hailed from pioneer stock, up with the roosters, toting pails...you get the idea. Women like his beloved Susan... and now Barbara. No. He just did not see the allure of the slutty types. Yet Wagner well knew he was in the minority.

Men went ga-ga over the Alice Crimmenses of the world. Maybe that was what separated him from other mortals.

Despite his personal predilections, Wagner would never attempt to sermonize to his flock. They had elected him mayor, not their lord and personal savior. Like other politicians of his generation, Wagner saw his job as making sure the buses and trains ran on time. Not discussing family values.

Indeed, if the masses craved wanton sexuality, Wagner would leave them be. As much as it appalled him, he would never try to eradicate the fleshpots, XXX theaters, red-light districts of the city, notably along Times Square. Or for those with deviant tastes, the not-so-secret but unmentionable spots in Greenwich Village.

Wagner thought of his late wife as he sipped his coffee. His last conversation with her in particular. Sighing, he put down his cup and rubbed at his eyes. First thing in the morning after a good night's sleep, and he felt exhausted. Something was wrong. Going into a campaign had never felt like this much drudgery. Well, he figured, he would shake it off, sooner or later. The old juices would kick in and he would be raring to go. For an unprecedented fourth term. Even now, after almost twelve years, to many New Yorkers it seemed as if Wagner had been mayor for life. That familiarity, that comfort level, was itself a powerful tool that should ease his path to reelection.

Yet he knew he could not rely on serendipity. Look at what happened to that fool Tom Dewey. Dewey was so certain of victory he engaged in a Rose Garden campaign before occupying said Garden. Only to be upended by the feisty Harry Truman with his whistle stop, Give 'em Hell campaign. Hence the reason for this morning's meeting. Wagner's chief allies and strategists would be arriving shortly here at Gracie Mansion to begin plotting the race to retain City Hall. As Wagner glanced around his surroundings, he realized how much he loved the mansion…and being mayor, despite the crushing burdens and tribulations. It was not easy running a city of over eight million people, the largest city in the world.

The mayor looked at a family picture. "Even Dad would have to admit this is one helluva job," he whispered to the empty room as his fingers grazed the photograph of Robert F. Wagner, Sr. The elder Wagner had been the noted senator from New York who made his mark championing much of the New Deal legislation. His name would rightfully go down in history as the father of the Social Security Act, ensuring the gratitude of generations.

Wagner, Jr. had tried to reclaim his father's senate seat without success. Yet after serving as Manhattan borough president and ingratiating himself with the Party bosses, he took office after the 1953 election. Unfortunately, this was the same year his dad died. Despite never attaining national office, Wagner felt his tenure as mayor would have met with his father's approval.

There were so many things he had accomplished. When the Dodgers and Giants left for the West Coast, Wagner had championed a commission that ultimately led to the return of National League baseball to New York. The City embraced its lovable losers, as the Mets had taken hold of the public fancy. Wagner had expanded the City University system, highways and public housing. Lincoln Center rose under his watch. And with the coming of the World's Fair last year, concern over the city's image led Wagner to mount an all-out assault against the homos. Labor relations were solid. The buses and trains did indeed run. People had bread and circuses when they so desired. An enviable record, Wagner reflected. So good, he should not even have to undergo yet another baptism by electoral fire. The citizens should simply anoint him out of gratitude. A deep sigh. A tough campaign seemed to be in the offing. That in itself surprised the mayor more than anything, and contributed to his recent despondency.

Glancing at his watch, he saw it was time. Can't keep his top supporters waiting. Wagner bounded down the hall. Just before he entered the conference room, he marshaled a bonhomie he did not feel and glued a smile onto his face.

In the conference room, he saw the table was almost full. "Hail! Hail! The gang's all here!" he exclaimed, greeting each individual by name and with a hearty handshake and in some cases a backslap to boot.

There was his running mate, the tall, dignified-looking Paul Screvane. Screvane had been city council president, the number two elected official in the city, and the one who would succeed to the mayoralty if anything happened to Wagner. Screvane was one of three on the ticket, but the third slot remained an issue for now.

Next to Screvane sat the two labor leaders, Harry Van Arsdale of the electricians' union, and Mike Quill of the transit workers'. These two represented the combined voice of Big Labor, totaling a score of unions in all.

Dave Dubinsky was there in his capacity as deputy chair of the Liberal Party of New York. "Where's Alex?" Wagner asked.

"Previous commitment," Dubinsky answered, although it rankled Wagner that the chairman himself could not break his other engagement, especially after all Wagner had done to provide patronage jobs to the Liberals.

Three of the so-called "Party bosses" were there. That is, three of the Democratic Party borough chieftains. Five of the state's 62 counties were in the city, where they were referred to as boroughs. Charlie Buckley of the Bronx machine was here as were Moses Weinstein of Queens and J. Raymond Jones from Manhattan. Staten Island rarely figured in the Democratic calculus, being so tiny and Republican in orientation. Nor was Brooklyn here, a troubling fact that would have to be dealt with.

The group took their seats, following the mayor's lead. Looking at the assembled chieftains Wagner said, "The Magnificent Seven!" in a reference to the blockbuster western movie that had come out a couple of years ago. A few smiles.

"Well," Wagner said, patting the table with both palms, "how do we look for reelection?"

The smiles vanished. Most looked down at their papers.

"As John Nance Garner used to say," Buckley offered, "'You want it with the bark on or the bark off?'"

"Give it to me straight," the mayor urged.

"It's going to be a tough race," Buckley said. "You're just a little ahead of Lindsay, an' he hasn't started campaigning yet. Factor in what the pollsters call the margin of error, an' it's a dead heat."

"We can still win this thing," Van Arsdale roared. "We can get the labor vote out, the bosses get the machine to turn out...we'll round up the traditional votes, don't you worry!"

"I'm just saying it will be hard. No walk in the park this time," Buckley countered.

"We'll do it," Wagner said, a little morosely. "After all, who ever heard of a Republican winning in New York City?"

"This guy Lindsay is different," Jones cautioned.

"Bullshit!" Quill shot back. "We'll see how tough Lindslee is!"

The group laughed at Quill's mangling the congressman's name; from then on the name would be pronounced "Lindslee" by everyone present.

Wagner admitted he was surprised things seemed that dire. "How did we get here?" he asked.

Moses Weinstein said there were two things. To start with, the organization was not enthralled with the mayor. He had been the bosses' choice back in '53. However, in the last election in 1961 when the reform movement of the Democratic Party challenged the regular faction, Wagner tacked to the left and condemned "bossism."

"That's why you don't see Stan here," Buckley groused. Stan was Stanley Steingut, the Brooklyn boss.

"You seem a little miffed, too," Wagner told Buckley.

"'Course I am. You don't treat friends that way."

"Oh, Charlie, it was just politics. After the election, we all came together."

Buckley was having none of it. "You don't treat people like that," he reiterated. "Now you want us again. I'm here 'cause I'm a loyal Democrat. Dig up FDR and I'd campaign for his corpse, so long as he's still a Democrat. But I have to tell you, my heart is not in it this time. An' Stan's definitely ain't."

"He'll come around," Dubinsky said. "He's got nowhere else to go."

"Don't be so sure," Buckley retorted.

"The other problem," Dubinsky noted, "is that in addition to the regulars, there is a dampening of enthusiasm among the reform factions."

Wagner immediately conjured a mental image of the two lionized progressives, Mrs. Roosevelt, FDR's widow, and the former progressive governor, Herbert Lehman. "I always had Mrs. R and Governor Lehman to run interference for me with their reform-minded friends," he said. "Unfortunately, they've both passed away. There's no one of comparable stature who can command the reformers' loyalties."

"It is a lot like herding cats," Dubinsky agreed.

The mayor told the group he had an appointment scheduled with one of the new reform leaders. Guy by the name of Ed Koch.

"Frickin' queer," Quill spat out of the side of his mouth.

"All right, so we have some organizational problems we have to shore up," Screvane said, speaking for the first time. Looking at the Queens leader, he said, "Moses, you mentioned two problems. What's the other one?"

Weinstein shifted in his seat. Unlike Charlie Buckley, he did not relish being the bearer of bad news. "There is a sense… out there…," he waved his hand as if to take in the electorate beyond Gracie Mansion's walls, "…of what I would call incumbent fatigue. People are a little tired of you, see you as yesterday's news, Mr. Mayor. They're worried the City's in decline and your administration has not taken strong enough action to halt the slide."

"Ridiculous!" Wagner's voice rose. "I dare you to find a mayor anywhere in the country whose accomplishments match mine!"

Dubinsky said the problem was the perception that the problems were growing faster than the solutions. "And in politics," he said, "perception becomes reality." After a lull, Dubinsky added that people want the mayor to act on city issues more quickly.

"Sounds like more of the reformist bullcrap!" Quill commented as his fellow labor leader Van Arsdale nodded.

Wagner pointed to Quill. "That's so right, Mike. These problems take time to solve. Rome wasn't built in a day."

"We're not building Rome," Dubinsky countered.

The mayor frowned. "The point is, I can't just snap my fingers and make everything come up roses!"

"The worst are the Negroes," Jones added.

Wagner nodded. "I've done more for them than all of my predecessors combined. Housing, jobs, ended discrimination…yet the more they get, the more they seem to want. Don't they realize these things take time to correct?"

"The problem is," Dubinsky said as he chewed on the stem of his glasses, "they feel they've been waiting for three hundred years."

"*I* didn't torture them three hundred years ago," Wagner answered. "The times sure are changing. I remember when the Negroes were respectful. They knew their place. You could work with them. But this new bunch? Too uppity. Like that big-mouthed fighter, Cassius Clay. Not what I'd call a credit to the race.

"Hoo boy! Where is John Christenberry when we need him?"

Everyone laughed. Christenberry was Wagner's Republican opponent in the 1957 quadrennial elections. His chief charge was that Wagner's police department was too corrupt and not active enough in enforcing the laws. The police then raided the hotel Christenberry owned, where they found an illegal gambling den in the basement. Pffffft went Christenberry's law-and-order bona fides, and along with them his chances. He polled a minuscule 25 percent of the vote as Hizzoner romped to reelection.

Wagner asked sarcastically if the group had any other good news.

Jones said they had to decide on the third spot on the ticket, the comptroller position. Usually the Party chose candidates based on ethnic and geographic balance. "Unfortunately, we got balance but also a pain in the ass," Screvane uncharacteristically chimed in. He was clearly not a fan of the incumbent, Abe Beame.

"He is a damn Hebe," the mayor reflected. Looking at Weinstein, he said, "No offense, Moses."

The Queens boss held up his hands. "None taken. I've been called worse." Plus, he knew Beame had strayed off the reservation. The comptroller had issued several statements critical of the fiscal stability of the Wagner administration. Was this a sign of Beame's appetite for higher office, or a sign of the mayor's growing weakness? In any event, Screvane suggested they nudge Beame off the ticket. The problem was, who to replace him with? There were no obvious candidates. Buckley urged they stand pat with the diminutive comptroller, distasteful as it was. He, Jones and Weinstein all made three perceptive comments indicating unanimity among the bosses.

"We need to capture the Jew vote."

"We need to capture Brooklyn."

"We need to make Stan Steingut happy."

"Aw'right," Wagner summarized. "We stick with the schmuck—for the time being."

Next, talk turned to tactics. Dubinsky suggested starting right away.

"Too soon," the mayor demurred. He believed the voters did not engage until the fall. September was time enough to kick the campaign into high gear. A few of the others disagreed. They thought Lindsay would re-enter the race and would come flying out of the gate. Not wise to wait until Labor Day and give Lindsay that much time to stake a lead. Having said that, it was indeed a tired, unenthusiastic group. They were not young chickens any longer and did not have the energy for a lengthy campaign. So the consensus was to defer to Wagner and hold off on overt campaigning until the fall. They did urge Wagner to select his campaign manager. Contact an advertising guru. Think about the kind of campaign he wanted to run.

Wagner said he would time his formal announcement for June.

The only thing that could upset the calendar was if there was a primary challenge. If so, the primary would be in early September and Wagner would have to begin his campaign earlier.

Incumbents were rarely challenged in primaries. However, the early talk was that this year could be different. A Democratic congressman, William Fitts Ryan, was making noises of going against the mayor.

As the group broke, they agreed the first order of business was to discover if Ryan was for real. He hailed from the reform wing. Hence it was decided that Wagner would discern the progressives' intentions when he spoke with reform leader Koch. As the group broke, Van Arsdale remarked, "Better the mayor talk to that faggot than me."

The mayor asked Screvane to stay behind. "Is it all that bad, Paul?" he asked after the others had left.

Screvane shrugged. "We have such an overwhelming advantage, it is hard to imagine any Republican defeating us. It does seem, however, that this will be our most challenging race yet."

Wagner grimaced. "I'm only 53, but I feel like I'm 103. I didn't want to have to fight for it this time."

"Unfortunately," his running mate said, "we don't have a choice."

"There are always choices," Wagner replied.

When he was alone, the mayor took a few moments to peruse the morning's newspapers. A necessary evil for a politician, but of late Wagner dreaded the press more than most. It seemed the editors were only interested in negative news. Rather than extol the accomplishments of his administration, they accentuated the negative. Hardly a day went by when he did not read some attack on his stewardship. Today's *Tribune* offered up such an example. Wagner's stomach did back flips as he read.

"For the poor, the aged, the Negro, the Puerto Rican, and the blue-collar worker who is unemployed because of automation and the exodus of business, New York today is a nightmare—a hopeless city whose administration offers promises and handouts but little in the way of rehabilitation and retraining.

"For the young and the middle-class white and Negro, New York has become a terrible place to live because of unsafe streets, poor schools, and inadequate housing. They have been driven out to the suburbs just when the city needs them most.

"And even for the wealthy—those who can afford the best—the air pollution, the traffic-clogged streets, and the violence have come to outweigh the delights afforded by New York's stores, restaurants, and cultural events."

• • •

Later in the day when Wagner chanced to pass the press room, the *Herald Tribune* reporter responsible for the story buttonholed the mayor. "Any comment on our story?" the smirking scribe said.

"Yeah," Wagner replied. "Shove it up your ass."

The mayor had a genuinely low regard for the fourth estate. To his way of thinking, all reporters did was collect hand-outs from the press offices and regurgitate same. It was hardly work.

Yet in this regard, the mayor's old-fashioned attitude was truly behind the times. The coming generation of correspondents strove to dig deeper beneath each story and unearth the nuggets under the layers handed out by the press agents.

One such scribe was in the early stages of her craft. At the same moment when Wagner was insulting a *Tribune* reporter, Nancy Dickerson was consulting with Chuck Scarborough, who was back at NBC News from his flu hiatus.

Scarborough had told Nancy there were three available interns, two of whom Scarborough highly recommended.

"Why is that?" Nancy asked.

"Excellent pedigrees. One is from Harvard, the other Columbia."

Nancy inquired as to the third.

"University of Chicago."

"Also an excellent school."

Scarborough shrugged. "I suppose it's all right for a Midwestern college."

Nancy, who hailed from the Midwest, pursed her lips. She asked the manager of the intern pool what else distinguished the two candidates from the third.

He explained that the two he rated higher had more experience in the newsroom covering events.

Nancy could see why that would be helpful. She asked Scarborough why the third one was a laggard. He made a noncommittal gesture.

Nancy next asked if there was anything else that differentiated the three, and Scarborough said simply that the two appeared to be more serious newspeople.

"I suppose you'll want to meet my top two?" he asked.

A funny idea struck Nancy. "If you don't mind, I would like to interview all three. Send the top two in first."

The first candidate was all joviality and confidence. "Nancy," he said, "I'm Thad Richards." He proceeded to tell "Nancy" how familiar he was with the city scene and how much he could do for her.

Next was Tom Dolan, the Harvard. That was easy to tell, for Tom worked the fact into just about every sentence he spoke. He also asked Nancy if she had an Ivy League background. Upon hearing she did not, he made a slight face. Clearly, working for Nancy would be beneath him.

The third candidate, as Nancy suspected, belonged to the female persuasion. "Mrs. Dickerson," the intern said, "this is an honor. I have seen some of your on-air reports. My name is Emma Thornton. It would be an honor to work for you. I will do my best; certainly there is so much I can learn from you."

When Nancy inquired as to her news background, Emma admitted she had far less experience with hard news than either Thad or Tom.

"Why?" Nancy asked.

Emma was reluctant to venture a guess.

"What did Thad cover yesterday?" Nancy asked.

"The police beat."

"And Tom?"

"FDNY."

"And you?"

"I cleaned the supply room," Emma said in a very quiet voice.

"Good Lord! Why...? Don't tell me, I know."

Emma shrugged. "It comes with the territory," she said. "But I know if I keep plugging, sooner or later my break will come."

Scarborough was shocked when Nancy chose Emma.

"But she's...she's...," he stammered.

"A girl?" Nancy helped.

"Well, yeah…." He recovered and said, "And only the product of a Midwestern education."

"I'm from Wisconsin."

Scarborough looked puzzled. "That's in the Midwest?"

"Last time I checked."

Nancy didn't miss a beat. "Look, Chuck. The young lady deserves a chance. She interviewed the best of the three. She's the only one who did not condescend to me. Emma appears every bit as bright as the Ivy Leaguers. The problem is, she cannot show it cleaning the supply room. I'll go with her."

Scarborough shrugged. "Suit yourself."

When Nancy informed Emma, the intern teared up a bit. "You won't regret this, Mrs. Dickerson."

"Now that we shall be working together, please call me Nancy. And I know you will meet my expectations—or else!" When she said this last with a grin, Emma's widening eyes retracted to normal size.

Based on her conversations with Lindsay and Price, Nancy had been the first to break the story of Lindsay's re-entry into the race.

"Tomorrow, you'll come with me," Nancy told her new red-haired assistant. "We're covering the Lindsay for Mayor rally."

"And you want me to go with you?" Emma exclaimed.

Nancy stretched out her arm. "The news is out there, not inside this newsroom. Heaven forbid if the time should come when the on air personalities conflate their own importance with the events of the day."

· · ·

Price had brought in an advance man, Jerry Bruno, to stage manage massive Lindsay rallies. The next day had all the earmarks of a festival as Lindsay prepared to announce his candidacy "to restore greatness to the city."

When Nancy entered the press area, Emma with her, all the reporters turned to stare at Nancy, a gesture to which she'd grown inured. This time, however, a cluster noticed Emma a split second later. The intern's reddish mane sent off waves.

"Look!" one of the scribes shouted. "It's Alice Crimmens!"

As the pack raced toward her and Emma, Nancy treated the herd as a bunch of poorly trained pooches. "No! No! No!" she cried out. "Down boys! She is not Alice Crimmens!"

The pack came to an abrupt halt and, after eyeing—or more accurately, ogling—Emma and Nancy, finally retreated.

"Do I really look like a cocktail waitress?" Emma whispered to Nancy.

"Don't worry," Nancy responded. "This happens to me a lot."

What Nancy did not realize was that the lustful looks directed her way were mixed with a growing admiration and, in some cases, jealousy. She'd been the first to break the story of Lindsay's reemergence. Price had offered "exclusives" to the *Times*, the *Trib* and the *Post*, yet Nancy had scooped them all by a few hours. In the news business, that was eons. Arthur Haller had personally congratulated her, adding that he'd "made sure the suits upstairs and in Washington knew."

Even Emma was impressed. She knew Nancy had gotten the congressman and his campaign manager to open up, but not on the record. How had she scored the scoop?

"I developed another source," Nancy said, but offered nothing more.

Emma was about to press her, but there was a flurry of activity as cameramen jostled for position and cheers spontaneously arose from the crowd Jerry Bruno had corralled.

John Lindsay strode purposefully onto the stage, soaking in the growing crowd's adulation. He gave an acknowledging wave.

Nancy and Emma watched. Both had already read the advance copies of Lindsay's remarks. In addition, there would be a press conference following the rally. In fact, there would be a press conference after each of the rallies to be held that day in the five different boroughs of New York.

As carefully as Nancy watched Congressman Lindsay to see how he performed as a candidate, she also scanned the crowd. How did they respond to their would-be leader? As part of her story, Nancy intended to pick a few who struck her fancy. She would interview these people, using the choicest lines to be spliced into her voiceover. There was one spectator neither Nancy nor Emma could see, however, and yet in many ways he was the most important of all. In a small room off his City Hall office, Robert Wagner fiddled with the rabbit ears on his television set in order to improve the reception.

There were only three national networks in 1965: ABC, CBS and NBC. During the mid-day hours, all were deep into broadcasting the lucrative and vapid afternoon soap operas. Short of a presidential assassination, not one of the networks would dare cut away to cover anything, especially a local news item, regardless of its significance.

In addition to the national networks, there were just three other stations Wagner could reach on his dial. Channel 5, a loose affiliation of stations known as Metromedia that primarily aired children's programming with hosts like Sandy Becker and Sonny Fox as well as old, old movies; Channel 11, WPIX, one of two truly independent stations, wholly unaffiliated (and with the resources and audience to match); and WNET, Channel 13, which strove to offset what former FEC chairman Newton Minnow had called "the vast wasteland" by offering programming for more highbrow tastes. There was also a UHF station, marked by inordinate amounts of snow, whose hallmark was to broadcast foreign soccer games that appealed only to people referred to by many as "the ethnics."

Of the six New York alternatives to the national networks, only Channel 11 deigned to cover the Lindsay event. Wagner cursed mildly as he jiggled the antenna to improve its reception. He longed for a day when there would be a plethora of TV outlets covering a 24-hour news cycle with the technology to allow for crisp, clear images, but suspected such advances would never be possible. Technology was already so advanced; TV could never offer more than it did at present.

Satisfied that his television's reception was the best it would be, Wagner settled down and watched Lindsay every bit as carefully as Nancy Dickerson was watching the congressman. Curiously, both the on-scene reporter and backroom television-watching mayor battling for another chance had virtually identical reactions to the spectacle they were observing.

"He's good," they both thought.

Deep of voice and golden of looks, Lindsay had that undeniable "charisma," a word that had been coined of late. He projected a dedication and an energy Wagner thought he himself had once summoned. More compelling, however, was the reaction Lindsay inspired among the masses. He was Lochinvar from the Sir Walter Scott poem, come to slay the demons of urban decay. This guy was a far cry from Christenberry, Lefkowitz, Gerosa...any of the opponents Wagner had faced. Wagner's mouth formed a thin, grim line as he pondered the effort it would take to turn back the momentum being created by one Congressman Lindsay.

Nor was the overwhelming response to the Lindsay boomlet restricted to the one event's live audience. Without fail, the city's newspapers could have been waterlogged, so covered in drool was their reportage of "this exciting event in city history," as one of the next day editorials proclaimed. Too many, for Wagner's taste, took up the chant. "He is fresh and everyone else is tired," they all seemed to proclaim.

"Everyone else is full of shit," the mayor sadly whispered to himself.

· · ·

Speaking of one of those everyone else's Wagner had in mind, not two weeks later he found himself across the desk from reform leader Edward I. Koch.

Koch had gained his spurs leading the Village Independent Democrats (VID) in unseating long-time Tammany kingpin Carmine DeSapio. DeSapio's defeat marked the end of the century-and-a-half reign of Tammany Hall. Koch was as telegenic in a quintessentially New York sense as Lindsay was charismatic. An odd duck to say the least, Koch was rumored to have electoral aspirations of his own. A congressional seat loomed on his immediate horizon. For now, as Wagner entered the reception area to greet his visitor, Koch was calling out to two janitors across the hall, "How'm I doin'?" Which to Wagner made no sense at all. He was all affability, however, as he escorted Koch to his private office. Koch looked about, as if taking his measure of the room and its contents.

The mayor began his pitch for the reformer's support. Began, that is, but never got far, for the newcomer took to lecturing the veteran politician on how he should act. Try as Wagner might, there was no shutting up the voluble Koch, who had ideas, some cockamamie, about almost everything.

The balding young man started his riff by instructing Wagner to come out foursquare against the Vietnam War. One of the few times he gave Wagner a chance to reply, the mayor explained that city officials have no power over foreign affairs. Moreover, it was political suicide as the president had assured victory in the short term. Coming off his landslide mandate, LBJ would emasculate anyone daring to dispute him.

Koch dismissed Wagner—arrogantly, in fact—as he expostulated on the morality people expected from their elected leaders. Wagner grinned and bore it. Had he not needed reformist support, he would have thrown this faintly effeminate windbag out the window.

Oblivious of his audience's reaction, Koch was on a full rant about morality. He told, no he *lectured*, Wagner on the need to root out corruption in all forms. "If I was mayor, you'd never see a city commissioner, or a party leader, engage in any nefarious activities."

The moralistic sermon went on. About the plight of the Negroes, women, environmental concerns, economic injustice.... On and on it went. A few times, Wagner had to force himself to listen and not nod off.

Finally, mercifully, Koch stopped for air, but not before asking in a condescending tone if the mayor "had got all that."

Wagner answered that he was committed to the same principles. He asked the VID leader flat out: "Can I count on your endorsement?"

Koch made a wry face. "It's not mine to give. I'll have to go back and see if there's a consensus among the Village Independents. I'll get back to you."

"That'll be the day," the mayor thought, recognizing a brush-off when he heard one. As Wagner escorted the VID potentate to the door, the moralistic Koch made one last observation. "Of course, if there was a spot on your ticket for the comptroller position, now that could be a different story."

Wagner was glad to be rid of the windbag...and to see that the reformer's virginity was as besotted as any politician's.

True to his brush-off if not his word, Koch never did get back in touch.

Congressman William Fitts Ryan, meanwhile, did announce his candidacy. Wagner cursed the day, for now a primary was certain, as was the need to work harder, earlier.

•   •   •

Others greeted news of the pending Democratic primary with pleasure. For the reform wing, a primary represented a chance to flex their growing muscle. Price in the Lindsay camp was ecstatic. He anticipated no comparable challenge on the GOP side; Rockefeller's state chair, L. Judson Morhouse, would see to that. Only good could come from the opposition cutting each other up, Price believed. The third group elated over Congressman Ryan's announcement of candidacy was the working press. It gave added meaning to their existence. As Nancy put it to Emma, "Journalistic nature abhors a political vacuum."

"Since we're covering the Lindsay campaign," Emma said, "does the split in Democratic ranks mean anything to us?"

"Absolutely," Nancy said. "It alters the dynamics of Lindsay's campaign. Gives him a reason to chime in on any inter-party squabble among the Democrats, which adds to his public profile. In other words, he will get free publicity without any risk of loss. As my Wisconsin farm friends would say, he's likely in hog heaven right now."

"May I ask you something bordering on the personal?" Emma asked.

Nancy nodded. From the outset, she'd challenged the young woman to ask any and all questions.

"If the primary is a good thing, and increased exposure for Lindsay should equate to increased exposure for you, why don't you seem all that happy?"

Nancy's brow creased. "It's one of the two things that most bother me about the job. Professionally, it does make me happy. Personally, it means more time away from my family. You have to really love this business if you want to make a career out of it, Emma, because it exerts quite a toll. Especially for us. If a male reporter leaves early or files a haphazard report because his son has a Little League game he's leaving to watch, that's accepted. If we do it, it shows that women aren't serious enough to succeed in the business world. That's why we make so much less money for the same work. There is an inordinate double standard."

"Do you think it will ever change?"

"Yes, but not in my professional lifetime."

"What's the other thing about the business that annoys you? You said there were two things."

Nancy gave a derisive laugh. "If you're a woman and you win a scoop or do something that's a generally accepted success, you know what they say?"

Emma shook her head.

Nancy affected a mocking male voice, "'She must have slept with someone.' When I scooped everyone with the news last year that Johnson was selecting Hubert Humphrey as his running mate, you would not believe how many people asked me how Hubert was in bed."

"How do you deal with that kind of treatment?"

Nancy shrugged. "Ignore it. If you dignify it with an answer, you bestow credibility on the charge. Although...."

Emma stared at Nancy, who was grinning. "What?"

"The last time I heard that, I did kind of lose my cool. I walked up to the guy who said it and told him if he ever repeated that, I would tie his penis in knots."

Emma laughed. "Wow! How did that work out?"

"Not so good. The jerk got aroused. Do you know how awkward it is to be standing in a roomful of male reporters with one of them at attention before you?"

"How did you handle *that*?"

"I told him he should let his '*little* man' be at ease. That did the trick."

. . .

So as the Democrats strategized and the Lindsayites publicized, the reporters organized. Nancy turned Emma loose to develop her own contacts in the Lindsay camp, then went off to do same. One was easy for Emma to want to cultivate. He was a young post-graduate who was tall, lean, blonde. Looked so much like a younger version of Congressman Lindsay that many people on the campaign trail mistook him for the congressman's son. His name was Jeff Chamberlain, and he was a volunteer set up as a deputy under campaign manager Price. Emma felt her knees wobble the first time she approached him, he was so good looking. Her confidence grew as she noticed his quite open, and interested, appraisal of her own physical attributes, and the two wanna-be's hit it off.

Before one of the rallies started, Nancy watched sparks fly between the two.

When Emma took her seat next to Nancy, just before the congressman was to speak, Nancy whispered, "All that glitters...."

Emma frowned, but said nothing.

"Just be careful," Nancy added. "And choose wisely."

No sooner had Nancy whispered her bit of wisdom than the reporter to Emma's left spilled coffee on Emma's shoe.

"So sorry!" he gushed in a hushed voice. Producing a handkerchief, he mopped Emma's shoe.

While the gesture was kind, Emma also found it a bit creepy at first and was relieved that the reporter did not dab at the drops of coffee that had trickled onto her leg. His press pass identified him as Clark Mackenzie. He was just out of school, in his first year at the *Journal American*. The young man was especially skitterish, though Emma couldn't tell if this was due to his cub reporter status, or whether he always grew tongue-tied around women. He introduced himself to her as "Mark Clackenzie...I mean Clark Clenzie..." before finally getting it right, and spilling more coffee, this time on himself.

His face red, Clark mopped up the mess and then leaned over to greet Nancy, who advised him to invest in rain gear. Emma was pleased to see Clark had a sense of humor and didn't hesitate to laugh at himself. She also noticed that he had an endearingly crooked smile. He was pleasant looking, she noted, immediately comparing him to Jeff. Clark was average in build to Jeff's muscular physique, medium in size to Jeff's tall height, and cute to Jeff's Adonis-like looks. Clark also reminded Emma of someone, but she couldn't quite place it.

As Lindsay finally took the stage, Emma reflected on her good fortune. Not only was she working with a shrewd pioneer in network journalism who had kindly taken her under her wing, but an Adonis in the Lindsay camp fancied her, and she was meeting colleagues like the sincere Clark. Plus, she was on the ground floor of what could be the most exciting election ever.

If only she knew.

. . .

The night of the Lindsay rally, Mayor Wagner and his two sons paid a visit, a very private one. The three knelt in the twilight before a simple stone marker. "Beloved Wife and Mother" read the memorial to Susan Edwards Wagner. When the three stood, the youngest wiped at tears. "I miss her so much, Dad." Robert Wagner hugged his son, Duncan, and then hugged Robert III, also somber but older at 21 and able to hold it in. After a moment, the father asked his boys to wait by the car for the ride back from Woodside, Queens. He wanted a moment alone.

Mayor Wagner fingered his fedora nervously. Susan's death from cancer was still not easy to comprehend. A drawn-out affair, as is common with most cancers, at least it had given them time for a long goodbye. During that period, Susan had asked her husband to do several things such as move on with his life and find another woman. That he had, with the sister of his police commissioner. They were soon to be married. Barbara had been a help, a shoulder to cry on when Susan passed.

The other thing Susan had requested was harder, however. "It's in my bones, Honey," Wagner told her now. "I know I promised...that this would be my last term. But it's all I know. What should I do?"

He looked over to where his son Robert III was comforting his younger brother. Then Wagner turned back to the grave. "All right, I know. The boys need a full-time father now more than ever." He played with the rim of his hat some more, then looked deep into it, his own private felt...if not crystal...ball.

"Yes," he continued, "I'm so tired...so very tired. And things are not lining up right. Besides, when the boys are older and my... marriage with Barbara is settled, I can always run again. With distance, the people will appreciate me even more. Dad always said that happens, especially when he spoke of Harry Truman.

"Don't worry, Susan," he said. "I know what I have to do."

• • •

The next day, the press was summoned to City Hall for a hastily assembled news conference. At her cubicle, Nancy stared at her desk calendar. June 8. She fretted over how to handle this, having gotten the tip from her secret source. Gabe Pressman was aflutter, getting himself ready along with a cameraman for the rushed summons.

"Oh, hell," Nancy muttered. "It's the right thing to do." She bustled out of her cube. "Gabe! A moment, please."

"Don't have much time. Wagner called a press conference. I'm guessing it's his announcement for a fourth term. I have to be there. Funny, though. Deb Myers, Wagner's press secretary, told us the mayor wouldn't field questions after. Something's up."

"Gabe," Nancy said, pulling him aside and lowering her voice, "he's not going to run."

"What!" the young man said. "No way. It's all he knows. Where did you get this?"

"I cannot tell you that, but I have it from an unimpeachable source."

Pressman looked at Nancy suspiciously. "Why don't you go forward with the news?" he said. "It'd be the exclusive of the campaign so far."

She gave a sardonic laugh. "Don't think I wasn't tempted. Wagner is *your* beat, however. If we are to function as a team.... Well, you run with it. Good luck."

Pressman was silent. He nodded, then hurried off.

Over the next hour and a half, Nancy checked with Haller a few times to see if Gabe had phoned in a report. To her puzzlement, he had not.

"Why the concern?" Haller asked, but Nancy waved him off.

"It's nothing."

• • •

At the press conference, members of the press were flummoxed, Pressman only slightly less so, as Robert F. Wagner, 102nd mayor of New York City, announced that under no circumstances would he be a candidate for the mayoralty in 1965. Citing "personal reasons," the mayor kept his statement brief, stopping several times during the session to wipe his eyes.

As soon as Wagner finished speaking, the press fled the room in a stampede. The print journalists phoned in their stories, the afternoons trying desperately to get in under deadline. The radio newsmen called in hastily prepared remarks of scratchy quality, the state of current technology allowing for no more. The television men filed rushed head shots with City Hall in the background, and the camera crews then scurried at warp speed (in a phrase making the rounds from a new NBC sci-fi series, *Star Trek,* whose pilot had just been previewed) to get the reports on air.

• • •

Back in his private office, Wagner ran his handkerchief across his eyes one last time, composing himself. Then his tall city council president embraced him.

"You will go down in history as one of the greats," Paul Screvane quietly consoled the mayor.

"Thank you, Paul. Now it's up to you. Keep up what we've accomplished. Oh, and Paul?"

"Yes, sir?"

"Be sure to win this thing."

Screvane smiled broadly. "Absolutely."

• • •

In Midtown at Lindsay headquarters, Price uncharacteristically hugged John Lindsay. "You chased him out of the race, Jay Vie-el! Now it's Screvane. We run against him the same way, saying he's part of a losing team that's losing the city. And Screvane won't have the advantages of incumbency. Even bookies in Vegas have boosted the odds in your favor!"

. . .

Also in Midtown, a third encounter occurred, one that would entail no embrace or physical contact of any sort for a multitude of reasons. A glum Gabe Pressman stood outside Nancy's cubicle, his hat in hand.

"You didn't run with it." Nancy's voice was ice.

"I thought you might be setting me up."

Both reporters knew there was a lot of gamesmanship in their industry as many journalists believed the best way to get ahead was to tear their competition down.

"I just have one question, Gabe," Nancy said as she looked at him sternly. "If I had done what you've done, what would you be saying to me right now?"

"That it just goes to show a woman's place is not in the newsroom," he said quietly.

At that moment, Arthur Haller happened over. "Nice piece, Gabe. It would have been nicer if we'd scooped the rest of the pack, though. You two keep that in mind as this campaign gears up. I want to flex the muscle of NBC News."

Nancy and Gabe nodded, fully aware that CBS had been the acknowledged leader in network news for years. That was one reason why Nancy was here. She'd been lured from CBS just a few years ago. Gradually, however, NBC News had been bulking up. Edward R. Murrow and his generation at CBS were departing the scene, while NBC's *Huntley-Brinkley Report* was leading the national ratings race. And local NBC newscasts were scoring heavily. This was part of the reason the network had committed resources to the likes of Gabe Pressman and Nancy Dickerson.

"Uh, Arthur," Pressman said, "we did have advance word of Wagner's withdrawal from the race. Nancy did, that is."

Haller's eyes widened and his voice rose a notch, which for him was as close to a temper tantrum as he got. "And you didn't go with it!"

"Arthur, the source wasn't confirmed," Nancy said.

Haller harrumphed unhappily. "All right, carry on, but let's try to get on top of things. By the time I retire, I want CBS well in our rearview mirror."

When Haller was safely out of earshot, Pressman thanked his coworker. "I was wrong about you."

Nancy gave a sly grin. "You mean you didn't think I was a nice person?"

Pressman nodded. "There is that. But what I meant is I didn't think you were as good a reporter as you obviously are." He held out his hand. Nancy took it and they shook, two professionals who in that second had forged what would be a lasting bond.

"You know," Pressman said quietly, "after this, you have my balls in your pocket."

Nancy looked aghast. "Why in the world would I ever want a pair of smelly, sweaty genitals in my pocket?"

"Could come in useful someday."

"For what?" she retorted. "Badminton?"

For the first time in recorded memory, the newsroom was interrupted by gales of laughter emanating from the usually dour Gabe Pressman.

CHAPTER IV

LIKE THE FOUR MARX BROTHERS, BUT WITHOUT THE BRILLIANCE

"Oh my God!" Nancy thought to herself. "He's going to declare for Lindsay!"

"He" was Alex Rose, head of the Liberal Party of the State of New York. Though a statewide party, practically speaking, the Liberals' influence was restricted to the five boroughs of New York City. There was not a lot of far-left sentiment upstate. Indeed, if Republicans like Rockefeller and Javits were to succeed in statewide races, they would have to pull overwhelming majorities upstate, enough to offset the drubbing they would take in the city.

Of course, there were four political parties in the state. Any party polling at least 50,000 votes in the gubernatorial election was accorded on-going ballot position, in relation to their vote standings. Other parties could gain ballot access, but only if they produced the requisite number of petition signatures, a difficult chore. Hence, since Nelson Rockefeller had been elected governor, the Republicans held Row A. The next-highest polling party was the Democrats, who held Row B on the ballots. Then Alex Rose's Liberals. An upstart party, the Conservative Party, had been launched in 1962 largely out of chagrin with Rockefeller's progressivism. Their nominee, David Jaquith, had polled enough votes in the 1962 governor's race to achieve Row D.

Ballot position was considered important. The prevailing view among pundits and politicos was that the electorate was unsophisticated and would vote the first name it saw. Hence the GOP on Row A held a built-in advantage.

Even though it was the third party (there were fringe parties, the Socialists, Socialist Workers, Prohibition, Communist, etc., but they were so far down the line as to be inconsequential), the Liberals had outsized influence. In many important races, they had provided the margin of victory. In the razor-thin Kennedy-Nixon 1960 presidential contest, New York's massive trove of 45 electoral votes went to JFK, who won the Empire State by 400,000 votes—the number of ballots he polled on the Liberal line. The Liberal Party had endorsed Kennedy, as had the Democratic Party. In so many races besides JFK's, the Liberals had provided the difference.

It was not just numbers the Liberals commanded. Donations flowed through their coffers. Moreover, the party leadership, chiefly Alex Rose and his deputy David Dubinsky, were almost without question better strategists than the Democratic or Republican career political technocrats. When Alex Rose spoke, politicians of all stripes listened. When Rose was in your corner, you had best take his advice—if you wanted to win.

The Liberals had come of age with the New Deal, and had been rewarded by FDR with key patronage posts, also a source of their power. Rose shrewdly parlayed his political acumen to secure patronage posts for his followers.

Usually the Liberals supported Democratic candidates, their ideology most often synching up. To the benefit of the Democratic-Liberal alliance, there was no comparable rapprochement between the Republicans and Conservatives. This was due to Rockefeller's firm resolve to crush the rebellion on the right—and the Conservatives' implacable anger over Rocky's derailing of Goldwater's candidacy. Goldwater, after all, was the father of modern conservatism. The only saving grace for the Rockefeller Republicans thus far was that conservatism was as yet a newborn, with barely any muscle to flex. A number of conservative spokesmen were determined to see this change, however.

Most experts, of course, believed the conservative movement moribund after the Goldwater debacle. Indeed, some went so far as to say the Republican Party would face extinction, like the Whigs of old, if they remained yoked to the conservative team.

At this moment, the person delivering the most trenchant analysis of the plight of conservative Republicanism was the most prominent member of the Liberal Party.

Since Haller had mentioned to Nancy that Alex Rose could be the key to the election, she had taken up the bureau chief's recommendation to get to know the Liberal Party kingmaker. A single phone call to one of his handlers got her a meeting the next day. Nancy had interviewed many notable figures, some charming (JFK), some coarse (LBJ), some randy (both JFK and LBJ), some colorless (Nixon), and some quite intelligent (Adlai Stevenson). Rarely was she as captivated as she was by Alex Rose's command of his state's political scene.

"You know why there's so much excitement over Lindsay?" the kingmaker asked Nancy rhetorically midway into their meeting in his sparse office. "'Cause if he can win in the city, that creates a blueprint for Republicans everywhere. They will no longer be restricted to finding candidates who appeal to the rural or suburban areas. A Republican who can carry the cities would be an unstoppable force."

"Is John Lindsay that man?" Nancy asked.

"Could be. He does have liberal instincts, which any Republican would have to have to be a potent vote-getting force in the urban areas. You've seen his ADA score?"

Nancy had and knew Rose was referring to the Americans for Democratic Action, a far-left group that rated congressmen and senators based on their votes on progressive issues. Lindsay ran well ahead of most Democrats on social issues. Moreover, though not a leading voice, he was one of the few to come out against the Vietnam War.

"You sound like you're flirting with Congressman Lindsay," Nancy tossed out.

The elder strategist smiled. "Are you flirting with me, Mrs. Dickerson?"

Nancy batted her lashes coyly, and both laughed. "You always supported Mayor Wagner," she continued.

"Mayor Wagner was good to us. Reliably liberal in his policies, and he rewarded us with enough jobs and influence in his administration. Had he stayed in the race, we would have supported him still. I believe in loyalty, Mrs. Dickerson."

"And now?"

"Now, Mr. Wagner is not in the race."

"And Mr. Screvane is his heir apparent."

"Is he?" Rose's eyes twinkled mischievously.

"Does that mean you are not supporting Screvane?"

"I have not spoken to him yet."

"Really!" Nancy was dumbfounded. Screvane had not asked for Rose's support! "Perhaps he assumes it."

"You know what they say about assuming?"

Nancy nodded. "It can make an ass out of u and me. Well."

"Look," Rose explained, "let's just say the Liberal Party is actively looking at all the candidates."

"You're intrigued by Lindsay, however...?"

Another enigmatic smile. "This off the record...?"

Nancy again nodded.

"It would be fascinating to take a step that alters the dynamic of Republican politics, and politics in general, for a generation. Imagine if both parties became dedicated liberal, progressive parties, and the Republicans severed any dalliance with the conservatives."

Nancy thought about it. "Imagine, indeed."

Nancy left the meeting with Rose resolved to find another way to corroborate what he'd told her so she could go public and yet not violate the confidence she'd agreed to honor with the Liberal Party chieftain.

That afternoon, Nancy shared the news that Screvane had not asked for Rose's support with only one other person, Emma, and encouraged her young assistant to try to find out more from any ties she could develop in the Lindsay campaign. One thing Nancy did uncover as she worked the phones, calling her growing number of New York contacts as well as people she trusted in Washington, was that—unlike Screvane—Bob Price had met with Alex Rose several times already since the Wagner withdrawal.

That weekend, Nancy did not return to Northern Virginia. Dick and the children visited her for the long-promised visit to the World's Fair.

Dick and Nancy enjoyed the Fair, and were fairly blown away by some of the futuristic exhibits. They found it doubly pleasing, however, to see the Fair through the eyes of their children. John was actually open-mouthed at many of the halls, so staggering in scope was the entertainment, at least in a small child's eyes.

It was not hard to tell that what most intrigued the youngster was the State of Illinois pavilion. The chief attraction there was a robotic Abraham Lincoln who moved and spoke his iconic words of the ages. It was as if Lincoln still lived, which in some sense he did. Though it was Illinois-sponsored, the exhibit (as with many at the World's Fair) had been developed by the Walt Disney Company.

Nancy knew of Disney, of course. He was a familiar household face, the avuncular host of *The Wonderful World of Disney* each Sunday night, which both John and Jane watched without fail. Nancy was surprised that Disney had built his empire essentially from a mouse. And she had to admit what Disney called the audioanimatronic Lincoln (the kids could not pronounce the word; Jane kept saying "audio-aminalman") was a spectacular technological achievement.

A better world through technology was the theme of the Fair. Some of the promises of the future seemed fanciful. Like the Carousel of Progress, also Disney-inspired, which suggested everyone one day would have color televisions and be able to communicate through small screens.

Aside from the emphasis on technology, the Fair had some of the usual hallmarks of a major festival. Bucket rides, souvenir hawkers, food stalls. John and Jane tried a new food for the first time that was fast becoming the culinary sensation of the Fair: Belgian waffles topped with ice cream. Dick and Nancy wondered where they could purchase a waffle iron. The Unisphere was the central point of the Fair, a sculptural marvel that Nancy believed and hoped would survive when the Fair was long gone. She rather hoped it would not get torn down to provide more parking for the state-of-the-art stadium that had just opened, Shea Stadium, home of the baseball Mets and the football Jets.

As enjoyable as the futuristic exhibits were, the one exhibit that registered the deepest impact on Nancy had the least to do with technology. She was mesmerized in the Vatican pavilion, where Michelangelo's "Pieta" was on display. "How do you make that?" she marveled, to which Dick said, "Don't ask me; I can't even draw stickmen."

While the beauty of the sculpture captivated Nancy, the right side of her brain pondered a different facet of the Vatican's contribution to the Fair. Namely, the fact that the "Pieta" was here at all.

"I wonder why the Catholic Church would risk harm to one of the crown jewels of Christendom?" she said.

"It had to have been highly insured," Dick surmised.

"Fat lot of good the insurance proceeds would do if tragedy struck and Michelangelo's masterpiece was at the bottom of the Atlantic."

"Maybe it's part of the new Church," Dick said.

"Lord knows we could use that."

Though she still attended Mass and said the rosary, Nancy had strayed from her strict Catholic upbringing. Somehow it seemed to her that the Church with its antiquated dictatorial methods was losing its relevance. And as the polls showed, she was far from alone in this regard. Not by a long shot. Such a shame, Nancy thought. For the essence of the Church's teaching, the message of love, was one the world desperately needed. Yet the Catholic Church had lost itself, as well as thousands of followers, by supplanting ritualism for love. Maybe there was hope. Good Pope John, who had recently passed away after a bout with cancer, had thrown open the windows to let fresh air into his creaking edifice. The council he'd called promised many things. Rumor had it that the priests would stop turning their backs to the congregation, figuratively and literally, and would say Mass in each country's native language. A modern Church? "I'll believe it when I see it," Nancy had told Dick. Though she remained transfixed by the spiritual ardor that had inspired the "Pieta."

On Sunday afternoon when her family's visit ended, Nancy wiped at a tear as she watched their train leave Penn Station—and kept watching until it was completely vanished from her sight. Taking solace in the fact that she had only five months until this assignment was over, she had a quiet dinner that evening and then read an Allen Drury novel about the machinations of political Washington until sleep came.

Bright and early the next morning, Nancy and Emma headed out to see labor leader Harry Van Arsdale, who was allied with Screvane. Nancy wanted to get some perspective by looking into the opposition camps. Though she was covering Lindsay, she felt that understanding the other candidates could only enhance her reporting on Lindsay campaign developments. As a matter of fact, she and Gabe had agreed to an exchange of sorts for the week, so each could peek into the tents on the other side. Their newfound friendship had also led Gabe to share with Nancy insights into the Screvane campaign, and into the other Democratic campaigns.

Gabe had imparted three valuable nuggets to Nancy so far. For one, Screvane was supremely confident of victory, a sentiment shared by pundits all over the city. This included the Lindsay brain trust, which was taking aim in its daily pronouncements at the city council president. Indeed, largely because of his optimism that Screvane would emerge from the pack, Bob Price had adopted a slight mid-course correction. He was now going after the Jewish vote. New York City Jews were notoriously liberal in their outlook and tribal in their voting patterns. Without an incumbent and since Screvane was not a member of the tribe, Price believed Lindsay's liberalism left him well positioned to grab a goodly percentage of traditionally Democratic Jewish voters. Significant resources had already been funneled into this initiative.

Gabe's second tidbit was that there was not much going on in Screvane-land. The camp's chief strategists had assured their candidate that effort now was effort wasted. People would not pay attention until after Labor Day. No need to waste resources on the primary, since Screvane's nomination was assured. "Save your energy, Paul," one of his top aides emphasized, "we're going to need it to go after Lindsay." With Wagner's withdrawal, Lindsay had eked slightly ahead of Screvane in the polls.

Third, Gabe told Nancy, the reason for such supreme confidence was reliance on the powerful Democratic machine. Screvane and all knowledgeable insiders knew that the combined party and labor coalition could deliver bucketloads of votes at the drop of a hat. It was thus virtually impossible for an insurgent to topple the establishment candidate.

Screvane and his people were keeping things so under wraps it was hard to schedule time alone with any of them.

"Mostly they sit around evenings at the club, talking about how they're going to win," Gabe confided.

"Perhaps they should get out of the club and do something about it, instead," Nancy suggested.

Gabe agreed but allowed as to how he could understand Screvane's desire to marshal his energy for the general election campaign. The veteran, though still young, reporter advised Nancy to talk to one of the labor leaders. They would be more likely to open up and would be more available. Hence Nancy and Emma's session with Van Arsdale.

The head of the electrical workers' union repeated the party line: that Screvane as heir apparent to Wagner held the loyalties of the machine—and as such was sure to be the winner. This was the reason why the unions would support Screvane: because they wanted to be with a winner. That and the expectation that, as under Wagner and other victorious Democrats, Big Labor stood to be rewarded come municipal contract time for its fealty.

"Do you think the entire traditional Democratic coalition will line up behind Mr. Screvane?" Nancy asked.

Van Arsdale opined that they would.

"How about the Liberals?"

"Of course."

Nancy had to tread carefully. She wanted to inquire as to the source of Screvane's optimism, but she could not do it in a way that tipped them off to Alex Rose's inclinations, thereby violating his confidence.

"Is it not dangerous to take any bloc for granted?" she said.

"Not in this case," Van Arsdale answered smugly. "Who else the Liberals going to support? Not Lindsay. You ever heard of a liberal endorsing a Republican? That's just crazy talk. Next you'll be telling me we could get a non-Italian pope or a Negro president."

"It could happen," Nancy said.

"Not in my lifetime. Probably not in anyone's." Van Arsdale shrugged. "Look, Screvane's gonna' inherit the Wagner coalition intact. Negroes, Jews, Labor, old New Deal Democrats, Liberals. Wagner's allies will just transfer over to Paul. Should be easy enough for him to win."

Nancy commented that, in her experience, one's enemies readily transferred, but not so one's friends.

"Trust me. They got nowhere else ta' go. The reformers? Gimme a break. Those two clowns..." (Nancy knew the union leader was talking about Ryan and O'Dwyer, a late entrant) "...are out in left field. They're not serious candidates. An' Beame? He's just a schmuck. No, Screvane will win in a cake walk. It'll be like Wagner's fourth term. You want proof? Bobby Kennedy is supportin' Screvane. You ever know the Kennedys to back a loser?"

Nancy had to admit she did not. From what she knew of Senator Kennedy, his backing of Screvane was mildly surprising. She made a mental note to check on this.

Van Arsdale went on to extol his candidate's virtues. Much of it came out of the campaign's brochures, but Nancy gave him his leash. Let him wax poetic if it made him happy, she reasoned. Admittedly, the 51-year-old candidate did have some of the rags-to-riches aura. Screvane had been forced to drop out of college and find employment when his mother became seriously ill. The best job he could land was as an eighteen-dollar-a-week clerk. This was hardly a satisfactory sinecure, so when Screvane's uncle urged him to apply for a job with the city sanitation department, Screvane did so with alacrity. The job was driving a garbage truck, but the pay was double his current salary. More importantly, the department promoted based on merit tests. Confident in his own abilities, Screvane saw opportunity for rapid advancement.

This did in fact occur, with a helpful break in service while Screvane served his country in the Second World War. Going in a private and coming out a colonel with a Silver Star and two Bronze Stars said a lot about the future city council president.

True to form, the young vet rose rapidly once he was back at Sanitation. So much so that he caught Mayor Wagner's eye. The mayor appointed Screvane commissioner, the youngest in Sanitation history. From there, he was an easy choice when Wagner cast about for a new, competent running mate. Hence Screvane's elevation to the city council presidency and his current status as Wagner's heir apparent. There had been a few occasions when Wagner went on vacations with his family that Screvane served as acting mayor, stamping him in the public mind as next in line for the mayoralty when Wagner departed the scene.

On the way out of Van Arsdale's office, Emma reflected to Nancy on Screvane's admirable traits. "Self-made man, war hero, capable public servant. Do you think Van Arsdale is right about his elevation being a foregone conclusion?"

Nancy smoothed a stray lock of hair away from her face. "One funny thing about politics, Emma. In our system of government, it is not a meritocracy."

"Meaning?"

"Meaning who knows what will strike the public fancy. If elections were decided solely on merit, Nixon would have crushed Kennedy, the former vice president's resume was so superior. But the people were taken with JFK."

"So you think Screvane will lose?"

"I did not say that. I think he has his work cut out for him. A lot of people are unhappy with the current administration. If Mr. Screvane is campaigning as the heir apparent, well, he's going to have to take the bad with the good."

• • •

Later in the day at a Lindsay event, Nancy and Emma met up with Gabe. To Nancy's inquiry about Robert Kennedy's support of Screvane, Gabe replied that the city council president had served as co-chair of Kennedy's senate campaign the previous year. "It's probably a loyalty thing," he said.

"The Kennedys are loyal only to a point," Nancy replied. "Loyalty stops when self-interest overrides. I wonder why the senator is taking an interest in this campaign."

Gabe said he'd like to know as well. Unfortunately, he added, although he'd covered the Kennedy-Keating race last year, he didn't have warm and fuzzy ties with RFK or his people. "I'd like to get closer to Bobby," he noted.

Nancy smiled. "It might help if you didn't refer to him as 'Bobby.' He much prefers 'Bob'."

Gabe was noticeably impressed. "You know him that well?"

"We're not best buds or anything, but yes, we have a reasonably good relationship. I dealt with him several times when I was at the White House when his brother was president. He and Ethel have also been to several of the parties Dick and I have thrown, and in turn we've been to Hickory Hill (RFK's Northern Virginia estate)."

"Say no more," Gabe instructed, urging Nancy to arrange a session with the senator. When she agreed, Gabe requested that she attend.

"So you can ride my coattails?" she asked with a smirk.

Gabe nodded. "Absolutely."

Nancy got a charge out of one other person she and Emma happened upon at the Lindsay event. Clark Mackenzie from the *Journal American* was there. He did not spill anything this time, chiefly because he was not holding a cup. He was still quite nervous, though. He was also polite but brief with Nancy. Clark had something else on his mind. "Happy Birthday!" he gushed to Emma, producing a single red rose for her.

"How sweet!" she said, pleased to accept the flower. "How did you know? I haven't told anyone."

This was a statement for which Nancy could vouch. She wished Emma many happy returns and told the intern that after the event, she should quit early and go out to enjoy her day.

"I don't have anything special planned," Emma said.

Clark gestured as though he was about to suggest something, but then Congressman Lindsay made his appearance, prompting the reporters to prepare to ask questions along with the rest of the working press. Nancy, who got in a few to the congressman, took extensive notes related to Lindsay's answers to hers and other reporters' questions.

When the crowd began to dwindle, Jeff Chamberlain approached. "What gives with the flower?" he asked Emma. "Special occasion?

Emma explained it was her birthday, leading Jeff to announce they should go out for an early happy hour. Turning toward two shapely blonde women who had been trailing in his wake, Jeff excused himself, then offered Emma his arm and walked with her out of the event space.

Nancy glanced at Clark as he quietly walked away. Then she shook her head and called it a day as well.

. . .

The next morning at work, Nancy asked Emma how her evening had been.

"Great!" the intern answered, stifling a yawn.

"Late night?"

"I guess you could say that," she said, this time giving a full-fledged yawn.

Nancy kept her gaze on Emma, so much so that the younger woman grew uncomfortable.

"Don't worry," Emma offered. "I'll function fine today. I've pulled all-nighters at school and was good as gold the next day."

"No, it's not that," Nancy replied. "Emma, you know I only have your best interests at heart, right?"

"Yes, and I'm so grateful."

"Well, this borders on the personal, but it's important. After you have a night of...intimacy...be sure to wear a high collar."

Emma's hand flew to her neck, where two red hickies were in plain sight. She reddened immediately. "We....we weren't intimate. Just a lot of necking."

"No matter. You know men will seize on anything to demonstrate we're not fit to occupy their world. And I mean anything. Do not give them any ammunition."

"I...I can't change now. My clothes are at home. Maybe I can cover it with make-up."

"Doesn't work. I tried...when I was thirteen. Caught holy hell from my mother. Hmm...." Nancy fiddled in her drawer and came out with a scarf.

"Always keep a silk scarf handy," she said, handing it over. "They are always in style. They dress you up, dress you down, and can hide something."

Emma tied the scarf around her neck, noting that she and Jeff had also talked volumes about the campaign during their celebration of her birthday. "He's not only convinced Lindsay will win, he sees him in the White House in '72. After LBJ's second term." That presumed Johnson's reelection, which would be in 1968. "He let me know if I played my cards right, I could be with him. Jeff fully expects to have a top position in the Lindsay presidency."

"My, my," Nancy proclaimed. "Aren't we getting a little ahead of ourselves? Perhaps they should go ask President Dewey how it all worked out."

"You don't see Congressman Lindsay making it all the way?"

Nancy shrugged. "Who's to say? Right now, he's just three points ahead in the polls, so the mayoralty is hardly a sure thing. Then he has to do well as mayor. Win a second term. By 1972, there may be other Republicans who have different ideas about who should occupy the Oval Office. Look at 1960. Kennedy won, but along the way he had to battle better known rivals. Johnson, Humphrey, Stevenson, Symington, and a dozen favorite sons hoping for lightning to strike. At some point, I am sure they each believed in their inevitability. The Lindsay people shouldn't put the cart before the horse."

Emma said that at least by 1972, after a dozen years of Democratic rule, the country would be ready for another Republican.

Nancy raised her eyebrows. "Who knows what will be in 1972? That's seven years from now, an eternity in both dog years and in politics. I'm sure on November 21, 1963 a lot of people would have assumed John Kennedy's reelection to be a foregone conclusion."

"But his assassination was such a fluke."

"The killing, yes, but not the tug of unexpected events. In the world of today, change is the universal constant."

Emma smiled as she took out her notepad.

"What?" Nancy asked, amused by the intern's reaction.

"You toss out these great pearls of wisdom so offhandedly. I have to begin jotting them down. Any other words of wisdom for right now?" Emma asked, her pen poised.

Nancy shrugged again and then said with a smile, "Always moisturize before bed...and always carve out private time for just you and your husband."

As the two burst out laughing, a number of heads in the newsroom popped up to see the cause of the frivolity. The heads, all male, then shook as if to say, "Women are so un-businesslike."

Nancy sat back in her chair. "There's nothing wrong with enjoying yourself while you work," she said, loudly for others to hear. Then, in a lower voice, she said to Emma, "These people take themselves entirely too seriously." She wrote something on a piece of paper. Handing it to Emma, she told her to read it out loud.

Emma was so taken aback that, in spite of herself, she blurted out in an unintentionally louder than normal voice, "Penis enhancers!" Only to find two dozen pairs of male ears trained above the cubicles in her direction—while Nancy studiously made the pretext of fiddling with her typewriter.

At last Nancy looked up...right into the eyes of Gabe Pressman. "Did you say something?" he asked.

"We were just talking about my cousin back in Wisconsin," Nancy answered. "Enos Perganser. Why? What did you think I said?"

"Uh, nothing," Gabe said as his and all other ears in the newsroom dipped back beneath the partitions. Emma, meanwhile, was bent over in silent hysterics, tears streaming from her eyes.

· · ·

The day's schedule had Nancy and Emma first with reform candidate William Fitts Ryan and then with the new entrant, reform candidate Paul O'Dwyer. Then they'd interview the last of the Democratic contenders, the current city comptroller Abraham D. Beame.

Congressman William Fitts Ryan had a reliably progressive record, just one reason why he appealed to the newly established reform movement. The other was the fact that he'd won election several times to the House. This represented a sterling credential, inasmuch as the reformers seemed to be interested only in making a statement. Success at the polls did not matter. Of course, that could have been so much grist for the mill. The reform movement was so much in its infancy, it was unable to win anything. Hence, when one reformer did improbably win, as had been the case with Ryan, his luster in reform circles jumped astronomically.

The other factor aiding Ryan as a prominent member in the movement was the fact that the progressives were currently bereft of leadership. As noted earlier, the two iconic figures, Eleanor Roosevelt and Herbert Lehman, had passed recently, and no one had yet emerged to take their place.

The interview began with Nancy asking Congressman Ryan what he considered to be the most important issue of the day. She expected the candidate to choose from prominent issues such as inadequate housing, the budget crisis, or even juvenile delinquency. What he said, though, was "the Negro problem."

From Ryan's voting record, this did not surprise Nancy at all. Nor did the fact that, as a Northeastern liberal, the congressman's approach was sympathetic. A Southern congressman could indeed agree there was a "Negro problem," but he would see it as the federal government meddling and not allowing the old Confederacy to coordinate race relations as "God intended it to be," meaning keeping the races separate and the darkies in their place. Or, as a Southern California congressman might have spoken of the "Negro problem" after the previous summer's Watts rioting, it involved blacks being unreasonable and demanding "too much, too soon," leading to disastrous results, as burnt-out areas of LA could attest. No, when Congressman Ryan spoke of the "Negro problem," to him it meant the plight of a race downtrodden for three hundred years and the need to redress same as soon as practicable.

So what surprised Nancy was not Ryan's placing the "Negro problem" as issue number one, nor his sensitivity on matters of race. What came as an unwelcome surprise was the congressman's sheer volubility on the issue. Not content to simply respond to her query with a short answer, or even a brief explanatory description appended to his short answer, Ryan went on. And on. And on.

Ordinarily reporters appreciate a certain amount of loquaciousness from their subjects. The press derides parsimony in speech because it usually presages a tough interview. The textbook illustration was the taciturn Calvin Coolidge. The country's thirtieth president was noted for his economy with words. Once at a formal function, his dinner companion playfully told Silent Cal, "I bet a friend I could get you to say more than two words."

"You lose," Coolidge replied before going back to his soup.

The reason reporters appreciate volubility is it renders their task so much easier. The more an interviewee talks, the more some newsworthy nugget is apt to get tossed out.

Not so this time with Congressman Ryan, however. His remarks following his mention of the "Negro problem" led into a recitation of facts and figures comparing racial income disparity, education statistics, housing, sentencing, and a gamut of other collateral points. Nor were there anecdotes to liven the talk. No warmth and no personality whatsoever. Just a monotone recitation of facts that went on for so long. There was no doubt Ryan was sympathetic to racial causes and was knowledgeable of the issue; it's just that there was no passion in his presentation.

When he was at last mercifully done, Nancy dreaded bringing up any other issues, for she sensed, correctly, that Ryan would go on in a similar long-winded fashion as he addressed each one.

Hence nearly two hours slogged on as Nancy and Emma fought the urge to mentally nod off.

• • •

After visiting Ryan, Nancy and Emma rode the subway to O'Dwyer's office, still recovering from their latest interview.

"I wanted to put knitting needles in my eyes to force myself awake," Nancy complained.

"Thank God!" Emma said. "I thought maybe it was just me."

"He might be the most boring person I've ever interviewed," Nancy added. "Check that. In my early days, I had to do a bit with Smokey the Bear, who didn't talk at all."

"That was worse than what we just went through?"

"I'm not sure," Nancy said, shaking her head. "All I know is if we'd shot Ryan at the outset of the interview, by now with good behavior we'd be set free."

Emma laughed. "He does seem to know his stuff."

"If intelligence was the sine qua non of elective office, Einstein would have been president," Nancy remarked. "There is a wonderful book by a professor, Richard Neustadt, that I recommend to you. It's on presidential leadership, and in it Professor Neustadt says that 'power is the power to persuade.' I fear Congressman Ryan will never persuade people with his approach. Do you know who preceded Abraham Lincoln on the dais at Gettysburg?"

Emma did not.

"Edward Everett, a noted orator of the day. He spoke for over two hours. Then Lincoln stood and in 238 words gave an address that will be remembered for the ages." Nancy gazed wistfully ahead as she repeated, "Power is the power to persuade."

"So you don't think Ryan can win?" Emma asked.

"Not unless it's for mayor of an insomniacs' convention."

• • •

At Paul O'Dwyer's office, neither Nancy nor Emma knew quite what to expect next. Both were pleasantly surprised at first when they met the charming and entertaining white-haired councilman-at-large.

O'Dwyer's elder brother, Bill, who had once been mayor, by all accounts had run a particularly venal, ineffective administration. Yet this brother's apple apparently fell far from that tree. To the contrary, Paul was known as a "goo-goo," the term in vogue for "good government" types.

In addition to the younger O'Dwyer's genuinely reformist instincts, Nancy and Emma were immediately impressed by his personality. The politician still had a touch of his old Irish brogue...and a bit of the blarney about him. Were this New England instead of New York, he could have been a character in *The Last Hurrah,* a bestselling novel penned in the late 1950s about Boston Irish politicos.

"So good to see a working lass," O'Dwyer said with a chuckle as he shook Nancy's hand. With an older man's harmless leer at Emma he added, "And a pretty Colleen, to boot."

Nancy explained they had just come from Ryan's office. O'Dwyer asked if Ryan had talked about the issues of the day, specifically rising crime, pollution, substandard education, civil rights, and the financial crisis. When Nancy indicated he had, O'Dwyer made a show of looking at his watch. "Ah, it's grand you were able to make it here at all. I would've thought to cover those topics it would've taken Congressman Ryan at least eight days. Yes, he's quite a remarkable man. Even God had to rest on the seventh day."

Nancy and Emma laughed knowingly.

Turning serious, O'Dwyer acknowledged that all the issues raised by his reform rival were valid. Moreover, the two held virtually identical positions. Which begged the question: why enter the race, if Ryan was already in?

"I'm a man of the people; it's in me bones," came the enigmatic reply.

Nancy asked if O'Dwyer believed he could deliver on the issues more effectively than Ryan. She wanted to toss this likeable man a lifeline so he could express some reason for running.

"Fer sure! Fer sure!" was all he offered.

Opting for a different route, Nancy tried for more specificity. She selected a precise issue. Education. How, she asked, would Mr. O'Dwyer deal with the mess in the public school system?

"As the kids today say, we are going to rock and roll!" he said with a chortle, then accompanied the pronouncement with a little jig.

"But what specifically will you do?" Nancy persisted.

"Ah, young lady, like I said, we are going to rock and roll!"

"Yes, Mr. O'Dwyer, but what exactly does that mean?"

"Ah, as my own sainted mother used to say, it's the working lasses who ask the best questions. You just wait and see that we are going to rock and roll!"

The rest of the interview went much the same way. Rock and roll may be here to stay, but it was only one of the buzz words or phrases O'Dwyer relied upon to express substantive policy points. Of necessity, the session was abbreviated. There is only so much a journalist can do with bromides such as rocking and rolling, the "slow gin fizz," "que sera sera," or "the luck o' the Irish."

Finally outside the jovial councilman's office, Emma remarked that O'Dwyer seemed to be the exact opposite of Ryan. "One guy is all specifics and no personality, and the other is all personality but no substance. Could O'Dwyer really do the job as mayor?"

Nancy gave her assistant an "Oh, honestly" look. "There's an old Groucho Marx line. 'Don't be confused by first impressions; this man really is an idiot.'"

"What's next?" Emma asked as they headed to their last stop.

"After hear no evil, see no evil, speak no evil?" Nancy quipped. "All that is left is evil."

As it turned out, city comptroller, Wagner gadfly and Democrat mayoral aspirant Abraham D. Beame was not evil personified. Actually, he came across as quite a nice man. Emma later told Nancy he reminded her of an old Jewish tailor her father had frequented in her younger days. Nancy had no frame of reference, as the Jewish residents of Wisconsin when she grew up had been outnumbered by the elk. Emma persisted that Abe Beame could just as easily wear a tape measure around his neck and hold pins in his mouth as don a suit. To her mind he was a warm, vaguely appealing figure.

To Beame, the issues that mattered most to him were the financial crisis and the better execution of Wagner's initiatives. As comptroller, Beame declared, he had the best experience to handle both.

With respect to the city's finances, Beame was troubled that, with the middle class tax base emigrating to suburbia, businesses voting with their feet, and the cost of social services rising, Wagner had resorted to bond issuance and budgetary gimmickry to balance his budget. To Beame, this had represented a recipe for fiscal collapse.

"How would you counter that?" Nancy asked.

"We have to live within our means," Beame said, "and if need be, go to the federal and state governments for greater assistance."

Nancy asked if it was realistic that the feds would add to their own financial woes by forking over money to the city of New York.

"Sure. They're not going to tell New York to drop dead. The strength of the country is bound up with the solvency of New York City."

"Would you cut services?"

"Not at this time. We need to attract people and businesses to the city, not risk losing them by reducing services."

He extolled aspects of his job as comptroller, which Beame believed set him apart as the man who could best manage the diverse city governmental bureaucracy.

Soliciting for federal handouts and managing effectively were hardly clarion calls to lure voters to join a crusade, however. Nor was Beame physically compelling. He was very short of stature. Even standing, he appeared to be seated. And his voice was unprepossessing, in stark contrast to the charismatic Lindsay's voice. The three things Beame had going for him was his tweaking of the Wagner record or, as he kept up the refrain, "the Wagner-Screvane administration." Point number two was that Beame had the solid backing of his native Brooklyn party organization, along with elements of the Bronx that were dissatisfied with Wagner for his affront four years ago. Finally Beame, if elected, would be the city's first Jewish mayor, and thus he expected that potent voting bloc to be solidly in his corner.

At the end of their allotted time, Comptroller Beame made a memorable peroration. "This city has been good to me. It has educated me, given me a home and a career. I want to return something to the city I love."

Afterward, as she walked with Nancy back toward their subway stop, Emma said, "Nice man, but is he a match for Screvane—or Lindsay?"

"Probably not," Nancy surmised, "but of the three anti-establishment candidates, he has the best chance of making inroads." After a pause, Nancy asked Emma her opinion of the four Democratic candidates.

Emma smiled. "Remember when you mentioned Groucho Marx? None of these four is especially impressive. They're like the four Marx Brothers, but without the brilliance."

Nancy agreed it was a sad commentary on the current state of political leadership.

After they'd walked a while, Emma queried, "A penny for your thoughts?"

Nancy sighed. "I'll be glad to return to the Lindsay campaign. There's much more excitement there. Yet I wish... something would transpire to ignite more interest in this campaign."

CHAPTER V

CONSERVATIVELY SPEAKING, I EXPECT TO GET ONE VOTE

At Rock Center, Arthur Haller looked out at what the reporters had taken to calling the "nights of the round table." This was a play on three things: the recent Broadway hit *Camelot*, NBC's own bureau chief "King Arthur"(Haller), and the fact that—in preparing for the evening newscast and the next morning's *Today* show—NBC reporters often labored into the night. For what it was worth, the table in Arthur's conference room was rectangular.

Arthur sat at the head, flanked by Gabe and Nancy, the two reporters formally assigned to cover the political beat. Other correspondents were there who covered the different, non-political areas of the news. All had a finger on the pulse of the city, so Arthur asserted that occasionally taking their temperature was a sound news-gathering practice. This meeting was only for the elite of the reporters; interns were not invited.

The lead reporter, who covered international affairs and by nature was an arrogant SOB, looked down his nose at the newcomer. "Nancy," he said in his affected upper-class accent, "why don't you act as scrivener for the group?"

Before Nancy or Arthur could say anything, Gabe interjected, "She's not your note taker, Jerome. Take your own effin' notes."

Jerome gave a look of marked disgust. "As you wish," for he had no desire to wrestle with the likes of street fighter Gabe.

The meeting was brief. The consensus was that Lindsay was the most exciting opposition candidate to emerge in many a year. That while the Democrats had a battle on their hands, by dint of electoral demographics, they were likely to prevail. And that Screvane was likely to be the next mayor by virtue of his inheritance of most of the Democratic machine and other parts of the Wagner coalition.

Afterward, Nancy thanked Gabe for leaping to her defense. The two, along with Emma, were headed to an important meeting. Gabe also had an intern for the duration of the campaign, but the lad was conflicted with another meeting Gabe had asked him to cover. Emma felt for the intern; she had long desired to see Bobby Kennedy. Even Gabe seemed a tad nervous as they entered the district office of the state's junior senator.

To their amazement, Kennedy greeted Nancy with an affectionate kiss on the cheek. "How are you?" he said with a grin.

"All the better for seeing you," Nancy replied with a ready smile of her own.

Kennedy then asked after her children and husband, and she in turn mentioned his family.

"Don't ask about all my kids," he jested. "Our household is larger than some third-world countries."

As Emma glanced around the senator's office, she was struck by the photographs that adorned it. Most politicians displayed pictures of themselves with presidents, popes, kings and assorted potentates. A testament to their vanity, if not their importance. Aside from a single framed portrait of himself with his brother Jack, the late President Kennedy, the senator's cluster of photographs depicted him with no other notables. Instead, one showed him alongside two Negroes in what appeared to be a tenement building, another showed him looking with concern at a malnourished child, and another showed him embracing Chicano farm laborers.

"The Senate? It agrees with you?" Nancy began. Kennedy had taken his seat just six months ago after a bruising, uphill battle for election.

"Sometimes I am tempted to give it back to your old beau," Kennedy quipped. His predecessor, the man he had defeated, was Kenneth Keating. Ironically, Nancy had dated Keating when he was a congressman and she had first arrived in Washington back in the '50s. Kennedy explained. "We don't do anything. Just a lot of talk. I'm more used to being at the center of the action." He had in fact been an activist attorney general and, as his brother's confidante, had been viewed as the true number two power player in Washington.

"It sounds like you crave executive responsibility," Gabe inserted. "Perhaps a return to the White House...in your own right?"

Kennedy looked wistful. "I don't know. I don't know. I don't know. Perhaps. Johnson (he almost spat out the name of the man he viewed as usurping his brother's rightful place) is likely to be reelected in '68. By '72...who knows where we will all be?" The senator shook his head. "Besides, Johnson hates me so much, he'll go to any lengths to stand in my way."

Nancy indicated the photos Emma had earlier observed. "You have a way with people. If they support you, no one's maneuvering can stop you."

Kennedy again looked wistful. "I don't know how much their support is for *me*, Nancy. I think really when they see me, they see Jack."

Nancy's voice expressed sympathy. "We are all still unable to get over it. He touched our lives."

Kennedy nodded. "What did the Greek poets say? 'Even in our sleep pain that cannot forget, falls drop by drop upon the heart and in our own despair, against our will, comes wisdom to us by the awful grace of God.'" He was silent then. Nancy had heard Bob sought solace in poetry and in some of the writings of the existentialists. Very gently, she said the purpose of the visit was to discuss the upcoming mayoral campaign.

That stirred Kennedy from his reverie. "Yes," he said, which sounded in his Massachusetts accent like 'Yaas.' "There is a very tough battle brewing in Corning, the small upstate New York city." Those in the office smiled at his humor.

Gabe got them back on track. "It surprised us that you would have a stake in this. Could it be that, as mayor, John Lindsay would be a potential rival down the road, and this is a way to head that off?"

Kennedy gave a wan smile. He looked at Emma. "Another one," he motioned to Gabe, "who thinks I'm ruthless. I'm really not that bad. At least my dog, Freckles, seems to know that." Then the senator grew serious. "This is not about Congressman Lindsay. Not really. No, this is about the Democratic Party, not the Republicans. I believe it's important to have control over the state party. Up to now, my only rival for influence has been Mayor Wagner. But with his departure, that leaves a void which I intend to fill. Controlling the party apparatus would be useful in selecting candidates who fit the Kennedy mold."

"Or in corralling a bloc of delegates at a future national convention?" Nancy suggested.

Kennedy gave a wry smile. "There is that."

"But why Screvane?" Gabe asked.

Nancy joined in. "Your politics seems to place your sympathies with the reformist factions."

Kennedy raised both his hands in a gesture of disgust. "Those reformers! Politics is about power. Action. Getting things done. This New York group is only interested in making a statement. I can't seem to get through to them.

"Look," he continued, "Screvane is not my ideal candidate. But he represents our best chance of winning. And I would rather have the mayor of New York, who will be the second-highest ranking elected Democratic official in this state, in my tent rather than outside."

"You know," Nancy said, smiling but with some trepidation, "that sounds exactly like something Lyndon Johnson would say."

Kennedy returned the smile. "Then perhaps I'd better reassess my position." He ran his hand through his hair. Emma noticed it seemed even longer in person than on camera. The length of the junior senator's hair often inspired barbs from those who felt it was not statesmanlike to adopt "hippie fashions."

Kennedy then turned to Gabe and, to Gabe's profound appreciation, made small talk for a moment, trying to find out more about the reporter's background, family and interests. Gabe had read of Kennedy's fondness for journalists and did not mind in the least being cultivated by a future president. He owed a huge debt to Nancy. Then Kennedy did the same with Emma. He saw her not as a journalist, but as a young person he could cultivate. Young people flocked to Kennedy. In the previous year's campaign, there had been hordes of screamers who would do anything to grab a piece of him. Bobby had seen this as a source of potential strength and zealously safeguarded his standing among college students. If in fact he ever had to go against LBJ and the establishment, the young would be his foot soldiers. Never would he let another politician lay claim to this support.

As the end of the allotted meeting time approached, Kennedy spoke words that were music to Gabe's ears. "Don't be a stranger, Mr. Pressman. Any friend of Nancy's...."

· · ·

The next day, Emma took Nancy to a baseball game. Nancy was not a huge fan of spectator sports, but this gave her a chance to round out her New York experience and fulfill one of the items D.C. sportscaster Dick Schaap had urged her to tackle. They went to a Mets game, since Emma hailed from Queens and Nancy wanted to see this Casey Stengel fellow. Emma explained that the Yankees were unwatchable. After a period of dominance stretching back to the Roaring Twenties of the Babe Ruth era, the team had aged overnight and was experiencing a precipitous fall. Despite being pennant winners in 1964, the team was currently mired in sixth place.

Baseball had been structured the same way for eons, it seemed. There were two leagues, the American and the National, and ten teams in each league (the result of a recent expansion, when two teams had been added, one of them being the Mets). After the regular season, the top two in each circuit squared off in the World Series. Anyway, the Yankees were so deplorable, at a recent game only 923 customers bothered to show. Quite a predicament when the team's stadium had been built to house 60,000.

Nancy was no fan, but even she could see the Mets were about as pathetic as Emma described the Yanks to be. Pitchers were getting torched, batters flailed and the fielding, well that was memorable, but not in a good way. In the sixth inning on a routine fly ball to right-center, the two outfielders collided with each other, allowing the ball to drop in and three runs to score.

"That's part of the charm," Emma said. "To see what new and imaginative ways they can come up with to lose." From the laughter in the stands, Nancy had to agree it was like a long-running comedy show. Feeding the comedic overtone was the skipper, Casey Stengel. Stengel had once managed the cross-town Yankees, and this helped fuel the inter-borough rivalry. Separate borough identity was strong in New York City. That was primarily why mayoral candidates selected running mates from different boroughs, for geographic balance. Indeed, Brooklyn had been part of the city proper for 60 years, and yet it still proudly proclaimed itself as "the fourth-largest city in America." Separate subway lines also fed separate tribal loyalties. Nor had much time passed when separate baseball teams from three boroughs, Manhattan (Giants), Brooklyn (Dodgers) and Bronx (Yankees) competed against each other annually for the world championship.

Anyway, Stengel was a comic in his own right. Before the game, Nancy had flashed her press credentials and Schaap's note to secure an interview with the septuagenarian. She marveled as she noted the spanking new, state-of-the-art Shea Stadium, so named for the attorney who had helped lure National League baseball back to New York. The multi-colored tiles gracing the outer façade of Shea lit up the horizon far in the distance as one approached. Inside were ads proclaiming the benefits of cigarettes and of the shapely Miss Rheingold, who represented the beer company sponsoring the Mets.

The interview with Stengel was perhaps the strangest Nancy had ever conducted. The "Ol' Perfesser," as he was called, talked volumes but was practically unintelligible. Disparate thoughts and grammatical oddities crashed into each other in the course of a single sentence. When Stengel did manage a lucid thought, there truly was wit.

An example of his incomprehensibility came when Nancy complimented the new stadium. Stengel remarked, "It sure is pretty but looks got nuthin' to do with this game as I tell the boys like that young Swoboda kid what hits so hard he could damage the seats but I tell him go easy on the night life it robs you of your strength not like Babe Ruth who could drink an' hit home runs with a rolled up newspaper an' he hit some at that there Forbes Field which has rocks."

Nancy smiled politely as she scribbled notes. In her mind she was saying, "Huh?" Eventually, she came to realize that Stengel interlaced multiple thoughts without any transitioning language, and he also assumed an intimate knowledge of facts on the part of the listener.

Throughout the interview, Stengel served up a few genuinely funny bits that came across in the unique language that sportswriters in the city had labeled "Stengelese." When

Nancy asked him when the Mets would become competitive, Stengel assured her that would happen through trades.

"Oh!" Nancy said. Now she had a logical nugget with which to work. "Is there a player you are trying to get who will build up this team?"

That was not what Stengel had meant. "When we trade enough of our shit and spread it across the whole league," he said, "all the other teams will get worse an' come down to our level. Then we'll start winning."

As to when the Mets could appear in the World Series, Stengel ventured no guess. "Never make predictions," he said, "especially about the future."

Even at his age, Stengel was a bit of a rogue and made several odd winks, touches and comments that Nancy and Emma assumed were passes. After the third such solicitation, Nancy said she thought athletes shied away from women, for fear they would sap their strength.

Case winked yet again. "Bein' with a woman never hurt a player. It's stayin' up all night lookin' for one that does the damage."

The Mets manager's clumsy attempt at a pass was not the only unexpected one made at the two women that day, though the next one was equally unwelcome. Nancy and Emma had seats along the first baseline, but they paid a brief visit to the press box. Through the haze of the cigarette smoke that filled the box, a bald man also visiting the scribes was holding forth about how his football team, the New York Jets (which also played at Shea), was poised for dominance. Sonny Werblin told the scribes it all rested on the right arm of "this amazing young man here." The dark-haired man Werblin indicated had the clearest blue eyes and an inviting smile. His hair seemed perpetually tousled, not unlike Bobby Kennedy's. He spoke with the trace of a Southern accent and in humble tones about what he could accomplish. When his impossibly blue eyes lit on Nancy and Emma, he dropped the cloak of humility. The man the writers called "Broadway Joe" Namath made clear his sexual intentions to Nancy and Emma, either one or both together. The writers laughingly put their pencils down. This was something they would not record for the body politic. Nancy said she was married, which Joe said was not a problem. But she held up her ring finger and proclaimed that she was "VERY married." Emma might have been more receptive but for two things: rumors of Namath's swordplay were already rampant, and Emma was a one-guy kind of woman. The second turn-off was the faint smell of alcohol, even this early in the day, on Namath's breath.

The two women beat a hasty retreat to their seats, where Nancy lit up, along with scores of fans. As she puffed on her cigarette, the right field ad encouraging her to "walk a mile for a Camel," her mind wandered. Baseball's pace allowed for free mental range. How would these people react to the likes of Lindsay and Screvane, she mused as she picked out different spectators and wondered about them. She had the idea to poll a select group sometime before the election. Perhaps even before the primary. Many in the crowd were well-dressed, in jacket and tie, much like they would be if attending Sunday church services. However, there was a growing number, especially the youth, in jeans and informal attire.

This was a double-header against the Dodgers. When the Dodgers and the Giants returned to town, they were by far the biggest draw for the young Mets franchise. New Yorkers were embittered that ownership had fled Ebbets Field and the Polo Grounds, yet they flocked to Shea to see the heroes who had provided decades of thrills. Willie Mays was a draw, for sure, as was the fireballing tandem of Don Drysdale and Sandy Koufax. The latter was a Jewish kid from New York who had just come into his own after the exodus to LA. Now Koufax was single-handedly carrying the team on his shoulders to the pennant.

After her fourth cigarette, Nancy realized how glad she was to be in an open-air venue. She had once covered a John F. Kennedy rally indoors. After several hours, the accumulated smoke filled the arena with a noticeable white haze. When she caught up to JFK, whom she had once dated, Nancy jokingly asked what all the white smoke meant. Quick as ever on his feet, Kennedy quipped, "Since we haven't elected a pope, I hope it means we're about to elect a president!"

The Kennedy wit would be recalled to her shortly. For now, Nancy leaned toward Emma and asked if people really stayed through both ends of a doubleheader.

"Are you kidding?" Emma answered. "People go out of their way to purchase these tickets."

"People really sit through this?" Nancy wondered.

"No more unusual than you sitting through gavel-to-gavel coverage of the Democratic National Convention last year."

Nancy had to admit that was a salient point.

Emma said she enjoyed baseball but was not a purist. One game a day was enough for her. So after the Dodgers mauled the home team 12-4—these were the hapless Mets, after all— the women left. In between games, they were allowed to walk onto the field to exit through the outfield gates. From there, one really got a perspective of the field dimensions. And what a feat it was to hit a 90-mile-per-hour fastball out of the park.

When Nancy and Emma reached the outfield bullpen area, a new Mets coach was working with the game-two pitchers. Emma politely interrupted and introduced Nancy. Both still wore their press passes.

The stumpy fortyish coach had a ready smile as he greeted the women.

"What an unusual name," Nancy said. "Yogi. Do you have Indian blood?"

Berra looked stumped. He scratched his head. "Gee, I dunno. I always preferred the cowboys." He asked if the women were leaving.

Nancy explained they had another engagement, to be followed by dinner. She mentioned the name of the restaurant.

"Oh, no one goes there anymore," Yogi observed. "It's always too crowded."

As during her chat with Stengel, Nancy had another "Huh?" moment.

Once out of Shea, Nancy and Emma did indeed have another engagement in Midtown Manhattan, so they rode the IRT subway line back. Nancy realized how much it would help the city if the three subway lines were fully consolidated into one.

"Perhaps you should ask the candidates about that," Emma urged. There were a few oddball, minor party candidates on the ballot, as there are in virtually every election in the United States. One of the fringe parties had made complete unification of the IRT, IND and BMT lines its mantra. Those parties and their candidates were so far out on the fringe, however, that they were not taken seriously.

This afternoon, one lesser candidate was announcing his candidacy. He would be taken more seriously that the rest of the also-rans, because he ran with the support of one of the four major party lines in New York, and because he had emerged as a leading spokesman for the nascent conservative movement in America. Credible conservative spokesmen were few and far between following the Goldwater disaster. This one was different, however. His name was William F. Buckley, Jr.

When they arrived, Nancy headed to the women's restroom while Emma headed to get them seats. She immediately noticed that, as usual at such events, members of the print media were placed several rows ahead of the electronic journalists. She'd always assumed that was because the noise from the bulky recording equipment distracted the print journalists, but this time this arrangement irritated her for some reason she couldn't peg.

As soon as Emma had settled into a seat, Clark stopped to say hello. Emma mentioned to Clark her consternation with the seating arrangements for different members of the press.

"I'm beginning to feel like a black person who's always shunted to the back of the bus," Emma said.

"I guess they reserve the first rows for the serious journalists," Clark good naturedly, if ill-advisedly, commented.

Emma could see he was not joking. Steam began to come out of her ears. Clark was too naïve to notice, however.

"What do you mean by that?" Emma hissed.

Now, too late, Clark noticed. "Ah, ah, well, you have to admit the newspapers are the thinking man's organ of communication."

That was not the organ Emma was thinking of stomping at this very minute.

Clark dug himself in deeper. "TV caters to the simple minded. Like soap operas for women."

"So television and women are less serious?" Emma challenged, menace in her voice. "What does that say about your opinion of me?"

"Uh, uh, you could be a good real journalist."

"I *could* be a good *real* journalist?"

"You know, working for a newspaper. Look, television is just a passing fad. Sort of like hula hoops or the clipper ships of old. As the country's education level rises, which is happening as more and more people go to college, the popularity of television is bound to decline."

"You are so wrong. Television is the wave of the future. I think it more likely newspapers will disappear."

Clark laughed. "Hardly. People always want to read."

"Then how do you explain the fact that New York once had fifteen newspapers and now has nine?"

Clark sloughed it off. "That's just the free market asserting itself. Well, I'd better be going."

"Yes, you'd better."

Nancy took her seat next to Emma just as Clark abruptly turned and walked away. She watched him depart with some amusement, then noted her intern's flushed face and severe frown.

"What's wrong?" she asked.

"Nothing!" Emma snapped.

"Boy trouble?" Nancy gently pushed.

"They are such immature jerks!"

Nancy nodded. "That is natural to their species. What did he say?"

"I don't want to talk about it!"

After a moment of silence, Emma said, "I can't believe he thinks we're not *real* journalists."

"Because we're women or because we work for a network?"

Emma looked up in surprise, and Nancy waved her hand dismissively. "I've heard it all before. Since we are not talking about it, though, let me just say that someday you will be vindicated. Television will eventually supplant newspapers, and women will figure more prominently on the public stage."

"He seemed like such a nice guy," Emma lamented.

"They all do."

Further conversation was curtailed by the approach of William F. Buckley, Jr. to the podium.

After a brief greeting, Buckley proceeded with the main business of the day. "I announce today my candidacy for the mayoralty of New York under the auspices of the Conservative Party of New York," he said. "I run because no one else is who matters. New York is a city in crisis, and I propose to offer innovative solutions consistent with conservative American principles.

"A modern Justine could, in New York City, wake up in the morning in a room she shares with her unemployed husband and two children, crowd into a subway in which she is hardly able to breathe, disembark at Grand Central and take a crosstown bus which takes twenty minutes to go the ten blocks to her textile loft, work a full day and receive her paycheck from which a sizeable deduction is withdrawn in taxes and union fees, return via the same ordeal, prepare supper for her family and tune up the radio to full blast to shield the children from the gamey denunciations her next-door neighbor is hurling at her husband, walk a few blocks past hideous buildings to the neighborhood park to breathe a little fresh air, and fall into a coughing fit as the sulphur dioxide excites her latent asthma, go home, and on the way lose her handbag to a purse-snatcher, sit down to oversee her son's homework only to trip over the fact that he doesn't really know the alphabet even though he had his fourteenth birthday yesterday, which he spent in the company of a well-known pusher. She hauls off and smacks him, but he dodges and she bangs her head against the table. The ambulance is slow in coming and at the hospital there is no doctor in attendance. An intern finally materializes and sticks her with a shot of morphine, and she dozes off to sleep. And dreams of John Lindsay."

Buckley grinned an elfish grin. Fairly tall, his hair parted and sloped down the left side of his forehead, Buckley frequently flashed his eyes and teeth, especially after he'd made a telling or humorous point. That was not what most stood out about Buckley's physical appearance, however. What stood out was his voice. A baritone with incredibly above-average intellect, he rolled his words in a voice that one commentator described as a "piquant blend of English upper class and Southern drawl." The last words of a Buckley sentence particularly were drawn out. Once heard, his voice was so distinctive it was never forgotten, and was often mimicked by comic impersonators.

Even more than the voice were two other staples of a Buckley speech. His rapier wit, as seen in the "Justine" comment, and his vocabulary. Reporters would soon discover the need to carry a pocket dictionary when covering Buckley; some of the verbiage he used was that obscure.

Many of the reporters had heard of Buckley but had never spoken to him. A few of the more literate of the old guard, like Murray Kempton of *The Post*, had and appreciated Buckley's intellectual contributions. Others who had no previous familiarity viewed Buckley as a right-wing nut job.

After Goldwater, a frequent assertion of the national media was that conservatism equated with neanderthalism. On both these points they were gravely mistaken, as Buckley set out to demonstrate.

After graduating from Yale, Buckley had written a tome, *God and Man at Yale,* that marked the beginning of his conservative gospel. After that, in the mid-1950s, Buckley founded a magazine called *The National Review.* It amounted to a conservative think tank and spearheaded the intellectual underpinnings that would lead to the future state of conservatism.

At the start of 1965, Buckley had penned a column for *The National Review* that dealt with the problems besetting New York City and suggested solutions, all of a rightist stripe. For the cover of that month's magazine, Buckley's wife Patricia had playfully suggested the headline "Buckley for Mayor." Conservative Party elders (actually not all that old) read it and thought "Why not?"—even though Buckley was a registered Republican. They approached Buckley, who—after a little convincing and the creation of an agreed set of principles (no baby kissing, etc.)—decided to run. Hence today's press conference. This was an unexpected development. The Conservative Party of New York had only mounted two notable campaigns since its 1962 founding: a race for governor in '62 and one for senator two years later. What's more, Buckley would be the first Conservative Party candidate with any public notoriety.

Nancy and Emma were in attendance at this event because the conservative challenge by registered Republican Buckley constituted a split in the GOP ranks. As such, it had direct consequences for the Lindsay campaign and became, for today at least, part of Nancy and Emma's beat.

Today was Buckley's opportunity to espouse his gospel. That gospel reflected a simple theoretical construct: that after the New Deal and liberalism's ascendancy, there was a need for a revitalized theory of government.

Buckley's chagrin was that, in the wake of Franklin Roosevelt's repeated landslide victories and the taint that had attached to conservatism as a result of Hoover and the Great Depression, Republicans had jettisoned their principles. Their campaign platform had evolved to nothing more than "me too." That is, the GOP would do the same thing as the liberal Democrats, only better. In Buckley's eyes, however, that did not amount to a meaningful choice. To Buckley's mind, the New Deal philosophy had bred reliance on centralized (federal) government action, which in turn inculcated a sense of entitlement on the part of the citizenry. The alternative Buckley proposed was a shift to localized control of issues save those impacting foreign affairs. Localization meant greater individual responsibility and restoring the balance of public power to the state and local governments.

Buckley espoused this philosophy further after his formal remarks when it came to the Q and A.

Q. "Mr. Buckley, what do you mean you are running 'because no one else is who matters'?"

A. "Certainly it matters to Mr. Lindsay. And to Mr. Beame, Mr. Ryan, Mr. O'Dwyer and Mr. Screvane. However, all of these gentlemen share the same theory of government. There is no significant difference on the major issues. I intend to provide that alternative."

Q. "Mr. Buckley, you have stated that at Yale you knew John Lindsay. However, Congressman Lindsay says you have not met and that you are suffering from, and I quote, 'delusions of grandeur.' Any comment?"

A. "When I was matriculated at Yale, grandeur was not defined as having knowledge of John Lindsay." (Laughter from the press) "In point of fact, we did know each other; indeed, my brother served as an usher at Mr. Lindsay's brother's wedding and is godfather to David Lindsay's daughter."

Q. "Did you and Congressman Lindsay engage in common activities and, if so, what did you do?"

A. "We ran through campus threatening to defenestrate any socialist sympathizers." (Laughter)

Q. "Isn't your true intention to siphon off GOP votes from Lindsay, harming his chances for election?"

A. "As I stated, my objective is to present a cogent series of policy alternatives to the issues facing this city. At the risk of being charged with failure to be civic-minded, my primary objective is not to deprive the city of New York of the brilliance of a Lindsay administration."

Q. "Why not run as a Republican in the primary?"

A. "Because the party as currently constituted in this state will admit of no material challenges. In addition, the respectable persons who presently chair the Conservative Party of New York have approached me, offering their endorsement and party designation."

Q. "As a registered Republican, which you are, does it not seem appropriate in the spirit of party unity to embrace Mr. Lindsay?"

A. "No more so than Mr. Lindsay's refusal to support the duly chosen Republican standard-bearer for the presidency last year, Mr. Goldwater."

Q. "As a minor party candidate, how many votes do you expect to receive, conservatively speaking?"

A. "Conservatively speaking, I expect to receive one vote." (Laughter)

Q. "Do you expect to be elected?"

A. "I am cognizant of the exigent circumstances facing a third- or fourth-party candidate and while I expect to poll well, I do not anticipate success at the polls."

Q. "If you do succeed, what will be the first thing you will do?"

A. "Demand a recount." (Laughter)

Q. "As the fourth party in New York, the Conservatives do not have the resources available to the Republican or Democratic candidates. How do you expect to compete?"

A. "Realizing that to professional politicians the statement I am about to make will appeal chiliastic in its implications…" (No laughter, since the scribes did not understand the meaning of the word, though they continued to scribble furiously) "…I unreservedly avow that I shall not visit Irish communities and dance a jig, visit Jewish areas and eat blintzes, or visit Italian precincts to eat Stromboli. Nor shall I endeavor to kiss babies, such as that might thwart their future civic aspirations." (Laughter) "My campaign will be based on ideas. I shall prepare the issuance of a series of detailed position papers addressing all the major issues of the day."

Two things happened as soon as the press conference ended. Most of the assembled reporters raced to buttonhole one of Buckley's top aides, chiefly his brother James Buckley and the chairman of the Conservative Party, Kieran O' Doherty. Not to uncover more of the story, however. Rather, they wanted to make sure they'd gotten some of the obscure words down correctly and to ask what they meant. This was where O' Doherty, only half in jest, suggested the reporters carry dictionaries with them, which from that day forward virtually all members of the fourth estate covering the Buckley campaign would do.

But wide-scale coverage of Buckley's campaign would not come until much later in the election calendar. What did happen immediately was the unofficial post-press conference, which on this day Nancy and Emma attended. This involved reporters gathering at a local watering hole, McHale's, to review the day's bidding. Gone were the days when journalists did little more than regurgitate the pablum handed out by corporations and candidates. Now, they gathered informally to decide what was newsworthy and how to play it. Some wags took to calling this the herd mentality.

At any rate, the consensus was that Buckley was an engaging and erudite fellow but, in the ultra-liberal precincts of New York City, he had nary a chance. Not just nary a chance of election, but also nary a chance of being heard and having an impact. True, he would siphon votes from Lindsay, but in all probability not enough to make a dent in the outcome. Before breaking and well before a number of additional rounds of libation, talk shifted to the upcoming contract talks between the pressman's union and management of *The New York Times*. Talks were currently stalled. The scuttlebutt was that the contract deadline was weeks away and, as had happened so often in the past, it was assumed the two sides would get together and hammer out an agreement at the last minute. The herd was clueless that these two points would intersect in a way that would profoundly alter the campaign dynamic.

As she walked out of the bar with Nancy, Emma asked why Nancy had frowned while the pundits minimized Buckley's chances.

"You don't accept the common wisdom on that front?"

"Perhaps because it's so common," Nancy said, stopping to light a cigarette. "Did Bill Buckley strike you as a stupid man?"

"Certainly not! Far from it."

"Compared to them?" Nancy indicated the bar they had just departed.

"My money's still on Buckley."

"Mine, too," Nancy responded.

"So, why are they so convinced otherwise?"

Nancy took a drag on her Winston. "It's all part of the herd mentality. Since Goldwater, they've preached the death of conservatism so often, they believe their own precepts. Self-made men worshipping their creator. They're also unable to see past their own foibles."

"How so?" Now it was Emma's turn to frown.

"Most of them, virtually all, covered the 1948 campaign. It wasn't that long ago. Harry Truman's negatives were so high, he was deemed unelectable. Plus, the Republicans were unified behind Thomas E. Dewey, who had run the strongest race ever against the invincible FDR. Here is the salient point. Unlike the united Republicans, the Democrats were split:

Henry Wallace bolted the party and ran as a Progressive; Strom Thurmond bolted on a segregationist platform and ran as a Dixiecrat. All of our esteemed colleagues reported that President Truman would not be reelected because of the split in his own party."

"But Truman did win."

"Precisely. Leaving egg the size of Humpty Dumpty on reporters' faces. In large part because the Democratic split failed to materialize, as the Wallace and Thurmond insurgencies imploded. Having been burned, these same reporters have now swung to the other side. They don't see that a splinter party can alter the equation."

"You think it can?"

"Wallace and Thurmond were idiots. Buckley is not. He may appeal to enough people. That remains to be seen. As of now, I do not see how, if he refuses to campaign actively. The voters are not savvy enough to really plow through dense position papers. However, if Mr. Buckley can find some way to get his message across, he can be a formidable foe."

Emma asked when they would know.

Nancy said that, in her expert opinion, they would know sometime late on November 2.

"But that's Election Day," Emma pointed out.

"There's a reason they hold elections," Nancy replied cryptically, taking another long drag on her cigarette.

CHAPTER VI

THIS DOES NOT FEEL LIKE THE DOG DAYS OF SUMMER; IT FEELS LIKE THE DOG YEARS

Reaction to William Buckley's entrance into the race was sharply divergent. The night of the formal announcement, the top Screvane brain trust gathered and actually popped a bottle of champagne. The prevailing view was that this sealed the deal. Despite what the press felt about Buckley's impact, Team Screvane held to the view that a split, even a minor one, would irreparably harm Republican Lindsay...and deliver the mayoralty to Screvane on a silver platter. "We will win in a cake walk," chuckled transit union chief Mike Quill as he raised his glass, though he would have preferred a Bud to the bubbly. "Linds-lee is toast."

Screvane mused over whom he should select to be his commissioners. Each of the assembled leaders had candidates they wanted to reward from within their own narrow constituencies. Screvane, of course, intended to accommodate all. This was putting the cart before the horse. There were more important selections to be made before the election. Such as the identity of Screvane's running mates, which still had to be fleshed out.

The group felt they needed a Jew on the ticket for ethnic balance and to blunt Abe Beame's potential appeal to Jewish voters. They found one in the person of Orin Lehman. Lehman was a great-nephew of Herbert Lehman, the beloved governor and senator practically canonized by the reform liberals. Thus, Orin might help with this tiny but vocal segment, blunting the Ryan and O'Dwyer challenges as well as Beame's. More importantly, Lehman was the great grandson of Mayer Lehman, who had founded the mega-rich Lehman Brothers investment house. The 35-year-old scion had worked in the family business for a while but decided early on he did not want to devote his life to making more money. He had more than enough. Instead, he opted for public service, beginning with a stint in the Truman administration overseeing Marshall Plan aid to Europe. Because of his background, Lehman was a natural candidate for the comptroller slot.

With that settled, the group turned to finding a candidate for city council president. They had earlier concluded an Irishman would give the ticket perfect ethnic balance, complementing Screvane's Italian heritage and Lehman's Judaism. It turned out Senator Kennedy had a candidate, Irish of course, that he was hawking. An academic by the name of Daniel Patrick Moynihan.

Moynihan had cut his teeth politically on the 1960 John F. Kennedy presidential campaign, serving as a Kennedy delegate. That election was where one proved his bona fides, as far as Bobby Kennedy was concerned, so Moynihan's stature as a New Frontiersman was secure. In the Johnson White House, Moynihan remained active in government in the Department of Agriculture. While most of his last decade had been spent in Washington, Moynihan did have New York ties. He'd started as a speechwriter for Mayor Wagner's first campaign in 1953 and later worked for Governor Averell Harriman. When Rockefeller ousted Democrat Harriman, Moynihan worked at Syracuse University, where he completed his Ph.D. before returning as a Kennedy man.

Bob Kennedy had earlier expressed preference for Moynihan as a mayoral candidate. However, Moynihan's profile was too low for so lofty a start in elective politics. Hence Kennedy, who soon became a Screvane supporter, pushed Moynihan for a spot on that ticket. This had the added advantage of giving Kennedy boots on the ground in the next mayoral administration, in addition to boosting his alliance with Screvane. Of course this annoyed the reformers but, as Kennedy noted, that wing of the party had too little clout to make a difference.

The Screvane group was not all that enamored with Moynihan but he was Irish and reliably Democratic, and if he could bring along some of the Kennedy machine, he would do.

The only one who groused was Quill. "The guy's too pedophantic," he said. That did send off alarm bells—until the group realized Quill's error and understood their putative candidate was not a child molester. Quill had meant to say pedantic, not pedophilic. The transit chief viewed Moynihan as too stuffy, too dry. Dull. Not someone who would elevate the electorate. The others convinced Quill this was not a concern, insisting that the second and third slots on the ticket did not require oratory descending from the likes of famous orator William Jennings Bryan. All they wanted was ethnic balance. The top of the ticket was what mostly mattered. With Screvane at the helm, and especially with the way events were breaking, the entire ticket would surely scoot their way into City Hall.

On the days when the Screvane team met that summer, it was to talk over the different ways the electoral map produced a victory for Team Screvane. They also dwelt on how to run the city when in office—and which scores to settle. Comptroller Beame in particular was singled out for retrograde treatment. The group routinely congratulated Screvane when events like the Buckley candidacy cropped up, as these augured well for Screvane's chances. A few times they addressed him as "Mr. Mayor," which never failed to bring a smile to Screvane's face.

So, Team Screvane was ecstatic over the Buckley challenge.

Team Beame, meanwhile, did not much care. They agreed it could hurt Lindsay but saw things as more of a mixed bag. They agreed that Bill Buckley would draw minimally, but would do so at Lindsay's expense. Ultimately, they would change their belief on both counts. For the most part, however, they remained fixated on the primary battle against Screvane and did not look past September 14. Lindsay and the Republicans could wait until later.

As with the Screvane high command, Team Beame did little in the way of significant campaigning during the early summer. They, too, would await the approach of Labor Day. There was a difference, however. Beame did make limited appearances before community groups, assailing the Wagner administration, whereas Screvane made none. Each time, Beame pounded home Screvane's ties to and endorsement by Mayor Wagner, gaining some newspaper coverage for the comptroller. The second nuance of difference involved the fact that Beame's lieutenants gathered nightly to review the bidding and, rather than convince each other of the victory to come, focused on strategy. Their discussions focused on honing the candidate's talking points, mapping out likely sources of votes, and determining the best ways to turn out that base. In short, the Beame team busied itself with crafting a game plan.

The reform camps were split in opinion. Ryan's supporters were outraged. To them, Buckley represented the worst impulses in American society including John Bircherism, segregationism, and antediluvian thinking. O'Dwyer, on the other hand, giddily welcomed Buckley to the race. "The more the merrier!" he proclaimed. His view was that there was room for diversity. The more fringe groups that sought a forum for their views, the better. Let the people decide.

In the boardrooms, specifically those housing the great newspapers, Buckleyism was seen as synonymous with the plague. As their respective papers had duly pounded into the body politic, the right was not might. Far from it. Conservatism was dead. "How dare Buckley try to prove us wrong, make us look like laughing stocks!" one of the publishers thundered to his directors. In short, Buckley would be given little space. When he was given treatment at all, he would be relegated to that of an amusing, albeit slightly freakish, circus sideshow.

There was an interesting clash in the newspaper world. Buckley was anathema (as he might have phrased it) to the suits in the boardroom. However, as we have seen, the employees of those suits, namely the reporters, had a different view. Though the working press did not believe Buckley or the conservative movement stood a chance, they enjoyed the new candidate's performances immensely. He was charming and funny and, when you stopped to think about it, many of his ideas made sense.

One *Times* reporter made the mistake back in the newsroom of gushing about how entertaining he found the candidate. This led to a protracted discussion where said journalist admitted he saw merit in some of Buckley's ideas. Shortly after this discussion, the reporter was reassigned and another, more malleable, fellow was chosen to cover the Buckley campaign.

This division in the journalism universe was not all that unusual. When JFK ran against Nixon, most of the papers endorsed Vice President Nixon, a sign of the staid establishmentarianism that ran rampant in editorial boardrooms. Reporters, however, had had enough of the churlish Nixon and were seduced by Kennedy's charm. Thus, while the papers' editorials endorsed Nixon, their day-to-day coverage lavished praise on Kennedy.

The split between editor/publisher and reporter was not as pronounced in the TV world. Unlike newspapers, networks did not endorse candidates. So the negative view of the right side of the political spectrum was not as pervasive in TV land. What mattered more at the networks was the "wow" factor, what would entertain the masses the most. Indeed, this was part of the reason why print journalists looked down their noses at their brethren of the electronic media. To the newspaper reporters, their counterparts were a bunch of pretty boys whose chief merit was looking good on camera. Broadcast "journalists" were more concerned with fluff than with being hard-hitting newsmen. This view was even harsher where Nancy Dickerson was concerned, she being the one pretty girl on campus.

・ ・ ・

At 30 Rock, Arthur Haller discussed Buckley with his top staff. They agreed Buckley was a sideshow but an amusing one, possibly a thought-provoking one, and he deserved some coverage. Not on the scale of Screvane or Lindsay, of course.

There were two dissenting views. Gabe thought Buckley had the makings of a solid protest vote and could thwart Lindsay. That in itself was a story line of some significance.

Nancy held the other disparate view. She thought the conservatives could gain traction. "Goldwater may have opened a door," she said.

"Yeah, to hell," one of the others remarked to much laughter. The jab was not all that funny, but it had been made at the expense of "the girl." All the reporters in the room looked at Nancy to see how she would react. All except Gabe, who was glaring at the colleague who'd made the remark. Arthur waved a hand to try to get the conversation back on track.

"As far as the network is concerned," he said, his voice stern, "the problem in coverage lies in a lack of resources." He added that while NBC was trying mightily to dethrone CBS as the news leader, there was only so much the suits would throw at the problem.

Nancy spoke up again. "Since the prevailing view is that the Buckley campaign is designed to derail Lindsay, and since I have an able assistant, why don't I cover both?"

All the men in the room, Gabe and Arthur included, gaped for a moment at Nancy's moxie. Then Arthur nodded. "Have at it," he said.

. . .

The party that should have been most interested in the Buckley candidacy, apart from Buckley and the conservatives, was John Lindsay. He did, in fact, feel a mild headache coming on when he first learned of the conservative's entry to the race. Price quickly calmed him down, though.

"Not to be Pollyannaish," Price assured his candidate, "but this is a very favorable development. It solidifies your liberal credentials. If the conservatives are going after you and not Screvane, that's because you are the true embodiment of progressive values."

"How should we attack Buckley, then?"

"By not attacking at all," Price said with a grin. "We're going to ignore him. Let him twist in the wind. By not dignifying his candidacy with any comment, we'll be more likely to see interest in him dry up."

This approach seemed counterintuitive, but Lindsay trusted his campaign manager implicitly. Price's assurance put the candidate immediately at ease.

"Right now we have more important things, Jay-viel," Price said. "Tomorrow is your interview with the Liberal Party organizing committee."

This meeting had been in the works ever since Wagner's withdrawal. Price assumed, correctly, that with Wagner out of the race, Alex Rose had no longstanding allegiances. Without Lindsay's knowledge, the campaign strategist had lunched with the Liberal Party chieftain. He began the lunch by reciting Lindsay's sterling progressive record in the House of Representatives. He need not have. Rose was all too familiar with Who's Who in American Politics and with politicians who backed liberal causes. Since Lindsay so clearly qualified, Rose had other motives in mind.

"If we support your guy, we want a commitment for half the positions in the administration," he said.

"Done," Price answered without batting an eye...or checking with his erstwhile boss.

The only thing remaining was for Lindsay to appear before the Party's organizing committee to answer their questions. This was perfunctory. As long as Lindsay did not completely mess up, the executive committee would follow Rose's lead. To be sure there would be no screw-ups, Rose had provided Price with the questions, and Price had tutored his charge assiduously. Going in, Lindsay felt confident. Partway through the session, he found the session was bordering on the surreal. Not only did he know each and every question, he knew the order in which they would be asked and their answers. Rose had also provided these to Price, who—without telling the congressman—had used them during the candidate's prep sessions.

Afterward, Lindsay whispered to Price, "Why is it I feel this has all been arranged?"

Price gave a noncommittal shrug.

"Good job, Bob," the congressman intoned.

Lindsay had in fact hit it out of the park. The Liberal Party organizing committee duly named John V. Lindsay its nominee for the mayoralty of New York. NBC was the first on air with the news, courtesy of the insight and follow-ups Nancy had gathered over the past weeks. "Damn fine reporting," Arthur told her, which pleased Nancy inordinately. A few of the other reporters on the campaign grumbled. They wondered what "favors" Nancy had bestowed in order to secure this news flash.

It was significant news, at that. A Liberal-Republican alliance was so unusual it pointed toward one avenue to Republican resurgence in the wake of the 1964 landslide loss. It also burnished Lindsay's credentials as a candidate with a real shot as a legitimate fusion candidate. That was how the Lindsay camp spun it, that he was a man who could cross party lines in constructing a winning coalition.

This scoop was one of two that Nancy secured in rapid succession, leading her to stand out among the press corps. When the second scoop hit, opinion was evenly divided as to whether she had traded sex for success, or whether she was that good a journalist.

The second news item that followed shortly after the Liberal Party anointing of Lindsay involved the identity of Lindsay's running mates. Screvane had already tabbed Moynihan and Lehman. Beame countered with his own form of balance to the ticket. To the Jewish-Brooklynite Beame were added Frank O'Connor, an Irishman from Queens for city council president, and Mario Procaccino, a Bronx Italian, for comptroller. Ryan and O'Dwyer's choices were marked solely by their choice of colored men for a spot on each reform ticket.

"A Negro winning citywide office?" one of the reporters questioned. "What kind of fantasy land are they living in?"

His colleague joined in. "Maybe it's a section in Freedomland," he said, referring to the amusement park in the city that competed with Northern Jersey's Palisades Amusement Park. "Or hey, maybe they think their guy is another Tim Pettigrew."

Both men laughed harshly at this one, a reference to a story one had told recently about a weekly reader publication his son had brought home from elementary school a few weeks earlier. The serialized cartoon series entitled "Pettigrew for President," which had been designed to teach about the nominating process, told the story of how Pettigrew, a major state governor, secured his party's nomination for the presidency. The candidate was only seen in shadow, behind obstructions or "off camera" until the very last panel—when it was revealed he was a black man. The revealed wisdom this taught to youngsters was that the election of a colored man in their lifetime to high office was so fantastic as to be absurd.

The only remaining ticket to be announced was Lindsay's, and newsmen were especially curious about what the candidate would announce on this front. There just were not that many Republicans of stature in the city.

On a fluke happenstance, a reporter for *The Herald Tribune* was heading home late one evening when he spied Nancy Dickerson leaving Lindsay's home. She looked a little disheveled. The newsman put two and two together and came up with 69. Lindsay was set to announce his ticket the next day. He did indeed do so: hours after Nancy had revealed it to NBC viewers. Despite her foreknowledge, Nancy (and Emma) attended Lindsay's press conference at which the running mates would be introduced. At the press conference, Lindsay even stated good-naturedly that his news was a "revelation to all, except Mrs. Dickerson." There were not a lot of guffaws, the male reporters disinclined to acknowledge Nancy's coup.

Just as she was about to leave the session, Nancy realized Emma was not by her side. A second later, Nancy turned her head at the sound of a familiar voice threatening to tear a *Trib* reporter's hind teeth out.

Nancy ran and pulled Emma, who looked about to dismantle the *Trib* reporter, away until they were outside. The intern's face was redder than her hair, and she was so angry she was shaking.

"All right," Nancy said, "what was that all about?"

Emma shook her head angrily. "He just...said something that got under my skin."

"What could he have said to provoke such an unprofessional reaction from you?"

Emma was silent.

"Out with it."

"He said you only got the news because you slept with John Lindsay!"

"Oh, honestly," Nancy said with a groan. "You'll hear these things all the time, Emma. You have to let them roll off your back."

"I threatened to rip his hind teeth out."

"That I heard, and I appreciate your offer to perform dental artistry on him, but it was quite unnecessary."

"He said he saw you coming out of Lindsay's home last night."

"I did," Nancy offered.

"Also that you look disheveled...you know, not made up."

"How does anyone look after a full day when it's near one in the morning?" Nancy said, trying to get Emma to see the humor in the situation. "How does *he* look, even on his best day?"

Emma looked momentarily crestfallen. "So...you were there?"

Nancy led Emma to a nearby bench. "Emma," she said, "how do you think I got the exclusive on Hubert Humphrey being chosen for vice president?"

"I don't know. President Johnson seems to be sweet on you. I mean, on TV he always makes a point of coming over to you and saying 'Hi Nancy!' even when there are other reporters around."

"I've known Lyndon Johnson since I worked for the Senate Foreign Relations Committee. And yes, I suppose he is a little smitten with me. One time on the campaign trail he did proposition me, awkwardly. But only that once."

"You didn't...?"

"Oh, good God, no! I was fortunate one of his aides, Bill Moyers, came down the hall and got LBJ to stop pestering me." Nancy paused at the memory. "I was doing a special on Lady Bird. So I happened to be at the White House to go over a few details with the First Lady, and who do I happen to see there but Muriel Humphrey. Why, I asked myself, would Senator Humphrey's wife be there the day the convention opened, unless.... Well, I did a little more digging and got it confirmed...and the rest is history.

"You see, it was my relationship with *Mrs.* Johnson that allowed me to get that scoop. Reporters chase after the candidates all the time and treat the wives as little more than hood ornaments. Not too different from what you and I have to deal with. But wives are people, too. I found out long ago that by buddying up with the women behind the men, you could learn a lot of important information. Many of these women are lonely. And afraid. They did not bargain for the spotlight when they exchanged vows. I remember meeting John Glenn's wife for the first time when he was about to become the first American in orbit. Anne was very nervous because she had a terrible stutter and was afraid the public would ridicule her.

"Just by showing some common decency and treating candidates' wives, and other women, as people, you can amass an enormous reservoir of good will. Besides, it's the right thing, the compassionate thing, to do."

Emma stared at Nancy, admiration and perhaps a little awe in her eyes. "So you were there to see *Mary* Lindsay."

Nancy smiled. "A very charming woman who is a little overwhelmed by all this. She will make a delightful first lady of the city, if it comes to that. Mind you, Emma, I would not share my source or my secret unless I had...a warm spot for you." Nancy grew suddenly introspective. "Emotion...displaying emotion...does not come easily for me. My parents were not very demonstrative in their affections."

Emma nodded. "I...I feel privileged," she said, "almost like Helen Keller in the presence of Annie Sullivan."

Nancy's smile broadened. "Just so long as you don't grab food off my plate," a reference to the iconic scene from the blockbuster movie of a few years ago.

• • •

The women arrived back at Rockefeller Center in time to view the evening news broadcast, which included Nancy's taped piece about the Lindsay ticket. The congressman had tabbed a Jew and an Italian to counterbalance his Waspishness. There was much more to the story than that, however. The two gentlemen hailed from different political parties than Lindsay's Republican. Milton Mollen, the comptroller candidate, was a card-carrying Democrat who presently held a position in the Wagner administration. Some Screvane aides cried foul, for Mollen had sat in on some of the early strategy sessions for their man. The other running mate, Timothy Costello, was a member of the Liberal Party. In one fell swoop, Lindsay demonstrated in graphic terms that he was in fact a fusion candidate.

After this announcement, the pace of the campaign slowed as if the entire city, candidates included, were wilting in the hot, humid summer months. Since they had a little more free time, Nancy and Emma indulged in a few recreational outlets. To repay Emma for the Mets game, Nancy sprang for tickets to plays that had just premiered on Broadway. Each was acclaimed by the critics, and long runs lasting for years as well as future revivals were anticipated.

The women enjoyed both, Nancy expressing slight preference for the first and Emma the second. The first, *Man of La Mancha,* had been a musical based on Cervantes' classic *Don Quixote*. The original book had been an immediate classic, and so was this show's music. Nancy liked to sing, though she had trouble carrying a tune. That did not stop her, however. For much of the summer she would spontaneously break into "The Impossible Dream" and "I Don Quixote." She wrote in her journal that the play "expressed idealism masterfully. This is how I felt when I first left Wisconsin for Washington," she added, "like I could change the world, for the better, of course. That sprout is still deeply planted inside me, but how people make it so hard to nurture!"

The second Broadway opening was as far removed from the first as possible. Yet its depiction of New Yorkers, its use of genuinely funny lines, and the obvious chemistry between the two leading stars made *The Odd Couple* an immediate classic in its own right.

"If Neil Simon can write more plays like that, he will surely have a remarkable career," Nancy remarked.

During their down-time together, Nancy would talk to Emma about Washington, D.C., and the differences that existed between the nation's capital and New York. A favorite topic was the prevalence and value of Washington's salon society. Traditionally, a few society hostesses for each generation sponsored periodic dinners. One of the most noted at present was Alice Roosevelt Longworth, daughter of Teddy Roosevelt. She was a character, so much so that some felt she should be sculpted onto Mt. Rushmore alongside her famous father. Alice had a biting wit and appreciated flamboyant shows. She once invited Nancy to attend a boxing match, shouting "Bully" (her father's favorite expression) when one pugilist delivered a particularly telling blow. Other society matrons were Laura Gross, founder of the iconic F Street Club, and Katharine Graham, publisher of *The Washington Post*.

Emma could see where this might be fun, but important?

Nancy told her it was critical to understanding how Washington worked. D.C. in the mid-'60s was bereft of night life, and there was a dearth of five-star restaurants. It truly was a Southern town. At these social settings, much work was accomplished. Senators and congressmen, loosened by whatever elixir of choice was available, would say and do things they never would publicly in the halls of Congress.

Despite her own successes, Nancy was not paid nearly as much as her male coworkers. Since her husband was so successful, however, she had the financial wherewithal to throw her own D.C. parties. As such, she was breaking in as one of the coming generation of society benefactresses. When Emma wondered aloud what was in it for Nancy, the older woman explained she developed many contacts and learned of late-breaking developments she could not otherwise at such gatherings. In short, it aided her performance as a reporter.

Because of the demands of the New York mayoralty campaign and Nancy's part-time transfer, however, she'd had to cut back on entertaining. Not completely, however; she feared being gone from the scene too long. "Out of sight; out of mind," she said. So Nancy and Dick were hosting a gathering, and Nancy had invited Emma.

On the bus ride down, Nancy tried to sleep but did not have much luck. At one point, Emma put down her magazine. "You look a little green around the gills," she said.

Nancy waved her off. "I'm not good with planes, trains and automobiles. On occasion, a twinge of motion sickness develops."

"Travel is what we do," Emma pointed out. "Why didn't you choose a profession where you could be completely sedentary?"

"Because I was not cut out to live in a convent."

The rest of the ride proceeded without incident. When the Greyhound disgorged its passengers, Nancy hailed a cab for the ride to McLean in Northern Virginia. Her complexion did not improve noticeably, the cab being no improvement, to Nancy's way of thinking, than the bus. On the way, Emma reflected on what Nancy had taught her about great D.C. parties. She'd heard from Nancy that the Kennedys, Bob and Ethel, threw raucous get-togethers at their estate, Hickory Hill.

"They mean well," Nancy had said in her friends' defense. "The Kennedys work hard and party hard. A Hickory Hill gathering is not intended to facilitate statecraft. Just good clean fun."

"Like throwing guests in the pool fully clothed?" Emma had said, smiling at the image of the Hickory Hill parties' staple.

In short order, not long after passing the sign "Welcome to Virginia—Capital of the Confederacy," the cab taxied up a very long driveway to a mansion. Nancy and Emma got out, retrieving their bags from the trunk.

Emma gaped at the massive structure.

"This is Merrywood," Nancy said.

"Wow!" the younger lady gushed. "You rented a banquet hall for the occasion! I didn't expect this. Very impressive!"

Nancy smiled. "No. Merrywood is our home. Dick and I purchased it a few years ago."

"What! How large is this place?"

"Thirty-six rooms. Enough for a growing family." In addition to Nancy and Dick, there were five children, the two boys Michael and John and three daughters from Dick's first marriage, before the girls' mother succumbed to cancer.

"Enough for a growing family!" Emma repeated. "Why, it's enough to house the entire population of Guatemala."

"Why ever would I want to do that?" Nancy asked.

As the cab drove off, a tall blonde man came down the stairs and kissed Nancy affectionately. "Dick" Dickerson introduced himself to Emma, who was immediately smitten by his handsome looks. Reasoning that he was a little old for her, probably late thirties, and married, she began to wonder if the Dickerson sons might resemble their father. Then she realized the sons would still be very young. At this point, Emma realized she had not seen any children yet. Of course, the house was so big, they could be anywhere.

Dick asked if she wanted a tour.

"Is it possible to see it all in one day?"

Emma was still spellbound. Dick laughed good naturedly and summoned one of the household staff, who escorted Emma to her room and gave her a quick survey of the domain. Nancy was already off to say hello to the children and check on the caterer and the florist for the dinner party.

If Emma was surprised by her first view of Merrywood, that evening she was, to use the word she'd heard the British ambassador say, absolutely "gobsmacked." The reason for this was the star-studded nature of the event. Everywhere she turned during the cocktail hour, Emma bumped into people she'd only seen on TV including senators, congressmen, governors, the British ambassador, a Supreme Court justice, several cabinet members and assorted luminaries from outside the government sector. Emma had always placed such people on a pedestal, but after a short time of speaking with those in attendance, she began to feel they had feet of clay. The number of dignitaries who made not-so-subtle passes at her turned her off.

Two people stood out because they went against the grain. One was the balding, virile senator from Wisconsin, William Proxmire. Compared to the other guests, Proxmire was practically ascetic. His interest in good government was undeniable. When he learned of Emma's role as a reporter assigned to the Lindsay campaign, he peppered her with questions about the congressman. Beyond that, their conversation veered in another direction.

Proxmire was in fighting form. It turned out he was quite the health nut. When he told Emma he jogged five miles a day, Emma was surprised. "You run? For fun?" She had never heard of someone who was not on a school track team or in basic training with the armed forces jogging for the sake of their health and said as much to Senator Proxmire.

The senator confided his belief that, as the country's booming young population grew older, Americans would become more health conscious. "In time, I predict this country will undergo a health craze. On any given day, you'll see average people running along our streets." He added that he could envision health clubs, with exercise equipment, sprouting up on a wide scale. Emma did not see it. The only such clubs she knew of were Vic Tanney's, and they catered only to women desperate to keep some semblance of a figure. Most women Emma knew relied on girdles to hold in their excess weight.

Proxmire responded that there were two trends supporting his view. One was cultural. "Look at how rock 'n roll has infiltrated the mainstream. What is the number one song right now?"

Emma knew it was Sonny and Cher's "I Got You, Babe."

"Right," the senator said. "Not Bing Crosby, or Frank Sinatra, or Tommy Dorsey. Teenagers today are having an outsized influence. The other thing is, today's kids will remember when Kennedy was president. The idealism he preached will influence them, at least until they are a lot older and life's problems get in the way. It wouldn't surprise me to see many of them stage some sort of crusade in the next few years when they arrive on college campuses."

Emma still could not see it. It would take some major event, like a depression or a war, to energize American youth.

The other person to make an impact on Emma was a young astronaut. The Gemini V mission had just ended after setting an endurance record. Its two astronauts had spent eight days in space, the amount of time necessary for a trip to the moon and back. Like the rest of the country, Emma was enthralled by the heroics of the astronauts. There had been so many mishaps in the early days of the space race with rockets blowing up on the launch pad and so forth; it was incredibly brave for these men to strap themselves into what was essentially a can set atop a bomb.

Emma was seated next to the astronaut at dinner, so naturally the two spent much of the night conversing. The astronaut was in D.C. because NASA liked to have a spokesman in place during a mission. In case of emergency, someone knowledgeable had to be available to handle (i.e., lobby) the congressmen. The astronaut had also been selected to be the commander of the upcoming Gemini VIII mission. Accordingly, part of his mission was to debrief the space subcommittee on Capitol Hill in advance.

The earnest young man explained the purpose of the Gemini program was to develop the tools that would be needed to land a man on the moon. The specific goal of Gemini VIII was to have the two-man Gemini capsule rendezvous and dock with an Agena Target Vehicle in space. The eventual lunar mission blueprint called for a small landing craft to detach from the capsule in the moon's orbit and eventually return.

This rendezvous-and-docking was a critical component of the tool kit and would be tested by Gemini.

Emma followed that. She also knew President Kennedy had committed the country to a man on the moon by 1969. That was just four years away, and the space program, while having made strides, seemed so far from the goal. Moreover, the Soviets seemed to have a huge lead. Like most Americans, Emma remembered how frightening it had been when the U.S.S.R. launched Sputnik. The United States had been powerless as a Soviet rocket passed overhead every 90 minutes. She asked her dinner mate if it wasn't out of the question for NASA to co-opt the Russkies.

The young man tugged at his ear and gave a boyish grin. "They are ahead, there is no doubt. But their lead is in the fact that they have produced larger payloads." He explained the need for a more powerful booster rocket to launch the larger moon-landing craft to orbit and then onto a lunar trajectory. He thought with the development of a new rocket, the Saturn V, the U.S. would catch up in short order to Soviet rocketry. Moreover, he explained that the details of a moon landing required a series of "finesse steps," as he put it, like the rendezvous-and-docking maneuvers he would pilot on Gemini VIII. "You cannot do a lunar landing without that, and in that area, as best as our intelligence can tell us, the Soviets lag far behind. So yes, I believe we can get to the moon first. And by the end of the decade."

Emma felt reassured. His thought process was sound. Still, she was a bit skeptical. She asked who the first man on the moon would be.

"That's anyone's guess," he said with a grin. "NASA will not announce its crew selection until we get much closer to the actual date. Talk about playing your cards close to the vest."

"Any guess?" she prodded. "For what it's worth, I hope it's you." He seemed so nice and genuine.

"I don't know. But I'd give anything to be the man to take that one small step. It would really be a giant leap for mankind." Emma made a mental note to track Gemini VIII's progress and to keep tabs on her new contact, Neil Armstrong.

After dinner, the guests wandered from the tables to the patio and grounds for drinks. Emma was dreadfully thirsty. Rather than pester one of the wait staff, her Jeffersonian instincts led her to the kitchen, where she would fill her own glass of tap water. There she saw several of the catering staff, who in turn were surprised that one of the guests deigned to enter the realm of the common man. Emma also saw two young children. Immaculately dressed, the boy and girl were munching on sandwiches.

"Hi! I'm Emma!" she said brightly, offering her hand. Each child took it, reluctantly. "And you are…?" she prompted.

The boy, whom she learned was six, was John. His sister, slightly older Jane, just stared at her.

"Dinner?" Emma beckoned at the sandwiches. Jane nodded.

"But everyone else had sole stuffed with crabmeat," Emma said.

"Yuck! Fish!" John said, and Jane also made a distasteful expression.

Emma complimented each on how well turned out they were.

"That's because we're supposed to answer the door and greet each guest," John said.

"Mom says it's cute," Jane offered.

"Well, it certainly is. You are adorable children. It must be exciting meeting all these famous people."

"I guess," Jane said with a shrug.

"I'd rather be upstairs listening to my transistor radio," John said.

"And I would like to be at Cathy's. She's my bestest friend in the whole world. I can get dirty there."

Emma giggled. "I can see how that would be more exciting."

"You don't have to talk to us," John said. "People don't pay attention to kids. Unless they want something. Like these people want to get close to my mother. She's a famous TV reporter."

"Perhaps I'm different," Emma replied. "I'm not a politician, so I'm not looking for anything. In fact, I work with your mother. I want to talk to you because I want to talk to you. Do you like to play games?" She fished in her purse and took out a penny. Placing it on the table, Emma explained, "You hit the penny with the tip of your finger. You get three tries. The idea is to put it over the edge of the table without letting it fall off." Emma gave the Lincoln head a hard nudge. Then another. It was near the end on the children's side of the table. Then another light tap. The coin inched past the lip of the table. "That's one point for me. Now you try."

John went first. His second shot was too hard, and the coin flew off the table. Jane's three shots fell far short. By their third joint attempt however, the children were getting the knack.

"First to eleven wins," Emma proclaimed.

The youngsters prevailed, 11-9. "But there are two of us, so we got two chances for every one of yours," John pointed out.

"That's the age handicap," Emma said, "so it all evens out in the end. Since you won, you each get a penny." She fished again in her purse for another one. The kids regarded them as if they had just earned Olympic gold.

"What's a handiddlycop?" John inquired, and Emma explained about how a 'handicap' worked.

Just then, Nancy came in. "Armand, we're ready for dessert…. Oh, children, you shouldn't be pestering our guests."

Emma explained they were playing a game and she thoroughly enjoyed spending time with John and Jane.

Nancy smiled. "They are my pride and joy."

"Mother, look what we won!" Jane enthused.

"Oh, children, don't take Emma's money."

"Really, Nancy," Emma held up a hand. "It's all right."

"Wanna' play, Mother?" Jane asked. She demonstrated how to maneuver the coin.

"You mean, 'Would you like to play, Mother?'" Nancy said, and then gave it a whirl. The penny flew sideways, off the table and onto the stovetop, where Armand was fussing with the baked Alaska.

"Klutz," John whispered as Jane giggled.

"Oh, honestly," Nancy said. "Finish your sandwiches, now. Armand will return the penny to you when he has a moment." She signaled to Emma to follow her back to the living room.

"All right, Mother," John said. "Emma is a gas!"

"We have ginger ale if you need some," Nancy offered.

Emma smiled. "No. In their lingo, someone who's a gas is a fun person, not one afflicted with flatulence."

"What's fat-enz, Mother?" John asked.

Nancy shook her head but smiled at her son. "Not fat-enz...Flatulence. F-L-A-T-U-L-E-N-C-E."

"What's that?" Jane asked again, this time of her brother.

"Don't ask me. You know I can't spell."

Emma turned toward them before following Nancy out the kitchen door. "It means farting," she whispered. That cracked the children up, even more so when they saw the funny face that Armand made.

At midnight, the party broke up, and Emma wondered if her clothes would turn to rags and the house staff to mice and pumpkins. Blissfully, they did not.

The entire family slept in the next day, Saturday. For the rest of the bucolic weekend, Emma played tennis with Dick, horsed around with John and Jane and their other siblings, and attended early Sunday Mass and brunch with the Dickersons. Late Sunday, it was time for Nancy and Emma to do the reverse commute via Greyhound back to New York City.

As they prepared to leave, the younger children hugged Emma. "Please visit again!" Jane exhorted. "She's nice!" John exclaimed to Nancy. The two gave their mother perfunctory kisses then waved goodbye once more to Emma and ran off to play.

Outside with Dick, Nancy observed to Emma as their cab pulled up, "You were quite a hit with Jane and John."

"They're lovely children," Emma said.

Nancy and Dick nodded, and then Nancy gave her husband a playful poke. "Don't get any ideas about hiring Emma as a governess, now," she said, referring to that summer's hit movie *The Sound of Music*.

"Wouldn't think of it, Baroness," Dick replied, winking at his wife.

. . .

On Monday, Nancy and Emma were back at Rockefeller Center bright and early, the grime of their return bus ride washed and slept off. The first person to stop by Nancy's desk that morning was Herb Pennock, who said hello and told Nancy that he'd flown in the night before. "They *flew* you?" Nancy asked, rubbing at the crick in her neck from the uncomfortable bus head rest.

"Yeah. I have a meeting with Brannigan."

Brannigan was the president of the news division. Nancy feared that meant Herb was getting canned. Even at this early hour, his breath reeked of alcohol. She had nothing against Herb and actually felt bad at the thought that he might be about to lose his job. He'd once been a good newsman. Whether his demise had been caused by the bottle or age or a combination of the two, he was no longer competent. He had seniority, but little else that she could see.

Herb had also started out in the Washington bureau. Though she'd been in New York longer than Herb, Nancy was still surprised that the other reporters in the newsroom seemed to treat Herb with warmth and familiarity. With a shrug, she chalked that up to the tendency of men to prefer to work with other men, regardless of the circumstances.

There was no time to stick around to witness the outcome of Herb's visit. Nancy and Emma were headed out to one of the new storefronts being opened by the Lindsay campaign. As the summer wore on, Lindsay campaign manager Bob Price had launched a two-pronged interrelated strategy. Because the city was congenitally Democratic, Price felt he had to demonstrate that Lindsay, though nominally a Republican, did not wear any horns. The Liberal Party designation helped in that regard, but by itself was not enough. Increased exposure would do the trick. Ancillary to this was Price's decision to wage a retail campaign. That is, he opened "Lindsay for Mayor" storefronts in as many accessible locations as possible to put his candidate, or at least his candidate's campaign offices, in the public eye every day. This was also largely the reason why Price scaled back the television budget David Garth had envisioned.

Lindsay storefronts had begun to pop up with relative frequency and in highly visible locations, where there was a lot of pedestrian traffic. Lindsay, of course, was on hand to do meet-and-greets at each grand opening. The candidate kept showing up at all sorts of locations. In the Rockaways, he could be seen walking along the beach in swim trunks, potential voters in his wake. Or he could be photographed taking a swan dive off the high board at one of the city park system's community pools. These had the added benefit of displaying Lindsay's athletic physique, which Price told Nancy the "girls" (i.e., female voters) would swoon over.

Oddly, the emphasis of these campaign efforts was not on what Lindsay had to say. Indeed, his off-the-cuff talks were mere bromides about the city in crisis and the need to look to the future and work together. And his talks always included the obligatory swing at the tired Wagner administration and its candidate, Paul Screvane. Price seemed to care less about what Jay-viel had to say, as long as people could see him in the flesh or, at a minimum, in an attractive newspaper photo.

Despite having a candidate who presented himself as the face of the future, Price was using a curiously old-fashioned campaign style.

Opponents ridiculed this approach. William F. Buckley likened a Lindsay campaign speech to the intellectual consistency of oatmeal. While Lindsay slogged the streets, Buckley was ensconced indoors, fashioning the position papers he would deliver in the fall. He viewed ten major issues as critical and planned to present solutions to those issues that were substantively different from the solutions offered by the major party candidates. He confided to insiders that the "major party candidates would differ from each other only in the appoggiaturas."

The one issue that caused Buckley to bang his head against the wall most involved traffic and transit. Problem was, there was so much vehicular traffic clogging the city streets that it impeded commerce. Congestion kept people away from the city, hence less money was spent in the city on goods and services.

Part of Buckley's idea was to create a bikeway down Second Avenue from 125th Street to 1st Street. This would ease the traffic problem, provide New Yorkers an opportunity for exercise and provide an outlet for pleasure. Buckley had the devil's own time with justifying the idea, however. One obstacle was...you guessed it...intellectual. Article I of the Constitution vested Congress with the exclusive power to regulate interstate traffic, so how to "drive" around that? In the end, he surmounted that obstacle by defining it away. Since the bikeway would solely be within city borders, it was intra-and not inter-state. Ex hypothesi, the constitutional impediment dissolved.

An interesting postscript: once revealed, the plan was ridiculed by many "in the know." "You will never see bike lanes in this city," one editorial writer assured his readership. "Buckley's idea is too fanciful."

Of course, most voters paid no attention to this sort of granularity. That was why candidates, except Buckley, routinely bumper-stickered their messages. Moreover, the public was so busy as to leave little, if any, time to grow more politically sophisticated. Positions and candidates often became transposed. A few days after outlining his plan, the candidate himself ran across the daughter-in-law of an associate who confided, "I was for John Lindsay until I heard about his ridiculous bike plan."

"Yes that *was* ridiculous, wasn't it?" Buckley said, then quickly changed the subject. It was at that moment, he later confided to a friend, that he felt he had the makings of a politician. Then the Catholic Buckley added, "How would I formulate *that* sin at my next session with my confessor?"

On the Democratic side, O'Dwyer kept appearing at community events, lambasting the tired old policies of the Wagner administration and, implicitly, of Wagner's chosen successor, Screvane. The other reformer, Ryan, spoke primarily to reform clubs while his growing cadre of volunteers popped up on his behalf at community events, pounding home the same theme as O'Dwyer (and, to an extent, as Lindsay and Beame).

The last of the gadflies of the incumbent administration, Beame also appeared at a few chosen forums castigating "the tired policies of the Wagner-Screvane team." While he did so, the bosses of Brooklyn and the Bronx who were supporting his insurgency strategized how to get the vote out.

In all, there was not much going on. For the press, this was the dullest period of the campaign. One reporter commiserated on a sweltering day with a colleague after a particularly uninspiring performance by the bland Beame. Mopping the sweat from his brow, he remarked, "Now I see why they call this the dog days of summer."

His friend snorted. "You just sat through that," he said, pointing back at Beame's podium. "This doesn't feel like the dog days of summer; it feels like the dog *years*."

The calmest camp in the race was at the air-conditioned and genteel Screvane headquarters. Firm in their conviction of inevitability, able to rationalize away any negative development with the statement that no one paid attention until after Labor Day, they let the others sweat while they coolly prepared for a leisurely run up to primary day.

And then Labor Day arrived.

CHAPTER VII

WAIT UNTIL THE SUBWAY FARE GOES UP TO 20 CENTS

"Hoo boy! Let's get on the Screvane Train!" shouted Harry Van Arsdale. The labor leader, Screvane and Manhattan party boss J. Raymond Jones were in their car on the way to Screvane headquarters. Everywhere they drove, they saw multiple "Screvane for Mayor" posters. Far more than those touting Beame.

"The boys did a great job gettin' them up," Van Arsdale said, giving himself a figurative pat on the back. His union, along with Quill's transit men and a couple of others, had spent Labor Day weekend plastering Screvane's image all over the city.

Despite Van Arsdale's euphoria, the troika was headed to campaign headquarters to discuss the latest poll results, which showed the race tightening.

Much earlier in the year, the polls on the Democratic side had not favored any of the present combatants. Screvane had placed second; Beame a distant fifth. The leader was Franklin Roosevelt, Jr. That result was a function of Roosevelt's legendary namesake. No way would anyone in his right mind entrust any serious task to FDR Junior. The late president's son had perhaps more sense than those asking the poll questions, however, for in the end he did not make the race.

Screvane was the leading pol in the city after Wagner; after all, he was city council president and acting mayor in Wagner's absence. Thus, his name recognition led to his placing close to 60 percent in the next round of polls once the FDR Jr. foolishness was dismissed. Beame languished in the high twenties. The reformers registered asterisks, with the rest undecided. Of greater note to Screvane's strategists, their man pulled in more than 80 percent of those who believed he would become the next top dog. It was this air of inevitability they believed helped their man. People like to be with a winner, so this finding meant each of the also-rans would have a much tougher time securing support for what was perceived by many to be a lost cause.

Of late, however, a number of chinks in the armor of the Screvane campaign had appeared, culminating in negative poll trends right around Labor Day:

- While Big Labor was in Screvane's court, one of the major unions, the Central Labor Council, declined to endorse Screvane. Again, this led the campaign's preferred image of inevitability to fade more.
- Beame's ethnic roots cut into what otherwise would have been a solid Jewish bloc of support for Screvane.
- Having sat out the spring and summer, Screvane had not honed his message. Thus, he was far less sharp on the stump than his primary challengers.
- Mayor Wagner, having endorsed Screvane, did little by way of active campaigning. One of Screvane's aides suggested the mayor retire early, thereby placing Screvane in Gracie Mansion right away. As the new incumbent, he would benefit from an immediate

honeymoon period. This would certainly clinch his election. Wagner rubbed his tired eyes as he refused. "I'll not do anything gimmicky for Paul. Let the electoral process proceed of its own inertia."

Due to all these factors, the polls showed a tightening. Beame was coming on strong as the only palatable alternative. Screvane's and Beame's percentages were now 46 and 38, respectively. Screvane's lead still held, but it was slipping. Faced with this, the campaign's brain trust did what it did best: met to review the bidding and convince themselves their lead was insurmountable. "Everyone knows we're gonna' win," Mike Quill said. "That by itself will push our vote totals up."

The candidate asked what steps were being taken to get that vote out. "Oh, we'll make the calls the night before. Round up the usual suspects," Jones assured the mayor-to-be. There was not much time. Labor Day that year fell on September 6. The primary would be just eight days later, on Tuesday, September 14.

"Even if you give the little Jew some credit for making a fight of it," Quill said, "he can't make up eight points in a week. Everyone knows we're gonna' win," he repeated.

Reassured, the group met nightly to continue monitoring the situation. Now in the final week, the nightly strategy sessions were minus Screvane, for the candidate at last took to the hustings. His message, though not as refined as the rest, was to stick with the Wagner policies that had done so much for the city. In this appeal, Screvane's was a lone voice crying in the wilderness, and a boring one at that.

Ryan and O'Dwyer were like a couple of pesky gnats buzzing around Screvane's head. Their message was that it was time for a change, that more of Wagner was not what was called for. Of the two, Ryan was by far the more effective, though O'Dwyer had more color and spoke with a passion Ryan could not muster. O'Dwyer had no resources, however, and was not taken as seriously.

Ryan had the bodies, although their numbers were small, of the reform-minded activists. He did not have much in the way of a monetary war chest, though what he had dwarfed what O'Dwyer had. Ryan's message was the steady eroding drip-drip-drip of criticism of the Wagner-Screvane record.

Lindsay, of course, was not in this part of the race. He faced no primary challenge. However, he had been the most active campaigner during the summer, courtesy of Bob Price's retail strategy. As such, the press routinely sought him out for comment on what was happening on the Democratic side as the primary season neared its conclusion. For public consumption, Lindsay reserved his fire for the Wagner record, in which he claimed all the Democratic contenders were complicit.

Buckley had no horse in this race, either, and was ensconced in his study, crafting his position papers, so he had no comment. Not that he had opportunity to voice one. Since he was viewed as such a long shot and since he had taken a low profile, the fourth estate let him be. There was little coverage of Buckley's campaign aside from the original announcement and the occasional piece. Certainly Buckley garnered nowhere near the ink Lindsay, Screvane, Beame, and Ryan did.

Beame emerged as the scrappiest of the lot as he blasted "the Wagner-Screvane record of futility." Not to overstate Beame's scrappiness, however. He was no Harry Truman, after all. True, Truman's voice tended to monotone when he gave a set speech. Extemporaneously, however, the little man from Missouri became quite peppy in a way that connected him with his audience. Beame, on the other hand, was a walking tranquilizer gun whether he was giving a set speech or speaking off the cuff. His highest moments rhetorically came when he gave his close. "This city has given so much to me. It has provided me a home, an education, a job. Now I want to give back to it." Hardly on par with "Four score and seven years ago," but it was endearingly homespun and did the trick. As an establishment candidate—he was comptroller, after all, and certainly no reformist—Beame could launch attacks on the "Wagner-Screvane mess" that were perceived to be a tad more credible than his opponents'. As Beame was the man in charge of the purse, people assumed he must know what he was talking about. Also, as an establishment figure, he seemed the only Democrat who had a realistic shot at dethroning Screvane. Hence, his polls numbers rose, at Screvane's expense. With a week to go, the Beame team was excited that their man was closing the gap. At least they would not be embarrassed come primary day and could push their resumes for future jobs. They prayed the week left would be enough time, though privately many of the comptroller's aides doubted. They would strive mightily for their man. Indeed, Brooklyn boss Steingut demanded it. However, they, too, had bought into the aura of Screvane's inevitability.

The "Screvane is in" mantra was heard all over the city, with kudos to Beame for making it interesting. Newspapers were awash in their own ink with this story line. That and the fresh approach awaiting the primary victor in the form of John Lindsay. Lindsay's campaign had also partaken of this particular wash. "It's going to be Paul Screvane. Of that I have no doubt," the congressman told Nancy during a snippet of conversation after one of his events. Emma was not with Nancy. In order to cover more ground, and to give the intern a chance to excel on her own, Nancy had dispatched Emma to the Buckley camp. Since Buckley was not preoccupied with the labors of greeting the electorate, Emma's task of uncovering whatever she could was eminently more difficult. On the other hand, there were low expectations of newsworthiness to come from the Buckley campaign, so Nancy saw it as a perfect training ground for Emma, an opportunity for her to hone her skills with little risk. Covering such a campaign would be a lot easier than what Nancy had to endure when she first broke in—after scratching and clawing for years to get the break. "Kids today have it so easy," she said with a sigh.

Emma's assignment and the frenetic pace set by the Lindsay camp meant there had been little time for romance between Nancy's young assistant and Jeff Chamberlain. That realization struck Nancy when Emma reported back that

Clark Mackenzie, whom Emma had royally blown up at, had been assigned to cover Buckley as well, and was crestfallen about it; Clark thought the assignment said something about how the higher-ups viewed his journalistic abilities.

Overcoming her lingering annoyance with the young man, Emma tried to give Clark an ego boost. "This is a tremendous opportunity," she said.

"How?" Clark asked morosely. "Nothing is happening here."

"Nancy says that's where the news mostly strikes, out of the unexpected."

"Nothing is happening," he repeated in the same glum tone.

"Just pick yourself up!" Emma demanded. "Listen to yourself. 'Nothing is happening.' That's probably what they said on November 22, 1963, about five minutes before the shots in Dealey Plaza rang out."

"You're right," Clark said. "I have to go about my job. Prove to them what I can be. Thanks, Emma. You know, your Nancy has some sound advice. Not bad for a girl reporter."

Emma opened her eyes wide for a second, then shook her head as she said for the first time in her life, "Oh, honestly."

Clark explained that one of the senior guys had been assigned to the Lindsay campaign, though he had other responsibilities than reporting. This morning, the other reporter attended a union meeting. All the unions tied to the newspaper industry met periodically to discuss matters of common interest, Clark further explained. "Today, I gather the big topic is the state of the talks between *New York Times* management and the pressmen's union."

"I understand if all the typesetters and other pressmen walk out at *The Times,* all the other papers will be impacted," Emma said.

"Including mine," Clark said, frowning, "though we reporters will still cover our beats. There just won't be any papers printed. The union covers all the pressmen for all city-based newspapers. They have a lot of clout."

He paused as he took off his glasses to wipe their lenses clean. Emma looked at him strangely as he did so.

"That's why they'll get management to cave," Clark continued. "It's just a matter of time."

"Not much," Emma replied. "Doesn't the contract expire soon?"

"It always goes to the wire. That's how these things operate."

Emma felt inside her purse. "Darn. I'm out of dimes. Can I borrow one?"

Clark, of course, had a load. All the reporters did. They had to be able to reach the home office at a moment's notice. The surest way to do that was to feed Ma Bell at one of the omnipresent pay phones placed all over the metropolis.

Clark gave Emma a dime from a coin wrapper that contained nearly ten dollars' worth. He again took off his tortoiseshells as he handed it over.

Emma again looked at him closely and this time, she giggled.

"What? What is it?"

"Oh, nothing," she said. "I just thought of something funny."

She ran off before Clark could pursue the point. "Girls!" he muttered. He would not have found it amusing if he'd realized Emma had run off not to call her office but to call Jeff at the Lindsay offices in the Bronx. It took a few moments for the volunteer answering the phone to locate Jeff, who was all joviality as he spoke to Emma. "I see your boss is here."

"Nancy?"

"Yeah." Emma couldn't know, of course, but her love interest was at that moment leering at her boss's rear end from his vantage point about twenty feet away.

The conversation ended shortly after. Due to the time that had elapsed while the receptionist tried to find Jeff, the three minutes of the call quickly expired after he finally got on the phone. "Please deposit ten cents for another three minutes," the nasal operator's voice broke in.

Since she had no more dimes, Emma rang off with a "Miss you!" Jeff mumbled something that sounded like he missed her, too, but might not have been. When she hung up, Emma glared at the rotary dial. "Darn phone company!" she complained, turning to a reporter who was waiting to use the phone. "I hate the control they have. Ten cents for just three minutes! It's outrageous! Money doesn't grow on trees! Besides, I thought there was a law against monopolies."

"Fat chance of that ever happening," the reporter said as he deposited his own dime. "AT&T is far too powerful. She'll never be broken up into smaller phone companies. There are certain things that are so big, so monolithic, they will last forever. Like the telephone company. And the Soviet Union."

. . .

Then it was Tuesday, election day—that is to say, primary day. It was all over but the voting. Early checking at key polling stations indicated turnout was similar to the last contested election in 1953. Around 750,000 voters were expected at the polls.

As the evening started, the gayest place of all was the Manhattan ballroom rented out by the Screvane staff. They expected to party well into the night. Nancy and Emma were stationed at their respective candidates' headquarters, so they were on the outside for the Democratic race. Gabe Pressman was there, however, fulfilling his obligation. What the other two learned later about the evening came courtesy of Gabe's sharing.

The night started off well. The Manhattan districts reported in first, and Screvane held a small lead. Not as much as his aides had expected, but he was running about eight points ahead of Beame and way ahead of the two reformers. Ryan was showing surprising strength, however.

Then the precincts from Queens and Brooklyn started to come in, and Beame chipped away at the lead. By eleven o'clock, the votes were all in, and it was a rout. The final tally was as follows:

	MHTN	Bronx	Brook'n	Queens	Staten Is.	Totals
Beame	53,386	66,664	128,146	82,801	6,148	336,345
Screvane	66,444	54,260	79,485	63.680	7,512	271,381
Ryan	48,744	16,632	24,588	22,570	1,204	113,738
O'Dwyer	6,771	5,976	8,332	6,895	697	28,675
						750,139

The turnout was, in fact, about the same as in that last contested primary race in '53. The difference all came down to Brooklyn. In 1953, then Manhattan borough president Robert Wagner defeated incumbent mayor Vincent Impellitteri by 40,000 votes in Brooklyn alone. Now, the Wagner machine failed to produce as the insurgent Brooklyn and Bronx leaders came through for Beame. Thus, the earlier pro-Wagner bulge of 40,000 in Brooklyn turned into an anti-Wagner margin of almost 50,000.

Aside from the intra-party feud between party leaders and Wagner, the steady drumbeat of anti-Wagner rhetoric by all the campaigns except Screvane's had exacted a toll. As had Screvane's presiding over what turned out to be a poorly run campaign.

The soon-to-be-former city council president conceded gracefully. He pledged his support to the Beame ticket, which had won almost across the board. Beame's running mates Frank O'Connor and Mario Procaccino had been swept along in the tide. A reporter expressed regret that one of Screvane's ticket mates whom he felt was of superior ability would be consigned to political oblivion. Yet while crestfallen, Daniel

THE NATION'S HOPE

Patrick Moynihan had a resiliency and did not expect to remain counted out.

As the night wore on and the shocking upset became apparent, would-be revelers quietly slunk out of the Screvane party-turned-wake as members of the campaign's inner circle mouthed inanities.

"We have to fix this fuckin' thing!" Mike Quill shouted.

"How?" party leader Weinstein said. "The polls have closed; the votes are in, Mike."

"We have to fix this fuckin' thing," was Quill's not-so-helpful reply.

The only discordant note came when Mayor Wagner paid a visit to the funereal gathering. A reporter overheard Screvane tell one of his supporters, "There's the blankety-blank that caused me to lose." Whether Screvane's sentiment stemmed from Wagner's refusal to abdicate in his favor or campaign more actively, or because he'd helped foment the party split, the reporter could not say.

Curiously, while Screvane conceded and endorsed Beame, the reformers played coy, partly due to the influence of Alex Rose. There was a natural affinity between the reform wing of the Democratic Party and the Liberal Party. Rose had been working the phones assiduously primary night and urged them to follow his lead into the Lindsay camp. "If you want to send a message to the regular Democrats, this will do it. Make no mistake." The second part of his message was that Lindsay believed in the causes they did, more so than the regulars like Wagner, Screvane and Beame. Some reformers opted right away to cleave to the party of their ancestors and endorsed Beame. Others heeded Rose's advice and endorsed Lindsay flat out. Many remained aloof—for the time being. "We will have to see what we can get out of this," Village Independent Democrats leader Ed Koch advised.

Whereas the gloom in Screvane-land and the dichotomous reaction in the reform camps were palpable, the scene at Beame headquarters was riotously joyous. Several of the top echelon were drunk, so deep were they into celebrating their good fortune.

The diminutive comptroller grinned from ear to ear as, of necessity, he stood on a soap box placed behind the podium. He thanked supporters, especially the Brooklyn and Bronx leadership. He acknowledged Screvane's public service and welcomed him in the fight for "progressive principles." Then he lambasted Lindsay. Not by name, but there was no mistaking the reference. "We cannot allow the reactionary forces of Goldwaterism to pollute our city," he said, trying to tie Lindsay, despite his outspoken liberalism, to what was perceived as the GOP's albatross, the unpopular conservative movement. He closed, as always, with "New York City has done a lot for me...."

The people who were among the most snake bit by the primary were those who'd least expected to be, namely the Lindsay staff. Reporters assigned to Congressman Lindsay had expected a perfunctory statement after the primary results were in and the Screvane-Lindsay race was set to begin.

Now there would be none of that, courtesy of the Democratic voters. Lindsay made a brief appearance during which he congratulated Beame. "I look forward to discussing the issues with Comptroller Beame in the coming weeks, and letting New Yorkers choose if they want a change, or if they want to remain on the path set forth by the Wagner-Beame team." Then he was off like a shot as reporters shouted questions in his direction.

"Congressman! Are you surprised at Beame's showing?"

"No comment."

"Congressman Lindsay! Does this change your campaign strategy?"

"No comment."

"Mr. Lindsay, are you disappointed that your opponent has been equally critical of the Wagner administration?"

This time there was not even a "no comment" comment, as aides hustled the candidate away from the prying eyes of the cameramen and reporters. In the backroom, Lindsay, Price and others of their campaign's higher echelon huddled together. Beame's win represented a setback, to be sure, but they could not admit as much publicly. For the first time, the "new politics" of openness was welded shut. Nancy was able to piece together most of the story from a sympathetic aide to Price.

There was, in fact, much consternation in Lindsay-land, according to the aide. They fervently believed Wagner deserved to be discredited. When he stepped out, the mantle fell to Screvane, so in effect, a campaign against Screvane was still a campaign against the status quo. But now? Beame had run by attacking Wagnerism, thus removing one of their most effective tools.

Beame's ethnicity also compromised the Lindsay strategy. Heretofore, Price had intended to wage holy war in Jewish districts to secure otherwise Democratic votes. Now, with the emergence of Beame—who, if elected, would be the city' first Jewish mayor—that prong of the Lindsay campaign strategy was toppled over. This upset all of Price's carefully laid plans.

The person who rode to the rescue was Alex Rose, so much so that Price, who had a superior opinion of himself over all other tacticians on the planet, came to view Rose with admiration.

Rose was categorical in his belief that, run properly, the Lindsay campaign would prevail. There were three points he considered crucial:

- The need to tie Wagner around Beame's neck. The comptroller might try to talk his way out of claiming that albatross, but despite his words, he'd run with and served as comptroller under Wagner. Hence, he was as much a part of the Wagner administration as anyone. When Beame tried to break free, the Lindsay campaign should accuse him of being an untrustworthy flip-flopper.

- The fact that Beame was not an impressive-looking fellow. Certainly, he was not dynamic enough to handle a city slipping out of control. The Lindsay campaign should stay active in the Jewish areas and ask Jewish voters if Beame was the kind of person they would be proud to say represents their race. Moreover, if the city were to slide into bankruptcy, would Jews want Beame (and hence Jews generally) to get the blame? He would become the Jewish Hoover.
- The fact that there was nothing dynamic about Beame. The Lindsay campaign should capitalize on the youth, energy and enthusiasm Lindsay offered the city. As the saying goes, "He is fresh, and everyone else is tired."

So, with a modest mid-course correction, the Lindsay strategy stood. As part of demonstrating his aura of excitement, Lindsay came out swinging the next day. He trekked to all five boroughs, tagging Beame with the failures of the Wagner administration. The word used most often in connection with Wagner-Beame was "tired." Advance man Jerry Bruno had done his work. Crowds showed up at each event, eager to grab some part of the likeable, handsome congressman.

As part of their refined strategy, Lindsay challenged Beame to debate. Sponsorship would be under the aegis of an influential but nonpartisan group, the League of Women Voters. Faced with no choice, Beame accepted. No one thought many people would tune in to local programming on a Sunday afternoon to watch the mayoral candidates. That did not matter to Team Lindsay. The fact that they were calling for the debate set their man apart as a fresh face. In addition, even though few would see the debate directly, Price believed Lindsay's glamour would easily outclass Beame's blandness. What's more, the press would report on Lindsay's appearance favorably. And it was in the newspapers that voters got their news and formed their opinions. How the newspapers reported the debate was more important than the debate itself, largely because the actual viewing audience was expected to be so tiny. In 1964 when Bobby Kennedy debated Senator Kenneth Keating, the ratings were miniscule. The newspapers, however, trumpeted news of Kennedy's superior performance repeatedly, and that was how word got out.

Lindsay and Beame were obviously all about bells and whistles. Buckley, on the other hand, had substance, but his voice was akin to the sound of a tree falling in the forest. Except on primary night, there were two Zen novitiates, in a manner of speaking, who witnessed the sound.

. . .

Of the few reporters assigned to Buckley, all had left the area adjoining *The National Review* offices...except Emma and Clark. No one inside the offices had left, so the two young journalists determined to wait it out to get a sound bite from Buckley regarding Beame's success.

Nancy had intended to make a pit stop at Buckley's offices that night to see the candidate's reaction for herself. As much as she trusted Emma, at the core this was Nancy's assignment, and she was not one to abdicate responsibility. But it had been a hectic day that had started very early. Knowing that election nights often dragged on as returns came in, especially in close races, and wanting to develop warm relations with the male press corps, Nancy had decided the day prior to the primary to spring for a treat the morning of the big day. She had long felt it was important for her to find a way to bond with the men, but she was at a disadvantage since she was neither a sports enthusiast nor into heavy drinking. Moreover, inasmuch as the New York bureau was too far from Merrywood, it was not practical to invite the entire bureau to a luncheon or dinner.

In a Monday evening discussion of these impediments, Emma had said to her boss, "If the mountain cannot come to Mohammed...." Nancy brightened as she snapped her fingers, and then headed for the grocery store.

Tuesday morning, Nancy arrived before everyone else, busily going about her tasks. When Arthur, Gabe and the rest ambled in, their first stop was always at the coffee station. This time, however, they were shocked to see something that had never been in the food room before—Food! An array of bagels, donuts, butter, jams, cream cheese, lox, fresh-squeezed orange juice was laid out for all to enjoy. It did not take long for word to spread about the spread, and the newsmen herded to the food en masse. Nancy was at her hostess best, mingling and facilitating conversations.

One of the correspondents cried out in delight. "Oh! Cream cheese! I would love a schmear!"

Nancy told him to go right on and smear it on his bagel.

"Not smear. Schmear," he happily corrected her.

"Schmear?" Nancy questioned. "That's what the lady at the bakery said. I thought she had a speech impediment."

Emma, who had just arrived, was happy to see Nancy in her element. Truly, the breakfast could not have gone better. Emma also noticed Arthur taking it all in, especially when Nancy was stuck in a sports circle talking about Mickey Mantle's decline. "His legs are shot," one of the men said.

Another said the Mick was still solid muscle "up here" while gesturing to his upper torso.

Nancy said, "It seems to me a batter's strength comes from the waist down."

Emma could tell the men were impressed, and Nancy resolved to invite Dick Schaap to one of her dinners when she was back in Northern Virginia.

Arthur also witnessed many, though not all, of the newsmen thank Nancy as they left to start their work day, a few with enough bagels stuffed in their pockets to last until dinner. On the way out, one of the guys nudged Gabe. "You're right, Pressman. She's not bad at all!"

Another fell in step with Gabe and his comrade. "If she wasn't a girl, she could be one of the boys!"

One other told Nancy not to be a stranger and said she should join them for the nightly sessions at McHale's.

There were a few, however, who remained standoffish. No one was gauche enough to say anything such as "this only proved women belong in the kitchen," but Nancy was perceptive.

As the day progressed, Nancy worked the phones to get some Lindsay quotes in anticipation of the Screvane victory and went to several polling places and interviewed voters.

Late in the day, back at Rockefeller Center, Nancy went to the coffee room for a glass of water. There, she encountered a stooped figure who was strutting comically around the room. When he turned, she recognized him instantly.

Looking up, the man said, "I heard there was food in here, but all I see are some crumbs and this coffee here. If I was a bird, it would be sweet. Say," he added, leering at Nancy, "you could be my sweetener. What do you say?"

Nancy smiled pleasantly and replied the food had been put out in the morning.

"Oh, morning, noon, night, what does it matter? Let's run away and make love."

Nancy shook her head, assuming Groucho Marx was there because he would be a guest on that evening's *Tonight Show,* which would soon be taped.

"Why, Mr. Marx," she said, "I hardly know what to say."

"That's all right. I prefer the silent ones myself." He fingered his cigar and leered lasciviously.

"No. I mean I'm married."

Groucho's eyebrows darted up. "I won't tell."

He flung his arms around Nancy. "Marry me!"

"Certainly not!" she cried, though she could not disentangle herself.

"All right," he said, still holding her, "I'm all for by-passing the wedding and going right to bed."

Nancy was saved when *Tonight Show* producer Fred DeCordova came in search of his errant guest and pried Groucho loose. As he left, the Marx Brother called back, "Be sure to look me up! I'm in the book!" as he ogled a secretary who was passing him to enter the break room.

"Oh, honestly!" Nancy proclaimed. She must have looked flustered, for the secretary asked, "Is everything all right? How are you?"

Nancy replied with her trademark, "All the better for seeing you!"

Then it was back to work, though the episode exacted a toll as Nancy felt rattled and needed a few minutes and more than a few drinks of water to recuperate.

Of course, when Beame upset Screvane, he also upset all of Nancy's preparations for the evening. The late hours of the day were spent scampering after Lindsay's aides for comment, a task rendered more difficult because the Lindsay camp was in a mild panic after the loss of their anticipated opponent. Nancy would not stand down until she had buttonholed the congressman or Price, however, so there was no way could she enjoy the luxury of a field trip to Buckley's office.

Emma and Clark did not mind going solo at the candidate's office, however. As far as they were concerned, opportunity was knocking.

As the hours passed, fatigue and hunger set in. Between the two of them, they had 75 cents...not counting Clark's wad of dimes, which were sacrosanct. Emma offered to do a food run. There was no sexism involved, as Clark had earlier fetched three rounds of coffee for them. Emma felt it only fair that she offer to make the trip this time.

When she returned from a corner deli with two sandwiches, apples, cookies, chips and two coffees, Emma complained about costs getting out of control. "Can you believe it!" she fumed. "Just some lunch food for dinner, and all I got back from our 75 cents was four pennies change!"

"Wait until the subway fare goes up to twenty cents," Clark cautioned.

"Heaven forbid! That happens, and they'll lynch the mayor, whoever he is."

When they'd finished eating and were still lying in wait, Clark offered that the coffee had taken its toll. "Not to be crass," he said, "but I have to take a leak."

The two were startled when a familiar voice said, "I would be most sanguine if you did not perform any bodily functions in the hallway." As he spoke, William F. Buckley's eyes flashed at his quip. He directed Clark to a "lavatory" three doors down on the right. As Clark excused himself, two other gentlemen departed the *National Review* office. Emma recognized the candidate's brother James and Conservative Party chairman Kieran O'Doherty.

In the silence, Buckley tapped his fingernail against his teeth and looked at Emma. "I rather hope your friend is not in need of filling Lake Champlain. Otherwise, we can be in for a long night."

"Ye...yes...sir," Emma stammered.

Under the assumption the young lady was not afflicted with a stutter, Buckley grinned and asked, "Are you nervous? Of me?"

Emma felt foolish and, like an errant schoolchild, nodded.

"Why ever for? I shan't be cause for any harm. Aside from keeping you out past your bedtime," Buckley said, glancing at his watch.

"Oh, no sir," Emma said, "it's just that I'm nervous...."

Buckley feigned surprise. "You certainly hide it well."

Now Emma smiled at this pleasant man, the ice broken. "It's just that...I'm afraid I won't understand you."

"I promise not to spontaneously break into ancient Swahili," Buckley said with a disarming smile. Emma had no doubt he could.

Just then, Clark returned.

"I rather suspect it is time for interrogatories," Buckley surmised.

"Can we ask you a question?" Emma said.

"You just did," he smiled.

"Another one?"

"You have just done that as well."

Emma thought fast. "Two more?"

"Fortunately, I am not a genie, and you are not restricted to three questions."

Before the young journalists could pose their questions, Buckley spotted an unopened bag of potato chips on the hall table behind them. Emma noticed and asked if he would like some.

"I am famished," Buckley said. Re-opening the door to his office, he beckoned the reporters in, clutching the bag of snacks. The three sat around his office and, as Buckley munched on the chips, Clark asked for a comment on Beame's victory.

"Clearly congratulations are in order to Mr. Beame, if not to the electorate."

Emma asked if that meant he did not agree with the voters' choice.

"Oh, I have no quarrel personally with Mr. Beame or, for that matter, with Messrs. Screvane, Ryan or O'Dwyer. It is just that the voters could have written in the name 'William F. Buckley, Joon-yah,'" he stretched out the last syllable, "which, regretfully, they chose not to do. As I believe you shall see, the difference between Mr. Lindsay and Mr. Beame will be meaningless. Their solutions will all amount to either allocating greater government funding or designating a commission to study current problems. The only differences will be slight. I, on the other hand, shall offer meaningful choices. That is the object of the exercise. Allowing the voters to choose. One can hardly choose when there is no choice, can one?"

Emma next asked if the voters would take the time to study the alternatives.

Buckley admitted he was an optimist who believed people were smarter than the major parties gave them credit for. "I must, however, posit a caveat. This is the same country, after all, that is endlessly fascinated of late by the hula hoop."

Emma and Clark laughed, and Clark complimented the 39-year-old candidate. "If the election were based on wit, you would have a real chance," he said.

The candidate's smile faded. "Apparently not everyone appreciates my wit." He went on to explain the meeting that had just transpired dealt with the seriousness of his campaign. Specifically, the leadership of the Conservative Party was concerned Buckley was not taking things more seriously. They were squeamish because of his negligible standing in the polls, a mere blip in the low single digits. Buckley's continued pursuit of his other business interests and miniscule public campaigning profile fueled the perception. He was quite serious, however. He just did not believe in the efficacy of traditional campaigning. Buckley placed great store in the position papers to come. "As a compromise, I did agree to stage a few traditional events."

"Such as?" Emma prodded.

"I shall endeavor to kiss two babies a day."

All three laughed.

Emma asked if Buckley saw any path to victory.

"It all depends on how one defines victory, doesn't it? Shall I become the 103rd mayor of New York? Obviously not. However, if I can significantly improve on the showing of past conservative spokesmen, I believe that would indicate that conservatism as a political movement is a viable force in the United States."

Buckley noted that prior Conservative candidates for governor and senator in 1962 and 1964, respectively, had polled 100,000 votes in the city. He believed if he could increase that by 50,000, his efforts would be deemed a success. Nancy later agreed that would be a "win."

It was very late as Buckley bid his farewells to the young reporters and wished them well in their careers. "I like correspondents," he said. "Words are important to me, after all."

Out on the street, Emma plunked a subway token for the ride home. "Nice guy," she said.

Clark agreed. "A nice guy who's making me think Goldwater set conservatism back a generation."

.   .   .

When Emma relayed this exchange with Clark to Nancy the next morning after debriefing her boss on the Buckley interview, Nancy presented a different perspective.

"To the contrary," she said, "Goldwater may have opened the door to a revitalized conservatism. Remember the Solid South? No Republican could ever be victorious south of the Mason-Dixon Line. Well, the states old Barry won were in the South. Many unsuccessful campaigns sow the seeds for future harvest. Maybe the Goldwater movement was a way station that will allow Southern Democrats to actually enjoy a two-party system."

She continued to explain a similar dynamic had occurred in the 1928 election, when Al Smith was trounced by Republican Herbert Hoover. Though he lost, Smith had been the first Democrat to poll well in major urban areas, presaging Franklin Roosevelt's landslide just four years later and an era of Democratic dominance, especially in the cities, that still continued.

Nancy also called to mind the lesson of that actor, Ronald Reagan, who had spoken on a nationally televised fund appeal last fall for Goldwater. His speech resulted in record sums being raised. That indicated that conservatism was not dead, just looking for an appealing leader.

"So you think Buckley can be successful?" Emma queried.

"If he can poll 150,000 votes, yes, I think that would be the harbinger of things to come. On the other hand, if he does poorly and Lindsay succeeds, then it could be a nail in the right's coffin."

As the days progressed from September to October, Emma did notice an increase, small but nonetheless apparent, in Buckley's appearances. Nancy saw much more of Lindsay, meanwhile, for Price had placed the candidate on a rolling meat market, displaying his fit form as much as possible. The problem Nancy and most of the journalists covering Lindsay had was that the candidate was saying the same things over and over. This was a common affliction of all correspondents covering any campaign. By the end, they knew the candidate's stump speech by heart. In this case, however, it hurt Lindsay in two ways. First, his campaign placed so much emphasis on him being "fresh" that he could not afford to come across as staid. Second, because Lindsay had started so early and had been the most active campaigner in the spring and summer months, he ran the risk of becoming overexposed.

Beame, on the other hand, coming off his startling primary win, was something of a fresh face, oddly enough. He also did not have the direct taint of the Wagner administration that would've followed his primary opponent, had he won. And, because he was comptroller, people assumed he was the most knowledgeable regarding the city's fiscal affairs and would be well situated to steer the city out of any pending financial crisis. As such, Beame benefitted from a post-primary bump in the polls and now led Lindsay by four points.

There was excitement in the air, to be sure. In fact, the fall of 1965 in New York was a thrilling time. Events occurred that people never thought they would live to see, and all this added to the aura of magnificence surrounding the mayoralty race.

One of the manifestations of the season's nonpolitical events was the first visit to the city, in fact to the United States, of a pope of the Roman Catholic Church. The newly installed pope, Paul VI, spoke to the United Nations, bringing waves of onlookers into the city streets. It was unheard of for a pope to leave the Vatican. Paul was viewed as a progressive, so many American Catholics expected serious reform to occur in his papacy.

Of course, not all New York events outside politics were groundbreaking that fall. One traditional rite of passage unexpectedly took on serious religious overtones. The rite of passage was the annual national obsession with the number one sport in the land. Every October, afternoons were consumed by the World Series, and for decades, New York had been represented in this annual tradition. Now, however, with the collapse of the Yankee dynasty, the departure of the powerhouse Dodgers and Giants and the futility of the Mets, it could be eons before the national pastime's crown jewel returned to the city. Still, this year's World Series generated unusual interest among New Yorkers The despised Dodgers, who had fled Gotham, were in the fall classic. Their opponent, the Minnesota Twins, had themselves recently relocated from Washington, D.C. The Dodgers had gotten to the Series largely on the strong left arm of Sandy Koufax, who had emerged as the premier pitcher of his generation. The problem? Koufax was Jewish, and the Series began on one of the holiest of holy days in the Hebrew religion: Yom Kippur (or "Yom Kipper," as most non-ethnic New Yorkers pronounced it). Accordingly, Koufax had announced he would sit out the first two games of the Series in observance.

There being no forum for fans to talk sports on a mass scale, myriad small conversations occurred in bars, water coolers, schoolyards and newspaper columns as enormous amounts of energy were devoted to wondering how this man could let down his team, his fans and baseball purists everywhere. Surely the national pastime trumped some trivial religious observance. A tiny minority dissented, however. The man should abide his principles, they argued. Religion, even an outlying one like Judaism, deserved the same respect that would be accorded to Christianity when one of its faithful chose to refrain from playing a professional sport on Christmas or Easter. Though, of course, games would never be scheduled then because they were recognized widely by many Americans. The debate grew testier when the Dodgers lost the first two games of the best-of-seven Series. Fortunately, the holy day observation then ended, Koufax returned, and the Dodgers stormed back to prevail. And the furor around the pitcher's controversial decision died down.

When the furor was still in full swing, however, Nancy heard two somewhat inebriated fans going at it just outside Jack Dempsey's on her way from a Lindsay rally at Madison Square Garden. This was the third Garden and, oddly enough, the first one that was not located near Madison Square. This latest iteration stood at Eighth Avenue between 50th and 51st Streets, and several iconic restaurants and watering holes had sprouted up in the vicinity to service the Garden crowd. Toots Shors and Dempsey's, in particular, were highly popular. The latter was so named for its chief greeter and proprietor, the former heavyweight champion from the Roaring Twenties, Jack Dempsey. Since losing the infamous long count when he was clearly robbed of the title, Dempsey had become a beloved figure in his adopted city. Originally hailing from a tiny one-room house in equally tiny Manassa, Colorado, the "Manassa Mauler" retired to New York where, at the Garden, he had fought his most memorable fights and forged his (and some say the city's) identity.

Nancy stood outside Dempsey's and watched the "discussion" the two were having from a safe distance. Since they were swaying as they cursed each other out, it was safe to assume they had imbibed freely. Another sign was that, although they seemed to be on the same side of the issue, they were close to blows. From the derogatory references, which included words like jewboy, kike and hymie, Nancy gathered they were displeased with Koufax. It turned out one of the two had bet on the Dodgers at the behest of his colleague, and that fueled the source of the current friction, and the antagonism toward the Dodger southpaw.

When the pair finally gave up on their argument and went back into Dempsey's, Nancy went on her way. "Boys," she muttered. "If they keep watching instead of playing, this country is going to become quite obese." She never understood the near-total absorption men had with sports. It confused her almost as much as the fascination so many women shared with celebrities, especially celebrity romances.

Interest in the romantic lives of stars had run rampant in New York that summer and into the fall. Network television coverage and some of the newspapers, chiefly *The Daily News* and *The Post,* fueled this growing obsession as well as a burgeoning industry of fan magazines. A few of the noteworthy celebrity romances currently being covered were the August marriage of the young starlet-daughter of distinguished actor Henry Fonda (her name was Jane) to a much older French film director, Roger Vadim. The networks especially liked to project bikini-clad images of Mrs. Vadim. Another was a rising female tennis star, Billie Jean Moffitt, who married an attorney named Larry King in September. Interest in this romance was magnified because there were not a lot of female athletes who could claim the type of pop status Moffitt had already earned.

The third romance dominating the news was a tale of an on again-off again affair, namely the stormy marriage of Elizabeth Taylor and Richard Burton. There was an added reason why these two were in the headlines: they were embroiled in a fantastic legal battle with one of the major Hollywood movie studios, Twentieth Century Fox.

A few years earlier, Liz and Dick had met on the set of *Cleopatra,* had a torrid affair and married. The studio was now suing the two for breach of contract, and the suit was brought in the federal court system. The reason this case had taken on added notoriety in New York was because the federal district court was located in Manhattan, and the court had just ruled. The details were obscure, clouded in the mists of legal sophistry. Essentially, however, the suit was dismissed in Liz's favor. In order to bring an action in federal court, there must be diversity jurisdiction. That is, the litigants must be citizens of different states. Liz's attorneys argued that, although she was a citizen of the United States, she was not a resident of any particular state, since she had numerous homes and had never established permanent ties to any one state. Hence, there was no diversity, and the suit was thrown out.

At any rate, the case offered a pretext for the media to display revealing photos of the young beauty and to pore over, yet again, the salacious details of the Taylor-Burton relationship.

・　・　・

One summer romance that continued well into September that year but was not at all newsworthy was the one between Emma Thornton and Jeff Chamberlain. To Emma's delight, things with Jeff heated up during a rare lull that occurred when Congressman Lindsay had to return to Washington for a crucial vote.

One morning, an exhausted Emma confided in Nancy that she and Jeff had gone "well past first base," as she put it, the night before. By now, Nancy knew her protégé was old-fashioned, and that leaping into bed did not come naturally to Emma. She was not that kind of girl. Modesty seemed to be the norm, though it was hard to tell because such topics were never discussed in public. Indicative of this was the fact that on TV, husbands and wives all had separate beds, if not separate bedrooms. What Emma did not confide in Nancy was that Jeff had let it be known he expected to "go all the way" next time. Emma was definitely smitten and, since she now thought Jeff could be the one she would someday marry, she was slowly resolving in her mind the unshackling of her strict upbringing.

Later that day, Emma found herself half drifting off at a Buckley press conference. Snapping herself awake, she refocused on what the candidate was saying. This was the day Buckley planned to reveal his position paper on traffic and transit that included the Second Avenue bikeway idea, but went far beyond that. Buckley also called for an express commuter bus lane at all bridges and tunnels, increased tolls at bridges and tunnels for non-city registered vehicles, staggered even-odd days for deliveries into Midtown, lower costs and higher fares on city subways and buses, free transit tokens to the impoverished, the end of diplomatic immunity for traffic infractions, and the issuance of more taxi medallions.

As the city's mayoralty campaigns prepared to enter the second full week of September, Buckley was speaking to mostly empty audiences about the traffic and transit mess, Lindsay was addressing the need for fresh energy, Beame was pledging to give something back to the city, and the polls were showing:

Beame	44
Lindsay	39
Buckley	4
Fringe Candidates	1
Undecided	12

And then everything changed.

CHAPTER VIII

I WON'T INSULT YOUR INTELLIGENCE BY SUGGESTING THAT YOU REALLY BELIEVE WHAT YOU JUST SAID

On a hunch, Nancy was there the moment the clock stopped. She had been waiting outside the conference room of the Waldorf-Astoria. Since this impacted all the campaigns, Emma was in tow. Inside, representatives of the pressmen's union and management at *The New York Times* were hard at their task. Which at the moment seemed to be about not budging.

The crux of the problem was that, in order to contain costs, ownership wanted to mechanize more and more of the production process. Technology had advanced to the point where typeset did not have to be manually placed, as it had in Gutenberg's day. The union objected, for more mechanization meant less jobs. The owners contended that dollars were flying out of their pockets in droves. In response, labor played the world's tiniest violin. It was hard to generate sympathy when the millionaires and their hired legal mouthpieces were chauffeur driven to the hotel in mile-long cars.

(Of course, in America in 1965, almost all the cars were large, as they were manufactured by the Big Three in Detroit save for a few imports such as the downsized VW Beetles. The confident Big Three shrewdly marketed to never-changing tastes and thus designed cars that were enormous by European or Japanese standards and had tail fins rivaling the Titan rocket booster used in the Gemini space program.)

Compounding labor's unease, management refused to open their books for inspection. Their cries of poverty were deemed to be a sham. As to management's warning that this could be the end of (newspaper) life as we know it, the union negotiators cited Chicken Little. Everyone knew newspapers would be around forever. Any owner suggesting that some or all of New York's nine dailies would fold was branded a fool.

Yet despite the intransigence, both sides feared a strike. Memories of the 162-day strike in 1962 were still too raw. That walk-out had been prolonged for so long that, even after the settlement and increased pay, the workers never made up the lost wages. Nor did management recoup the enormous profits forfeited during the four-month stoppage. Of course, neither side cared back then that public opinion cast a pox on both their houses. "The people will come back when we are back online," both management and labor confidently predicted. "They have nowhere else to go. No alternative inexpensive entertainment outlets exist."

In that, they forgot that commercial television was free. Paid exclusively by advertisers, chief among which was the tobacco industry with its ever-present ads luring new generations to the health-inspiring benefits of nicotine. Television was coming of age as well, courtesy of two new inventions. Color TV, for one. And to lure people to purchase the more costly color TV sets, the networks broadcast series uniquely suited to display out-of-doors splendor. One such show was the number one hit *Bonanza,* which was set in Carson City, Nevada in the Old West. Citing the show's immense ratings, one critic waxed eloquent as to how *Bonanza* would likely be in production for at least 50 years.

The other TV-related technological development was the remote control, a tiny box that allowed a television viewer to change channels without leaving his couch. As with the rise of spectator sports, the remote control was contributing to the sedentary-ization of America as it helped spawn collateral industries, from *TV Guide* to snack foods.

Television strove to take up the slack in the 1962 strike. Children's show hosts like Captain Jack McCarthy and Officer Joe Bolton read comics to the kids (and those adults also forced to tune in to get their fix), as Mayor LaGuardia had done over the radio in years past. Newscasts were lengthened, featuring more local fare. Yet in the back rooms of the august Waldorf-Astoria, the negotiators blithely assumed life would go on as normal once past this logjam.

In any event, both sides agreed to "stop the clock" at a minute before midnight on the evening of September 13, 1965, the time the contract was set to expire, in order to avoid another strike. About four hours into the marathon bargaining session that followed the clock "stoppage," one of the management lawyers demonstrated either an incredible lack of tact or the arrogance for which the big law firms were known when he suggested to the union head that "the peons you represent are so ignorant, it is amazing to believe they are able to procreate." To this, the union chief responded with a pithier sexual reference of his own that started with the letter "f" and ended with the word "you."

This exchange effectively restarted the clock. The contract stopped, as did newspaper presses across the city. While technically the only paper imminently affected was *The Times,* union workers at all the other papers stood (or sat, depending on one's point of view) together.

The next morning, eight million residents of the city of New York saw nothing on their stoops or newsstands. They learned of the stoppage, and then the strike, from radio and TV. Increasingly they turned to television, accelerating a demographic trend for which the negotiators had not bargained, and which had been in the works since the early 1950s. Whereas before only one in ten Americans owned a television set, now eight in ten did. While only one in ten neighbors owning a set fostered community as groups would gather to witness major events, now the sheer number of sets bred isolation in the spatial sense. That is, people remained indoors and kept to themselves. Eventually in more affluent families, this trend would accelerate to where children might have their own TVs, keeping them in their rooms and away from the rest of their family. Conversely, a sense of electronic community arose as everyone shared the same news sources and entertainment, creating a common electronic culture.

On every day of the week, more people flocked to the tube for more hours each day. No more so than on Sundays, when the absence of the larger-edition newspapers with the magazine supplements was keenly felt.

Also because of the newspaper strike, New Yorkers were anxious to watch the debates on television, though many would not have done so otherwise. With the papers crippled, watching the debates was the only way to compare the candidates.

Indeed, this was the topic of conversation late on the third week of September in the Thornton household. As in the "Emma" Thornton household, more properly the Queens home of Emma's parents. Reciprocating Nancy's invitation for dinner at Merrywood, Emma's mother had brow beaten her daughter to extend a dinner invitation, which Nancy gracefully accepted. Mrs. Thornton was pleased. She had watched Nancy on TV. A real live star was going to be in her home!

Having been to Merrywood, Emma felt embarrassed. Nancy's 36-room estate was situated on acres and acres of land. Emma's Queens home had six rooms on a postage stamp sized plot. Nancy's husband looked like he could model for golf, tennis or business attire. Emma's dad watched the Mets on WOR-TV in his white Hanes undershirt. While "Dick" Dickerson was a titan of finance, Dad worked for the city

Transit Authority. He supervised maintenance on the subway cars. As for her younger brother, Randy in his torn jeans and perpetually smudged face could not live up to the fresh out of a magazine scrubbed good looks of the Dickerson children.

When Nancy arrived, Barbara Thornton had tasks to complete so the trio relocated to the kitchen. Then Randy came in. Warned by Emma under pain of death, he was on his best behavior. He asked Nancy if she wanted to try his skateboard. This was all the craze, "neat" as Randy characterized it in the vernacular. Nancy politely declined.

Just then they heard the front door slam and a low voice called out, "I'm home!"

Emma and Randy flew out of the kitchen, Barbara less hurriedly so. Nancy walked out to see what the commotion was all about. Mr. Thornton tousled the boy's hair, held his arms wide open for Emma and kissed his wife hello.

Emma stepped back and cast a long glance at her father. Something was off. Then she got it. In place of his tee, he was wearing a blue button down shirt. The one he wore on Thanksgiving, Christmas and Easter. He walked up to Nancy who extended her hand. Barbara had introduced "Dave", who took Nancy's hand, bowed down and kissed it. Emma wanted to crawl under the sofa. Nancy smiled broadly, curtsied, and told Dave, "Such a gallant gentleman!" Emma prayed for a quick death.

Dinner came out and it was just as delicious as it smelled. Chicken cacciatore. Nancy's mouth actually watered it was so good. The meat slid off the bone it was so tender.

During dinner in addition to Dave's dress shirt, Emma noticed other things that made her wonder if she had stumbled into the Twilight Zone. For one thing, the napkins. The Thorntons always ate with napkins to the left of the dinner plate, at the ready for quick mopping up of face and hands while eating. This evening however as soon as they were seated and grace was said, Nancy had taken her napkin, unfolded it and placed it down on her lap. Barbara caught this and immediately followed suit. She cleared her throat and Dave and Emma picked up the cue. It took Dave's look boring into Randy that persuaded the confused youngster to crumple his hand towel in a ball and toss it onto his lap. Throughout the meal the boy used the only thing handy to wipe himself, his hand.

Barbara had served coffee. When Dad lifted his cup Emma's eyes widened as he held it by the handle with his pinkie extended at about a 90-degree angle. Emma thought if she lived to be 9,000 years old she would never see Dad do such a thing. Mom was holding her cup at the same time. As soon as she saw Dad, she mentally reproached herself for her lower class manners and tried to recoup by quickly raising her pinkie finger. Randy thought it was good fun so he raised his as well. His cup was not filled with coffee but with that new chocolate drink that had just come on the market, Yoo Hoo. So as not to be a freak, or perhaps to hide her family's freakish ways, Emma followed the leader.

As Nancy raised her cup to her lips she noticed the weird way the family grasped their drinks. "It must be a New York thing," she figured. "Well, when in Rome..." and Nancy mimicked the rest. Strange as it seemed, for at least 30 years the story spread through the neighborhood of the time the Thorntons had a dinner guest so regal that the family drank their coffee with pinkies extended.

Nancy congratulated Dave on his return.

"Return? From where?" he wondered.

"Why, when you came home today, the way everyone greeted you, I assumed you had been away."

"Just to work. Yesterday I did have to go to Canarsie though. That took about 45 minutes."

"But the way the children and Barbara ran up to you when you arrived, I figured you must have been on an extended trip."

"No," Emma said. "That is just the way we greet Dad every night he comes home. We are happy he is here with us." Dave beamed.

Nancy nodded thoughtfully, her brow wrinkled as she buttered a biscuit.

Then talk turned to the election. Dave said we needed a change. "City's goin' to hell in a hand basket." The group talked about how hard it was to follow the election with the newspaper strike and how TV was taking up the slack. After dinner as Emma walked Nancy to the subway stop Nancy observed, "You are so lucky, Emma. Your family is wonderful! And your home...it is filled with love. It reminds me of my house growing up in Wisconsin, except my parents were not ones for displays of affection." She paused, looking at the stars, then repeated, "You are so lucky."

Barbara Thornton was pleased with how the evening had gone but she did tell Dave that Nancy "was so glamorous. And I...I am getting grayer. Finding more wrinkles, and gaining a little weight. I guess I need you to pay me a compliment."

"Your eyesight's perfect," Dave said as he ducked a pillow and the two were laughing and rassling on the bed.

On the ride home, Nancy reflected on how warm and genuine the Thorntons were, and also on the fact that because of the newspaper strike, the Thorntons and most New Yorkers were anxious to watch the debates on television, though many would not have done so otherwise. With the papers crippled, watching the debates was the only way to compare the candidates.

There were going to be a series of four debates starting this Sunday late morning after Church services, and continuing for the next three weeks. People would be home because of course the stores were closed on Sundays. Because Buckley was running on a regular party line, Row D, the League of Women Voters had invited him to debate. The Lindsay forces fought this. They wanted a two-man contest between their candidate and Beame. Buckley was just a minor irritant.

However, there were four permanent parties in New York, and Buckley had the endorsement of one of them. The League had feared a brouhaha with the FCC over unfair campaign practices if they did not extend the offer to Mr. Buckley. Hence they were adamant that it stand.

Nor did Lindsay get any help from the Beame team. The Democratic strategists reasoned that Buckley would take aim solely at Lindsay. After all, wasn't Buckley in the race to satisfy the conservative vendetta against Lindsay and his ilk for failing to support Goldwater?

In the end with no choice and unwilling to be stigmatized by pulling out of the debates, Lindsay capitulated. Price told him Buckley would be so marginalized, his presence would make no difference. In addition, Price was so enamored by Lindsay's telegenic appeal, he was confident that, side-by-side, his candidate would clobber Buckley without having to utter a word. The picture projected on television to millions of voters would be worth ten thousand of them.

• • •

The Saturday evening before the first debate, Nancy had dinner with Jim Brannigan, the president of NBC News, at his request. Because of his summons, Nancy had been forced to cancel yet another weekend with her family. She'd been instructed by his assistant to ask for his table at La Reserve, one of the city's poshest restaurants, which happened to be across the street from NBC studios. From the way the maître d' greeted the network executive when he arrived, it was apparent Brannigan was a regular.

After a few pleasantries, Brannigan got down to brass tacks. Nancy immediately realized this was her interview for the bureau job.

Brannigan asked the right questions. How effectively could Nancy work with an all-male staff beneath her? Did she have the "cojones" to fire a man? How did she evaluate the job Arthur had done? Did she have her own vision for where she would take NBC News?

The questions were good, but Nancy's answers were even better. She had thought long and hard about all of these issues and had anticipated each of these questions. The problem was not with the questions. Or the answers. The problem was with Brannigan's demeanor. At times, he seemed to lose focus, unable to follow what Nancy said. Twice she caught him looking past her as if to see if someone more important had arrived at the restaurant. Never having spent any time with the network chief, Nancy tried to excuse his behavior as an odd eccentricity of sorts. Much later, she wondered if the interview had been perfunctory. Had Brannigan merely gone through the motions so he could cross a candidate off the list?

The dinner ended pleasantly enough. Brannigan said Nancy had given him much to consider and he was glad she was in the "NBC stable." Nancy was not sure whether he'd meant she was just another piece of horseflesh, or if he saw her as an extra in this year's Nativity crèche scene.

If there was one thing Nancy could not abide, it was being played for a fool. So she sought out the one person she could trust who also had an excellent rapport with the NBC president.

That Monday, not two hours after the *Today* show aired, Nancy took a break from the post-debate story she'd been writing and headed to an early lunch with the new co-host of the network's franchise morning show. She had selected an out-of-the-way place on Ninth Avenue in order to be out of the range of prying eyes.

There was no one reputed to be better at the inside political game of network television than noted interviewer Barbara Walters. At lunch, Barbara told Nancy she'd heard nothing about the bureau chief role. She also added that, yes, Brannigan's eye had a tendency to wander when he was speaking with a person.

The two women talked about their boss's idiosyncrasies. And those of men in general, and how a man could get away with behavior that in a woman would be labeled aberrant. "I adore my male colleagues at *Today*," Barbara said, "but some of them are strange. They grow on you, however. There are two gentlemen here at NBC New York, let's just say they are the exception that proves the rule. One is a young correspondent just starting with us. Tom Brokaw. He could go places.

"The other is much more seasoned. Chet Huntley."

No sooner had Barbara uttered this than a familiar voice said, "Why are you taking my name in vain?" Both women turned, surprised to see Huntley sitting alone at the next table, a swirl of cigarette smoke wafting all about him. The co-anchor of the evening news broadcast, Huntley shared duties with David Brinkley in Washington. Barbara and Nancy insisted the newsman join them, and he happily moved to their table.

Huntley knew Barbara well and, though based in New York, was very familiar with Nancy's work from her pieces out of D.C. "I have not had the opportunity to tell you how pleased I was when you joined NBC News," he told Nancy. "Eric Sevareid...," legendary foreign correspondent for the rival network CBS and one of the famed Murrow Boys, as in Edward R., "...told me our luring you away was a malicious plot by NBC to destroy CBS News."

Nancy laughed. "I like Eric a lot."

"He's one of the best. Cronkite, too," Chet observed. "So why are you two breaking bread together so far from the home front? I thought this was my undiscovered hangout."

Barbara gave Nancy a "you can trust him" look, prompting Nancy to explain about her potential promotion and dinner with Brannigan.

Chet blew some smoke as he listened. "Personally," he said, "I'd love to see it. Too few women allowed into the club. But it is a club, a men's club, so I wouldn't hold my breath, if I were you. As for Brannigan's demeanor, the man is a poker player. Don't read anything into his mannerisms. There's a reason we call him 'Wild Eye.'"

"Does he know that?" Barbara asked.

"Goodness, no. Otherwise, there'd be a co-anchor position opening up real soon."

As Chet lit another cigarette, Barbara asked what tonight's lead story would be. Chet told her it was on the Surgeon General's recent warning about the harmful effects of smoking.

Barbara waved at the smoke all around them. "It doesn't appear to have harmed you."

"The science isn't all in. You know, when the settlers first came to Jamestown, they believed tobacco had incalculable medicinal benefits."

"Does it?" Nancy said as she, too, lit up. While a smoker, she had never smoked as much as Chet, who went through two packs a day.

"Don't ask me," he answered, "I'm really too sick to tell." He laughed. "The Surgeon General says it can cut ten years off your life, but I figure the last ten years are shit, anyway, pardon my French."

The conversation shifted to the first debate. All three had watched, Nancy the only one in person. And all three had the same verdict: Buckley had been the clear-cut winner.

While Beame had come across as what he was—an amiable, colorless accountant—Lindsay had generated some excitement via his good looks and stentorian voice. And his message was upbeat: the city is in rapid decline, and of the two major candidates, only he had the energy and the independence from the establishment that had caused this mess. In that, he was slightly appealing. The problem was, the congressman remained short on specifics. Many of his solutions were similar to Beame's. And by ignoring the third-party candidate, he may have made a tactical error. Buckley's ideas were fresher, if a little outside the mainstream, and his answers to the issues contained specificity, something that clearly differentiated him from the other two.

What also set Buckley apart were his wit and his vocabulary. Even when people did not understand what he was saying, he sounded impressive. Back to the humor, however.

It's been said that the gentle pinprick of sarcasm can burst the balloon of pomposity. As such, Buckley skewered the two major party candidates. When Beame went on about how much the city had done for him and how he wanted to repay his debt to the city, Buckley's response was: "If Mr. Beame really wishes to requite his obligation to New York, perhaps he should consider withdrawing from public life in favor of me."

And when Lindsay said, "I ask all New Yorkers to join me, to roll up their sleeves, to care, to adopt the view that there must be from now on *one hand* for the self, *one hand* for the family, and *one hand* for the city," Buckley quipped, "I find Mr. Lindsay's figure of speech biologically disconcerting, unless he aims to court the three-handed vote."

At another point, Beame grew testy over Lindsay's impugning his record. He rebutted by pointing out that Lindsay's campaign strategists had sounded him out to become part of the Lindsay fusion ticket well before his own declaration of candidacy for the mayoralty.

Lindsay denied that any such offer had been made. "We did in fact consider Mr. Beame," he noted, "and concluded he was not adequate to the task at hand."

The two volleyed back and forth. At last, the moderator turned to the third-party candidate. "Mr. Buckley? Any comment?"

Buckley's eyes flashed, and he grinned. "Sadly," he said, "I must acknowledge that despite my personal affection for Mr. Beame, I, too, did not offer him a place on my ticket."

Buckley's humor had the unintended consequence of throwing the others off their game. Beame was especially nervous throughout the debate. He kept his hands in his pockets and, though the viewers could not see this, those in the studio noted how much he was shaking. And while Lindsay strode to the podium purposefully and carefully arranged index cards across his space, his nervousness became apparent several times as he rearranged the cards and failed to make eye contact with the other candidates. Buckley later confessed with his typically impish grin that he'd had the urge to wander over when Lindsay turned away and mess up the order of his cards.

Buckley, in short, was the coolest one on stage. It was clear to everyone watching, whether on site or on television, that he was thoroughly enjoying himself. Some critics who agreed with this assessment attributed Buckley's serenity to the fact that, as a candidate who could not win, Buckley had less at stake. That oversimplified the equation, however. As a minor party candidate without funding and on whose shoulders rested the future of the conservative movement, Buckley actually had much more at stake than the loss of a single election.

One other facet of Buckley's approach had unnerved Lindsay and Beame, both of whom had been coached to speak over the moderator directly to the television audience. Buckley, on the other hand, treated the event exactly like a debate, pointing out flaws in his opponents' logic and addressing them directly. Oddly enough, this made more of an impression in establishing a connection with the viewer than did Lindsay or Beame's efforts to directly address the television monitors.

Buckley also continually assaulted Lindsay and Beame for having nothing original to contribute. Regardless of the issue, both had markedly similar solutions that included extra study or funding. Buckley believed the time for study had passed, and he provided detailed suggestions wherein government's role was limited and private responsibility encouraged. Equally stark was the difference on funding. Each time his opponents would call for a policy that would cost more money, Buckley asked where, with a deteriorating revenue base, would such money come from?

At one point, one of the few times he engaged Buckley, Lindsay smugly assured the viewers/voters that funds for a particular program would come from floating a bond issue, hence costing taxpayers nothing. Beame was on board with this suggestion.

Buckley turned to the other two and said, "I won't insult your intelligence by suggesting that you really believe what you just said." He went on to explain that once issued, bonds eventually matured, at which time public funds must be paid to satisfy the obligations. Where do the public funds come from? Increased taxes, naturally. "All my esteemed opponents are doing, it seems, is kicking the can down the road." Lindsay and Beame both looked as if they had ingested bad apples.

Reactions to the debate did vary, of course. Each camp afterward convinced itself and spun the narrative that their man had won. Between the two candidates considered to have a chance at winning, Lindsay was considered by viewers to be stronger. However, not by much—and that hurt. It was not Beame who had hurt Lindsay, however. Lindsay's inability to deflect Buckley's barbs had reduced his effectiveness. Going in, it had also been assumed the more energetic, youthful, telegenic, articulate Lindsay would make mincemeat of Beame. Yet Beame stayed on his feet and Lindsay faltered in the face of Buckley's barbs, so in the expectations game, Lindsay did not budge the meter much. Polls still showed him a few points behind Beame, though in all fairness he was within the margin of error.

To most viewers, however, the winner was Buckley, as the correspondents had readily concluded. Some voters did not pay full attention to the conservative gadfly, either because as a minor candidate he could not win or because it had been inculcated in them that a politician from the far right was out of touch. Many, however, reacted to Buckley's debate performance with something like, "I like this guy!" "He's funny as all get out!" "He showed up the other two!" "He's the only one who stands for real change!" And as more came to such conclusions, they moved the country to the right to the point where it would eventually become the new center.

Buckley supporters, a growing legion, were ecstatic, as reflected in the rise in attendance in the rallies he did begin to stage.

Reaction in the press was also varied. The reporters were giddy. There was a new element of excitement to the race. Those who had been assigned to cover Buckley and thought their careers had come to a screeching halt, were euphoric. More papers sent reporters to cover the emerging presence, and these newcomers were thrilled to include such a likeable presence in their coverage. As Nancy said to Emma, "A star is born."

In the backrooms of the media, publishers were glum. Here they had been convinced of the end of conservatism and, phoenix-like, it was rising from the ashes. As much as they hated to be proven wrong, they had no choice but to include Buckley in the daily reportage. For the first time, Buckley's poll numbers inched above four percent.

Emblematic of the new (right) reality in the campaign, as the papers considered their endorsements, they now had to factor in the conservative upstart. Newspaper endorsements would be a big deal. Television was costly and still unproven as a campaign tool, despite what up-and-coming political strategist David Garth and some others believed. Nor was there any other way to reach over the heads to the voters. So the recommendation of the papers received outsized influence. In the end, most New York papers would endorse Congressman Lindsay because he represented the greater break from the past. A few held that Comptroller Beame had the greater experience to deal with the city's crisis conditions. None endorsed Buckley, but all accorded him compliments, noting that he was not seriously considered for endorsement inasmuch as he did not have a chance of winning. Yet by paying him lip service, they furthered his cause.

The prospect of even considering such an outspoken conservative as Buckley resulted in considerable gnashing of teeth at *The New York Times*. The Old Gray Lady traditionally invited all city candidates to meet with the editorial board. The question-and-answer session would form the basis for the paper's arriving at its endorsement. *The Times* was reliably liberal, seeing progressive policies as the news most fit to print. Yet, after an internal debate, it was decided Buckley had to be invited to the board session. At least to provide the veneer of objectivity.

The meeting went well enough. In spite of themselves, the editors found they *liked* Buckley. Yet because he was from the wrong side of the political tracks, they would never dream of supporting him.

When Buckley left the offices on West 43rd, reporters asked him how it went. How would the editor react the morning after a Buckley victory?

The candidate flashed his smile and said, "In case of my victory, I shall hang a net outside the twenty-second floor of the city editor."

In the first Sunday paper after the three-week pressmen union strike ended, *The Times* would endorse John Lindsay for mayor. Elsewhere in the same edition, it would be noted that Buckley had risen in the latest Gallup poll, to six percent.

CHAPTER IX

AT THE GATE

In a race this close, Nancy told Emma, every vote counted. This race was so tight that mild panic had arisen in Camp Lindsay. For while Buckley had inched up another point, Lindsay had dropped one. What Nancy and one other reporter from *The Sun* had pieced together was a subtle shift in Lindsay's strategy. Price had broken the news to his man.

"Jay-viel, that damned Buckley is eating into our margin. He's been more resilient than we thought. So we're going to adjust our approach."

The congressman looked up in surprise. "You mean you want me to adopt some *conservative* positions?"

"Oh, no!" Price held up his hands in mock horror. "What we're going to do is point out that Buckley's in this race for one reason: to sabotage you. Why? Because *you're* the true liberal."

Indeed, a broadside came out later that day and was plastered everywhere. It showed Lindsay standing, his finger thrust forward as he made a point while Beame and Buckley sat glumly by. "Will the real Liberal please stand up?" blared the banner print. This was a play on the popular game show *To Tell the Truth,* which had three guests pretend to be a particular person. The guests were then interrogated by a celebrity panel that had to guess which of the three was the correct person. At the end, host Bud Collyer, who had played Superman on radio, asked would the real John Doe please stand up.

The copy of the Tell the Truth broadside bluntly asked why William Buckley was directing his fire at Lindsay. It answered its own question, because only Lindsay stood for true progressive principles, and included newspaper endorsements as validation of its claims. Thus, rather than having Lindsay tack to the right, Price positioned him further to the left.

The second prong of Price's refined strategy was to directly engage the conservative nuisance. "But I thought you wanted me to avoid mentioning him?" Lindsay asked.

"Things have changed. Campaigns are fluid. Now we have to go on the attack. He's gaining traction at our expense. I still don't want you to dignify his candidacy, however. We're going to use surrogates to do the dirty work."

Later that same day, Nancy sat at a press conference called by Lindsay headquarters. The congressman was not present, however. The speaker was a hero of a different stripe, a man Price called a "credit to his race." Jackie Robinson told reporters, "I am very much concerned. If Buckley gets a substantial number of votes here in this city, it could only mean that we have a lot more bigots than we figured that we did have in New York City, and we have already decided, with talk of the Klan coming into New York, that we've got to get ready and prepare ourselves for the ultimate." The pioneer who broke Major League Baseball's color barrier here in New York and had retired only eight years ago continued to say that, although subtle, Buckley's message and that of his supporters was clearly racist.

Nancy resisted the urge to race over to Buckley headquarters. Later, she would be glad she'd shown restraint and proud that Emma had buttonholed the candidate for a response.

Buckley, this time with no smile at all, said, "I believe nothing I have said is racially motivated, nor that of my supporters. But in case such a person does exist, I want to say something to him: 'Buster, I don't want your vote. You go off to the fever swamps and get yourself your own candidate, because I'm not your man.' There is no place for racism in New York City, which belongs to the Negroes as much as it belongs to any white man."

Next, Senator Jacob Javits charged Buckley with being the candidate of the far right and said Goldwater was running Buckley's campaign. The idea was to tar Buckley with the brush of the reviled Goldwater.

This time, Clark corralled Buckley, who replied, "The charge that Mr. Goldwater is running my campaign seems to me quaint. I don't know who is running Mr. Lindsay's campaign, but I certainly don't blame him for guarding anonymity. I have talked with Mr. Lindsay more frequently in Calendar 1965 than I have with Senator Goldwater, who in fact, as titular head of my party, the Republican Party, and as a personal friend, I have shamefully neglected and to whom, wherever he is, I take this opportunity, through the public media, to transmit my affectionate greetings."

Beame's advisors feared that the Lindsay campaign's new attack lines against Buckley made the congressman look more like a leader. They also feared conservative Democrats who were leaning toward the comptroller could be enticed to register a protest vote instead for Buckley. So they had Beame join in the attack. His comments were less personal and in no way hinted at racism, the new third rail of American politics. Beame referred to the right, to Goldwater, to forces of reaction, and to taking a step backward. His remarks were intended to ensure he did not cede ground to Lindsay, but it had nowhere near the level of animus that Lindsay's partisans displayed.

When next they met for the scheduled debate, Beame pulled Buckley aside and apologized for having to attack him. "Do what you have to, Mr. Beame, it shall not affect our personal regard," Buckley magnanimously offered.

Still, all was not well among members of the Beame team. Despite their steady lead, they sensed slippage. When Nancy and Emma shared breakfast with Gabe one morning, he reported on the doings of the other side, stating that Beame had wanted strong advocates from leading Democrats to counter Lindsay's edge in the newspaper endorsements. Of the top Dems, only Vice President Hubert Humphrey had issued a ringing statement of support.

Senator Kennedy, after his man Screvane lost, did campaign for Beame, but his effort seemed half-hearted. Courtesy of Nancy's introduction, Gabe was able to squirrel away some time with RFK. Later, he shared details about his meeting with the senator with Nancy.

"I don't understand how they are using me," Bobby Kennedy had complained. "I can do the most good in the black and Latino communities, but they have me scheduled in Jewish areas. Can you imagine? A Boston Irish Catholic wooing Jewish voters in New York. Wouldn't Beame, who last time I checked is a member of the tribe, do that more effectively himself? Go figure." Kennedy also confided that Beame was not his kind of candidate, as the comptroller was hardly the can-do take-charge personality cast in a New Frontier mold.

"So you're not excited?" Gabe probed.

Kennedy's answer was on background, meaning he could not be quoted as having said it. "It's better than having my tooth pulled, I suppose."

Other than their routine sharing of information, Gabe and Nancy talked for another reason: what they took to calling the White House factor. It was certainly understandable that President Lyndon Baines Johnson would not take sides in the primary fight. But now that a Democratic candidate was duly chosen, the silence emanating from 1600 Pennsylvania Avenue was deafening. Beame's people were growing frantic. Their messages were going unanswered. The opponent was liberal, but he was a *Republican.* Could it be that LBJ preferred Lindsay? Either way, it was a huge story that affected both Gabe's and Nancy's story lines. Gabe needed Nancy's help to get to the bottom of this issue. He did not have Nancy's clout with LBJ. No one did. She went back a long way with Johnson, back to when he was the Senate majority leader and she worked for the Foreign Relations committee.

She was efficiently put through by the White House switchboard operator.

"Hi, Nancy. How are ya, honey?" The president's soft Texas twang was unmistakable as Gabe leaned close to the earpiece.

Nancy quickly got to the nub of the matter.

"Ah heard you were covering the mayor's race up there. Ah sure do miss yore purty face down here. Y'all comin' back soon?"

Nancy assured the president it was a temporary assignment. Then LBJ said his piece.

"Our polls show the race tightening. This here Buckley fellow sure has thrown all the bales off the wagon. It's anyone's guess who'll win. Now if I back Beame and he loses, that could reflect poorly on me. You don' want to see me lose mah prestige, do you, Nancy dear?"

"You are so highly regarded, Mr. President," Nancy answered, "I cannot ever see that happening to you. I just reasoned that since Beame is a Democrat...."

"Yeah, hon, he is.... Oh, the burdens of this office are somethin' fierce. Oh, well, Ah guess Ah will have to issue a statement."

A terse release to that effect was produced by the White House press office later that afternoon, endorsing Abe Beame. Gabe was first on the air with the report. Beame's people were chagrined that it was not more effusive and that LBJ was not campaigning for their candidate in person. But it would have to do.

Before Nancy left the office for another day on the Lindsay campaign trail, she called in to the Washington NBC News bureau. Reaching a friendly secretary, she asked if any news had broken about the New York bureau chief role. It hadn't, but the office was abuzz over one internal piece of late-breaking news. Herb Pennock had abruptly cleared out his desk after announcing he was leaving to take a rest for a while.

Nancy abruptly finished her call, disheartened by this news. She recalled Herb as a wonderful newsman when she was just breaking in and hoped he'd get his life together somehow. On a whim, she then did something no one in the newsroom would have expected, though it was something Nancy did regularly. Before the next Lindsay event, she snuck into St. Patrick's Cathedral and found a small nook by the statue of Saint Jude. Nancy smiled when she realized she was praying to the patron saint of lost causes. She said a quiet rosary, praying both for Herb and for herself, hopeful that she would never end up so consumed by her career that it warped her personality and her health. As it was, life as one of the only newswomen on the planet took its toll. When Nancy got to the last decade of the rosary, she dedicated it to her family, specifically her children. "Please help me carve out more time for them," she prayed, "but more importantly than whatever I do, please help them grow up happy and well adjusted. No drugs, drink, or any other rubbish in their lives."

That day, Lindsay delivered another stump speech. By now, the reporters following his campaign could recite it by heart. Except today, there was a wrinkle. One that left everyone scratching his head. Congressman Lindsay talked about all the good things Mayor Wagner had done and how it was important to continue this progress. What? The man who had originally entered the race to do battle with Wagner was now lauding him? That was also part of Price's calculus, prodded by Rose. That there were surely pro-Wagner sentiments among the electorate. Might as well churn up a little sympathy with that bloc.

Lindsay continued to talk about the "crises" facing the city. However, he ceased personal references to Wagner, unless they were complimentary. His focus was on the need for a fresh direction—and toward that end, he attacked Beame as a tool of the bosses and the "old" politics. What that fresh direction would be was hard to say, for the Lindsay campaign was short on specifics, as has long been typical of most campaigns in the United States. In that, Buckley was the aberration. One the news people increasingly loved, because it gave them something new to chew over. New grist for the mill as they sought comment from Lindsay or Beame. It was in this light that the position papers came out. Each camp produced reams of paper on a number of issues. Yet aside from Buckley, the volume of paper contained little of substance. Much rhetoric and many catch phrases were cleverly dressed up to look like a detailed program. Both Lindsay and Beame were careful not to alienate any group. Part of this led to each potential "leader" of eight million citizens looking over his shoulder to see what the other one's take was on an issue. Thus caution dictated much of the me-tooism that Buckley correctly charged.

The major issues that justified sacrifice of a forest or two included traffic and transit, the current drought, welfare, education, fiscal policy, taxes, crime, housing, pollution (both air and water) and drugs. These ten covered much of what ailed the city and concerned its citizens. The next mayor would be expected on Day One to solve each. Hence, the need to address them now.

Rather than despoiling another forest in re-constructing all the papers devoted to these ten areas of concern, discussion of one will suffice to illustrate the differences among the candidates. Fiscal policy proposals are instructive. Buckley proposed a four-part plan.

- New York City must discontinue borrowing and must learn to live within its means by reducing services and reining in the unions before it goes bankrupt.
- Sound budgeting accounting principles must be enacted. Rather than lumping all services into one budget item, each public service offered by city government should carry its own price tag.
- All the nuisance taxes (commercial rent, gross receipts, miscellaneous fees, etc.) should be replaced by a single business tax.
- Welfare costs should be reduced by instituting a one-year residency requirement.

Lindsay vaguely proposed better housing, education and physical safety to improve the environment so more people and companies would relocate to the city and the tax base would expand. With no plan to pay for it, he also called for appealing to the federal government for greater funding to realize these improvements in housing, education and the like.

Beame urged adopting sounder accounting policies and approaching the federal government for more monies.

Buckley called the Lindsay and Beame papers "ten points of emptiness." The conservative looked to reduce the size and cost of government. His opponents sought an increase, Lindsay more so, and both told the taxpayers it would cost nothing because the feds would bail the city out. How they would persuade the congress and the president to release these federal funds was left unsaid.

Buckley's last sally occurred at one of the debates. Four were scheduled in all. Viewership was up for each one because of the newspaper strike, which was still on, in week two. Plus viewers were telling others how enlightening and entertaining it was to watch the debates on television, thanks to the Buckley presence. So an even greater number tuned in for week two. The strike would end after three weeks, but by then the debates would have become must-see TV. Accordingly, ratings remained high for the third and fourth rounds. The pattern of each held. Beame was nervous, plodding and earnest. Buckley was relaxed, witty, caustic in skewering his opponents' logic. And Lindsay called for freshness. The problem was, with hardly anything new to say, the congressman was overexposed and beginning to be viewed as old hat. This forfeited Lindsay's chief virtue. Hence, he remained stalled at 42 percent in the polls.

Lindsay's top strategists were concerned. Their man had been stuck at 42 percent for weeks now. Nothing they or he did seemed to budge the needle. After all this, so near and yet so far, Nancy knew there was near panic in the inner sanctum. She found out Price had come up with a new idea, and soon the Lindsay campaign charged that Buckley supporters had vandalized their storefronts. Swastikas were prominently mentioned. Jewish voters in particular might gravitate to the more energetic Lindsay to protect them rather than their own, weaker candidate, Beame. The press reported the allegations as news. It seemed so unlike the sort of campaign Buckley was running. Nancy and Emma paid a courtesy visit to police headquarters to run this one to ground.

The desk sergeant laughed. "Oh, that's just politics. We see it every four years or so."

"You mean no storefronts were trashed?"

"Oh, yeah, we had a squad car check it out."

"What did you find, if anything?"

"None of the Lindsay offices were damaged."

"But I thought you said there were signs of vandalism."

"Lady, there were. A few *Buckley* storefronts had rocks thrown through the windows. Not Lindsay ones."

"Well, that changes things," Nancy observed. "Did you tell the press?"

"Excuse me, ain't that what you are?"

Nancy smiled. "I meant the other reporters. The ones who wrote the stories about Buckley supporters vandalizing Lindsay property?"

He shook his head. "Nah. No one's been around about that. You'se two is the first we seen on this here story."

Nancy filed a report, but it never made it on air. It ended up on the cutting room floor. The campaign was moving on, and this episode seemed a tempest in a teapot. No one was interested in it anymore.

There were two other brainstorms, hatched from the fertile mind of Alex Rose. The first was to woo disaffected Democrats. Among Democrats, the likeliest base for Lindsay would be the reform wing. Reformers tended to be more liberal, more fed up with politics as usual, more inclined to send a message to the regular Democratic organization. Rose felt there could be a natural alliance with Lindsay, just as his Liberal party had teamed up with the congressman.

A few weeks back, there had been an intra-party spat in the Bronx over Democratic committee seating. At Rose's behest, Price freed up some Lindsay volunteers to aid the local reform group, headed by an ambitious young Democrat named Robert Abrams. This assistance also bolstered Lindsay's claim to the fusion mantle.

Armed with this and Lindsay's progressive voting record, Rose and Price went to work on one of the newest and more effective of the reform elders. They called him in for a private sit-down.

"I feel uncomfortable supporting a Republican," the man said. "I have never in my life voted for one."

"You can vote for Congressman Lindsay on the Liberal line," Rose pointed out.

"Yes, but he's still a Republican."

Price asked if there was a position in the new administration that the man would like, and if a guarantee of such a position would make his first-ever Republican vote more palatable?

He shook his head. "I can't see myself just yet as a City Hall kind of guy. Perhaps if I was in charge, but not as a low-level commissioner or something.... You know, I always wanted to sit in congress."

Price and Rose exchanged glances. Rose spoke. "What if we fixed things so when congress next stands for election in 1966, we were to support you? Make sure you have no opposition other than a sacrificial lamb, for the show of it?"

"Would you really make that commitment?"

"We would do so enthusiastically, Ed," Price assured the reformer.

The next day's *Daily News* headlined, "Dem Chief Koch Supports Lindsay."

It was a coup that sent subliminal messages to Democrats across the city, reformers and regulars alike, that it was acceptable to cross party lines.

But Rose's greatest contribution came the Friday before election day, when he met with Lindsay and Price. "If you want to win this thing," Rose said, "spend every remaining minute of the campaign in the Negro election districts."

Congressman Lindsay was surprised. He pointed out that blacks voted overwhelmingly Democratic. Over 90 percent. "We can never win them," he concluded.

"You don't have to," Rose countered. "All you need is to cut into Beame's margin. If you keep him under 70 percent, that will switch enough votes to guarantee your victory in a race this tight. Besides, we've tried every other avenue. There are no more votes to be squeezed out. Except among the Negroes."

The congressman looked to Price. On its face, it did not add up because, as Lindsay had noted, Negro precincts were hostile territory for Republicans. Even liberal ones. However, Price's respect for Rose had grown geometrically. Moreover, as he put it while shrugging his shoulders, "I got nothing else."

Nancy later learned of this meeting. For now, she witnessed a hurried effort as Emma's boyfriend, Jeff, and the squeaky-white advance team marched into Harlem, Bedford, Stuyvesant and other black enclaves, setting up meeting after meeting for Lindsay. It was a logistical effort that put D-Day to shame.

Meanwhile as word got around, a steady procession of black community leaders trooped into Price's office. The message was simple. "Do what you can for Congressman Lindsay. We will remember you later. And this," said while handing over an envelope, "is a little walking-around money for your troubles."

That weekend into Monday, the day before election day, Lindsay did nothing but speak to black voters in churches, town halls and along the streets of Negro neighborhoods. He even spent time with Wilbur Tatum's *New York Amsterdam News,* the respected black newspaper. Slowly word spread throughout these communities that this patrician white guy was "all right." By late Monday, Lindsay, with his politician's well-honed eye, could sense the bloc warming to him. Whether it was out of genuine conviction or merely out of politeness, he could not say. Nor could he tell if any such shift in attitudes would be enough.

Chasing after the Lindsay motorcade on a late Monday push into yet another black area, Nancy spotted the gleaming Unisphere, which would remain despite the closing of the World's Fair, its two-year run complete. Just before the fair closed, Nancy had ventured one last time to the Flushing Meadows site. She figured it was one place she could find a cross-section of New Yorkers, and there she corralled visitors for a brief survey of her own. If they lived in the city and intended to vote, she asked their preference. The result of Nancy's unofficial "poll" had Lindsay by a whisker, with Buckley showing surprising strength.

Of the major polls, the only one that predicted a (close) Lindsay win was the respected *Daily News* Straw Poll. It was respected because while its methodology was of dubious mathematical validity, the fact remained that in more than 20 years, the Straw Poll had never failed to forecast the outcome of a major election.

As for the leading established polls, Gallup and Harris, both predicted a (close) Beame win.

That night, Beame wrapped up his campaign with an old-fashioned motorcade tour through the streets of his native Brooklyn. Then he and his advisors went to sleep, fitfully, uncertain what the next day's outcome might be, but hopeful because of the polls and the historic demographic of overwhelming Democratic superiority in the city.

Buckley wrapped up with one of the rallies he'd originally said he disdained. And while he did not kiss any babies, he did allow a young woman, Arlene Luterman, to plant a kiss on his cheek. The image of this exchange was recorded on the front page of *The Daily News,* which summed up the campaign with the headline: "At The Gate."

As the city's reporters also signed off to rest up for what was expected to be a long election day and night, they retired one last time to McHale's. Most felt Beame would win; Lindsay had a future, however, having run an incredibly strong race...for a Republican in the city, that is.

The greatest topic of conversation dealt with the third man in the race. How would Buckley fare?

All believed he would do better than other conservative candidates who had run. They attributed this to William F.'s personal qualities and not to any latent conservative leanings in the land. Nor was the consensus that he would budge the needle too much.

If 100,000 votes was the benchmark, most guessed Buckley would surpass that. One-fifty was considered his likely vote total. Reaching that level would represent a huge personal accomplishment. A few pegged him at less. Two even felt the movement on the right was so dead that Buckley would barely surpass 100,000. On the other hand, a few thought he could do even better than 150,000. One reporter tossed out the 175,000 figure, and the group laughed at the "fool" who had obviously been so taken in by Buckley's charm that he could no longer think straight.

Nancy was an outlier to this conversation. At last Gabe sidled up to her. "What do you think?" he asked. He'd opted to do so privately, since her vibes indicated she did not want to join in the community discussion. Her thoughts were clearly elsewhere.

From her own "poll," her instincts and based on Emma's insights, for the young intern had been Nancy's eyes and ears at the Buckley events, Nancy said she thought Lindsay would squeak by and that Buckley would pass the 200,000 mark. Privately, she thought Buckley would do even better, but feared being branded a wild-eyed innocent if she was to say so. If wrong, she might never live it down. So she held herself in check at 200,000.

Gabe whistled. "A gutsy call. We'll have to see. By the way, I hear tomorrow an announcement will come out regarding Arthur's successor." He clinked his glass with hers. "Good luck and remember me when you're the boss."

Nancy smiled and told Gabe she wasn't counting her chickens, but she would love to continue working with him.

"Of course," he added with a grin. "And I won't share your 200,000 Buckley prediction with anyone in the office, lest they decide you're too unbalanced for the job." Nancy punched him playfully on the shoulder.

As they prepared to head out of the bar, Emma told Nancy that she seemed a million miles away. In a rare moment of vulnerability, Nancy said that now the campaign was effectively over, "all over but the counting," yes, she was preoccupied. About the bureau chief job...and her family.

Before Emma could say anything, Jeff caught up to them. He was now officially free as well, with no more Lindsay events to hawk. Not until the reelection in 1969, God willing. It was after one in the morning, but he was energized.

He whispered in Emma's ear that he felt like celebrating. She knew what that meant. As the intern leaned into her boyfriend for a lingering kiss, Nancy averted her gaze.

Jeff lived a few blocks from Nancy's temporary rental, so the three strolled out of the bar together.

Also averting his gaze was Clark. Though after the trio departed, Clark noticed that Emma had dropped her wristlet.

CHAPTER X

IT IS A FUN CITY

At this hour surrounded by Emma and Jeff, Nancy felt like a college kid herself. When Jeff related that Lindsay and Price were pulling an all-nighter in the Negro districts, looking for any voters they could find until the sun rose on election day, Nancy remarked on how pervasive the college lifestyle seemed to be. Lindsay spoke at a late-night black-operated station radio call-in. He hit a few bars. No drinks, and the discussion was less than scintillating. He also passed a pool hall but graciously declined a game, mainly because he was pressed for time…and didn't know how to hold a cue stick.

On the walk back to Hell's Kitchen, Nancy, Emma and Jeff passed by Holy Cross Church, which stood opposite the Port Authority Bus Terminal. The plaque outside read that the church had been founded in 1852 at the "crossroads of the world." Father Duffy, of WWI fame and who was immortalized in bronze in nearby Times Square, had been pastor of the church for many years, another plaque informed.

Nancy asked Emma and Jeff if they would wait a minute for her. "Thank God the churches are open all night," she said.

Emma noted that with the crime rate rising so alarmingly, she feared the day would come when even the churches would bar their doors come nightfall.

"Perish the thought," Nancy said. "Those are precisely the sort of people the church needs to be open for."

Inside, Nancy found the church to be blessedly quiet, save for the crackle of the candle in the Sanctuary Lamp on the altar. The only other congregants present were two winos who slept peacefully in the last pews.

Nancy genuflected and entered a pew, where she knelt and said a decade of the rosary, offering it up for her chances to be bureau chief. When she left, tiptoeing so as not to disturb the bums, she saw Emma and Jeff locked in a soulful kiss that showed no signs of ending. "I sure know what they have planned for tonight," Nancy thought. The two broke when Nancy cleared her throat, then all three resumed their walk.

After a few more blocks, when they got to Tenth Avenue in the high forties, the city was deserted. Almost, that is. Here and there in doorways and alleys, a few drunkards, streetwalkers and other low-lying denizens of the night stirred.

Apparently one of them did more than stir, as the trio heard a yelp. A high-pitched voice with a bit of a lisp cried out, "Get out of here! Get out of here!" Nancy was sure she'd heard that voice before. As they rounded the corner to Nancy's street, she, Emma and Jeff witnessed a frightful sight. The two men who roomed across the hall from Nancy were on their knees. One of them was Tiny, the person who'd been crying out. His mate, Edgar, was shaking visibly and whimpering.

The reason they were in that state stood menacingly over them. "This would be so touching if it weren't sickening to see you two faggots holding onto each other," the rather large, intimidating man said. "Now for the last time, give me your money!"

Instinctively, and showing tremendous courage or no common sense at all, Nancy cried out herself. "Leave those two men alone this instant!"

The felon turned, did a double-take and hurled a stream of curses in Nancy's direction. As he then grinned through a set of bad teeth, a dim streetlight glinted off the knife that only now Nancy and the others noticed. When the man took a step toward the three newcomers, Nancy reflexively dropped her purse.

Without a word, Jeff turned and sprinted back the way they had come.

Emma's mouth opened. She was too shocked and saddened to say anything, both by the would-be attacker and by her soiled knight. Immediately, thoughts of rape filled her mind and she began to feel faint.

"The gutless coward," Nancy said through clenched teeth as the sound of Jeff's swiftly receding footsteps faded in the distance.

The criminal saw Emma's look and leered at her. "What an unexpected bonus," he said.

"Please," Tiny pled, "take our money and just leave us alone."

At the sound of Tiny's voice, the attacker turned—and suddenly another pair of footsteps turned the corner and raced toward them. In a blur, someone grabbed Nancy's purse off the ground by its strap and hurled it with all his might at the attacker, connecting with the thug's temple. He stumbled, his knife clattering toward Edgar, who scrambled to pick it up, prompting the man to run from the scene just as quickly as Jeff had.

Nancy went to her two neighbors, both of whom had dissolved into a puddle of tears. Nancy gently stroked their backs, assuring them it was all over now, and the two gradually calmed.

Then Nancy picked up her bag and went to Emma...and their Good Samaritan. "Clark!" Nancy cried. "How did you think to hit him with my purse?"

Clark gave a goofy smile that both Nancy and Emma (and Nancy's neighbors) found quite endearing. "Everyone knows a woman's purse is the hardest substance known to man," Clark said.

"Well, you were magnificent," Nancy said.

Clark glanced down, and Nancy realized he wasn't wearing his glasses.

They had fallen off during the melee. Emma retrieved them and stood directly in front of Clark to place them back where they belonged. Then she paused and asked how Clark had happened on the scene.

"Oh!" he exclaimed, pulling Emma's wristlet out of his jacket pocket. "I realized a few minutes after you left the bar that you'd dropped your purse, and since I saw the direction you and Jeff were heading, I thought...."

"Don't mention his name to me ever again!" Emma cried. "And to think I was about to...."

"About to what?" Clark asked.

"Nothing," Emma said. "I was about to make a mistake." Now she gently affixed his glasses. "Remember a few weeks ago when you had your glasses off and I laughed?"

Clark nodded.

"I laughed because, when you don't have your glasses on, you look a little like Superman."

Suddenly Emma pulled Clark close and kissed him passionately. Nancy, Tiny and Edgar were all smiles as the kiss went on...and on.

When at last the couple came up for air, Clark said, a little breathlessly, "It was the honorable thing to do. I'm no Superman."

Still clutching him tightly so her body was firmly nestled against Clark's, Emma whispered, "That's funny, because I can tell part of you is turning into the Man of Steel." Even in the dim streetlight, Emma saw Clark turn beet red. "Don't be embarrassed," she said. "I'm flattered by it."

Now recovered but still a little unsteady on his feet, Tiny suggested they go inside for a little something to calm them down. In her neighbors' apartment, Nancy was surprised when Edgar brewed a pot of chamomile tea. She'd been expecting something a wee bit stronger.

"I've never heard of this," Emma said as she watched Tiny spoon green leaves into a tea infuser. "My mom just plops a bag of Tetley into her mug."

"Trust me, Sweetie," Tiny said, "this will soothe you like nobody's business. It works wonders for us all the time."

"Are you often in need of soothing?" Nancy asked.

Edgar's face lost its smile. "You would not believe what our type has to put up with, Nancy. That's why we hide it as best we can."

"At least there's Greenwich Village," Tiny said. "We can be ourselves there."

All sat in the living room with their tea, which in fact did the trick. Conversation flowed, beginning with the crime wave recently hitting the city. "We've had to start locking our door when we go out," Edgar said, saddened by this mournful development.

"I hope Lindsay can do something about the crime here. It's getting out of control!" Tiny said.

"I still think it'll be Beame who has to deal with it," Edgar commented.

Nancy marveled at the immaculate state of Tiny and Edgar's flat, thought back to Emma's home, and wondered if everyone else in the world was a spectacular housekeeper. Her apartment was orderly, chiefly because she spent so little time there. Merrywood was spotless, but that was due to the house staff. "Lord help me if I ever have to keep house," Nancy reflected when she finally returned to her own apartment for some much-needed rest.

Like most other reporters in the city that morning, Nancy was able to enjoy the luxury of a late sleep-in, because nothing was happening. No more campaigning. Just ballots being quietly cast. The real fun would start when the polls closed at nine. It was mid-afternoon when Nancy found her way back to Rockefeller Center.

It was still quiet, strangely so, but major elections only happened every other year. The mayoralty only every four years. Groundbreaking ones like Lindsay-Beame-Buckley once or twice a century.

Before Nancy settled in at her desk, she noticed the arrival in the newsroom of a woman she knew but not well. Twenty years older than Nancy, she was rarely in the newsroom because her beat was the United Nations. Nancy happily walked over to her.

"Pauline! So good to see you."

Pauline Frederick lit up at the sight of a kindred spirit in the testosterone-fueled atmosphere of a 1965 newsroom. "Nancy! How are you?"

"All the better for seeing you!"

The two grabbed some coffee from the break room and found a barren conference room to chat. Nancy was the first network female correspondent to cover the national conventions, and the inaugurations, and the space flights. Because of her looks, she was the first woman news media star. But for all her firsts, Nancy knew she owed a debt to Pauline, who was the first of firsts. In the 1940s, Pauline had started covering foreign affairs, which eventually led to the UN gig. She was the trailblazer at a time when no one thought women could handle the pressures of the newsroom, not to mention the world of big business.

Nancy once asked Pauline how she got into journalism. "The only two occupations open to women were nursing and teaching," Pauline had answered. "I can't stand the sight of blood and have no patience with brats, so I had to do something different."

Pauline had known back then that in many eyes she was an aberration. She was thus happy when Nancy eventually came along, and was more pleased when Nancy excelled and set the bar even higher. Nancy's coming meant Pauline was no longer the lone freak. Eventually, the two of them would pave the way for others of the female gender.

Because Nancy was based in D.C., other than for this historic campaign assignment, and Pauline was in New York, their paths rarely crossed. Even during this campaign, their rigorous schedules made it unlikely the two would develop a lasting friendship. Lasting respect, however—now that was another matter.

"I see another one has joined us," Pauline said. She did not have to identify the new co-host of *Today*, Barbara Walters. "Though what she covers is, shall I say, soft news."

"I agree," Nancy said, "but she is the best interviewer I have ever seen."

Pauline nodded in thought. "Good point. With that skill, she could eventually make it to the hard news side of the business."

"If the men who run the shop will allow it," Nancy said, daring to think of her own pending promotion.

Pauline smiled. "A few more of us who perform as well as the men, and in time they will have to let us at those top jobs." She then shared that she was filing a report of foreign attitudes toward today's election. "They want me to be on hand to talk to the anchors. New York City, after all, is home to the UN, so whoever runs the city has a profound impact on all the nations housed on East Forty-Fourth."

After a few more minutes of conversation, the women wrapped up and said farewell. Since there were no men around, they exchanged warm embraces before going to do their separate tasks.

Nancy and Emma, who by now had arrived, began working the phones. That exercise revealed voter turnout was unusually high. Eighty percent of eligible voters were casting ballots.

"Wow!" Nancy exclaimed. "Kennedy-Nixon set the modern record and they got 70 percent and Johnson-Goldwater far below that. Eighty is unheard of!"

Emma asked what it meant.

Nancy gave a mischievous grin. "It means a lot of people are going to the polls."

"No," Emma said with a laugh. "I mean, what does it mean to the outcome?"

"Who knows?" Nancy replied. "My guess is, this is good news for John Lindsay, but.... This is why when people ask me to make a prediction on any election, my stock answer is the winner will be the one who gets the most votes. You can never go wrong with that."

Through the afternoon and into the evening hours, the heavy turnout trend continued. At many polling stations, the lines snaked out the doors. People saw their city in crisis and this election as a seminal one.

As soon as the polls closed, Nancy left for Lindsay headquarters and Emma went to Buckley's. Gabe, of course, was at the hotel where Beame's supporters eagerly and nervously awaited the election's outcome.

For the first two hours, results see-sawed between Lindsay and Beame. Then, at about eleven o'clock, Lindsay took a slight lead and held on. More precincts reported in and the Lindsay lead, while small, grew little by little. In the early morning hours, it was clear John V. Lindsay was to be the 103rd mayor of New York. It was close, but a recount would not be warranted; Lindsay polled 45 percent of the vote, Beame 39 percent.

The loser appeared amid raucous cheering and graciously conceded. He congratulated the mayor-elect, pledged to do his part to help the new administration and promised supporters they had not heard the last of him.

At Lindsay headquarters, as Nancy reviewed the reporting precincts, she saw what a master stroke Rose's last weekend gambit had been. Lindsay polled 40 percent of the black vote. That shift of almost fifty points that would otherwise have gone Democratic precipitated the sudden drop in Beame's strength from the last Gallup poll. Correspondingly, it fueled the crucial three-point bulge that pushed Lindsay from 42 to 45 percent.

The candidate had pulled an all-nighter, but Nancy marveled at how fresh he looked. The ballroom exploded at his appearance. The new mayor hit all the right notes. He congratulated his opponents. Thanked Price, Rose and all others who had worked so hard and those who had voted for him. Pledged the new direction the city desperately needed. "This is the greatest city in the world!" he thundered to overwhelming cheers and applause. "With our vigor together, we shall make it even greater! It is a fun city, and we shall make it ever so!" He looked so Kennedyesque, Nancy thought. At that moment, great things seemed in store for New York.

It turned out to be a remarkable victory, but quite a personal one. Lindsay's running mates lost. Democrats Frank O'Connor and Mario Procaccino won city council president and comptroller, respectively. At his Fifty-Fifth Street condominium, Governor Rockefeller gnashed his teeth that Lindsay did not acknowledge the governor's support, and that the media was already boosting O'Connor as Rocky's likely opponent for the governorship next year.

As happy as the Lindsay forces were, there was euphoria in another part of town. William F. Buckley, Jr. had blown past the 100,000 mark. Past the pundits' anticipated 150,000 vote total. Past Nancy's expressed view of 200,000. Indeed, she now chided herself for being so cautious. The conservative would win about 14 percent of the vote, at an astounding 340,000! The candidate, his supporters, the voting public and Conservative Party kingpins were enthralled.

Buckley's remarks were brief, for his father-in-law had passed away just the day before. He expressed the conviction that the result vindicated the vibrancy of conservatism in America. Taking careful note was his chief advisor and brother James, who had his own eye on elective office somewhere down the road. The party roared on long after the Buckleys had departed.

"Who says conservatives don't know how to have fun?" Emma laughed with Clark. They were both euphoric, equal parts due to the good Buckley's campaign had done for their careers, equal parts for having found each other. The only serious note of the evening (though it was way past midnight) was when Emma remarked on the liberal bias in the media.

Clark said he hated to admit it, but it was true. "It's a shame there are only three networks," he observed. Looking around at the wild throng in the Buckley ballroom, he voiced the idea that a fourth network with a rightward bent could be hugely successful.

"Let's not get carried away," Emma said.

Oh, there was one other semi-serious note. Clark asked Emma if she remembered his belittling of television journalists, female ones in particular.

"You've been on a roll, so don't remind me, Buster," she warned.

"Well, I just want to say…I was wrong. You and Nancy have been spectacular."

"But how do you like my reporting?" she joked.

Clark continued. "And the newspaper strike opened up my eyes to the possibilities in TV. It just might have more of a future than I thought."

The surprise and euphoria at Buckley headquarters did not go unnoticed. In far-off California, the clock was just striking midnight. Two wealthy industrialists named Justin Dart and Holmes Tuttle both believed that Buckley's showing as a minor party candidate in the bastion of liberalism portended well for grassroots conservatism. They intended to bankroll a candidate for next year's governorship in the Golden State.

"We need a candidate," Dart said.

"How about that actor who spoke for Goldwater last year? Ronald Reagan?"

Not only in California but across the nation, political observers and wannabees took heart in Buckley's showing.

Enjoying down time in Florida even though he had relocated to New York, Richard Nixon believed conservative views proliferated in the South and West. He began to jot notes on a yellow legal pad. In time, his notes would coalesce into a "Southern Strategy" for capturing the White House. In like fashion, many hopefuls began to hone their message for the off-year elections in 1966.

It was well after three on the East Coast when the political cognoscenti crawled under their covers. That was also when Nancy and Emma caught up with each other in the NBC newsroom. Each had filed pieces from their respective sites. Now what was left to say? Each woman was filled with much emotion.

Neither had a chance to express their feelings because just then, Arthur asked Nancy to step into his office. He looked stricken, Emma thought, assuming that's what happens when you're his age and have to stay up this late. As Nancy got up from her desk, she crossed her fingers as Emma gave her a reassuring tap on her arm.

While Nancy was in the inner sanctum, Emma was so happy, she was actually giddy. She thought of where she could take Nancy to celebrate, late as it was. She hoped she would not have to wait long, for the hour was late and what watering holes might still be open were sure to close soon.

Emma did not have to wait long. Actually, the meeting was surprisingly short. Emma's broad smile evaporated the moment she saw Nancy, who was chalk white. As if in a fog, Nancy made her way to her chair and sank into it.

Emma's heart was in her throat. "You...you...didn't get it."

Nancy looked at her protégé. Her eyes were moist as she shook her head.

Averting her gaze, Nancy held her hand up to her forehead, revealing a slight tremble. Soon composed, she looked at Emma. "They named Herb Pennock the new bureau chief."

"What!" Emma exploded. "That old drunk! That's so unfair! Just because you're a woman! I'm...I'm...I'm so out of here! I want nothing to do with this place!"

Nancy was shaking her head. She took Emma's hands in both of hers and pulled the younger woman onto the adjacent chair. Nancy looked deeply into Emma's eyes, clutching her hands the whole time.

"Oh, Emma, you have a wonderful future in this business. Someone once said it is just as bad to be ahead of the times as to be behind the times. I was foolish not to see it, but this time is not for me. But it is changing. ABC News just hired Lisa Howard and Marlene Sanders. More will follow. Believe me," she squeezed Emma's hands so hard, "you will do very, very well. And if I had a small part in that...." Nancy stopped, for she was too choked up. Emma leaned over and hugged this woman she had come to cherish.

With a last sniffle, Nancy pulled back.

Emma gazed at her...friend...with concern. "How are you?"

Nancy gave a smile, a tiny one, but a smile nonetheless. "All the better for seeing you," she said in a hoarse whisper.

The two women rose, only to hear a small commotion down the hall. Gabe was throwing stuff from his desk into a large brown packing box.

"Gabe?" Nancy inquired.

"Clearing out my desk. I just gave notice."

"But Gabe...why?"

Gabe looked at her.

It hit Nancy. "No!" she cried out. "No! Don't do this for me!"

Gabe paused. When he spoke, his voice was very quiet. "I have a commitment to your heart...and also to what is right."

"But...but you can't throw away your career...."

"I'm not. I have an offer to join WNEW."

"Channel 5? But they're not a national network."

"They will be. They have ambitious growth objectives. In time, they could become the fourth nationwide network. What's more, they plan a fascinating innovation. A ten o'clock news program. They're bringing in a guy from Cleveland, Bill Jorgenson, to anchor. I know Jorgenson a little. He's a solid newsman. Besides, I'm not cutting all my ties. Who knows? I could end up back here someday."

"Oh, Gabe!" Nancy gave him a warm embrace.

Before she and Emma left, Nancy asked her assistant to go with her while she went to find Chuck Scarborough. She left Emma momentarily while she spoke earnestly to Chuck, who looked over at Emma for a moment during their discussion. From where she stood, Emma saw Chuck nod solemnly, then shake Nancy's hand.

"What was that about?" Emma asked upon Nancy's return.

Nancy cast a sideways glance at her protégé. "The future," was all she said.

That night, Emma crashed at Nancy's pad. They woke early after just a few hours' sleep. Emma helped Nancy pack, sadness in her heart. There was not much to get together for the trip. Then Nancy announced, "Today, I'm going to live like a human. No buses today." So they prepared to head to Penn Station. Just before they did, the phone in Nancy's apartment rang. Emma could hear most of the ensuing conversation, the speaker's voice was so loud.

"The White House for Nancy Dickerson," the operator said.

"Speaking."

"Please hold for the president."

"Hi, Nancy. How's mah favorite reporter? Now that damn election is over, and didn' Ah tell you Beame would lose an' make me look bad? Well, thass water down the Pedernales. Now just get back here right quick. Ah'm fixin' to increase our commitment in Vietnam to win this sucker once and for all and would like to give you the scoop." They made arrangements for her to interview the president the next day.

"Is that what you want to do?" Emma asked after Nancy had finished her call.

"It's what I do when something goes wrong," Nancy said. "Pick myself up and start anew. So I shall start with the major players for '68. President Johnson, for sure, as he is certainly going to run for a second term. I also set up a meeting with Richard Nixon. He's going to run also."

"Nixon?" Emma asked. "He's a two-time loser. Why waste your time with him? Isn't he finished?"

Nancy gave an "Oh, please" look. "Richard Nixon is like cancer. He is never finished."

Emma laughed. "Comparing the former vice president to a cancer is hardly complimentary."

Nancy looked at her evenly. "We are talking about Richard Nixon."

She looked around at her now-empty apartment. "Well, time to shove off."

Outside, they hailed a cab and snaked through the traffic.

At Penn Station, Nancy purchased her ticket, and the train to Washington arrived a few minutes later. Just before Nancy boarded, she looked at Emma, who was biting her lip.

"Are you all right?" Nancy asked.

Through teary eyes Emma smiled. "All the better for seeing you."

Nancy smiled broadly and pointed her index finger directly at Emma. "This is not goodbye," she stated. "Like Gabe said, I have a commitment to your heart." They hugged, and then the conductor shouted "All aboard!"

CHAPTER XI

SHE HAD A BIG AND MESSY IRISH HEART

Thirty-Two Years Later...

Breakfast with the affiliates had just ended and already David had a stack of pink message slips when his assigned exec rushed past. Holding one aloft as he trailed in her wake, he said, "Tom Brokaw wants to know if you agree the lead story should be the Clinton impeachment?"

Scanning papers as she strode briskly, she instructed David, "Tell him I agree."

Next piece of paper. "Katie Couric called. She wants to know why Matt Lauer's dressing room just received a fresh coat of paint."

"Oh, honestly. Tell her because of the kitchen fire and the water damage from the sprinkler system. Oh, when you send her the note in my name remind her her office is one-quarter larger than Matt's. She's welcome to switch, if she chooses."

"Chuck Scarborough called. Wants to thank you for the new contract."

"One of the ten lepers," she mused.

"Come again, Ma'am?"

"At least one returned to express gratitude."

"Quite so. Quite so," the admin said.

"Some guy named Karl Rove called. He's with Governor Bush down in Texas. Wants to discuss matters if they go for the White House in 2000."

"Another one," she said with a groan. "They all think ingratiating themselves will produce more favorable coverage." She stopped mid-stride. "Didn't he approach us last week?"

"No, that was someone from Al Gore's campaign-in-waiting."

"Not a dime's worth of difference," she muttered. Probably because of her next appointment, her mind went back to something she had not thought of in years. The Buckley campaign.

As to her last remark, David smiled, for that mirrored his views exactly. He then pulled yet another pink message slip from his stack while his boss busied herself stuffing things into her purse and putting her coat on to head back out. "This one," he waved the slip in the air, "might be the most important of all. The chairman's administrative assistant called. The chairman wants to have lunch with you today."

She spun around. "Didn't you tell her I have a pressing personal commitment today?"

"I did, most certainly. But the admin said didn't you know you were up for president of NBC and did you want to throw it away?"

"David, how long have we worked together?"

"Two and a half years."

"Have you ever known me to pull rank?"

"No, Ma'am. Well, just that one time you commandeered the corporate jet to fly those orphans stateside."

"Well, let's make today number two. Tell Her Officiousness last time I checked *I* outranked *her* on the corporate chart. Ask her how she likes having a job."

"It would give me great pleasure, Ms. Thornton."

Emma smiled. "If it costs me the network presidency, so be it. A dear friend long ago taught me that sometimes you have to put personal affairs before business. She did not practice it as well as she preached it, but nevertheless, she taught me well."

It was not far and the weather held, so Emma walked to St. Patrick's Cathedral. The first person she happened into just outside the entrance facing the statue of Atlas holding up the world was Leslie Stahl. The latter had been in the midst of filing a report for this coming Sunday's edition of *60 Minutes*. The two friends walked in together, then gravitated to a pew in the front left center aisle, where they saw other familiar faces.

Emma kissed the first on the cheek. "Nervous?" Emma asked.

Peggy Noonan smiled. "A little. I'm more used to writing speeches than giving them."

"You'll be marvelous!"

Next to Peggy sat an icon of journalism, the woman who had parlayed a career as master interviewer into the first-ever female network news anchor, then co-host, of ABC's answer to *60 Minutes,* and then pioneered a new morning show dedicated to stay-at-home moms. The show was called *The View,* and Barbara Walters was its heart and soul. Thirty-some years after she burst on the scene with the *Today* show, Barbara still looked fantastic and was still sharp as a whip. She also greeted Emma affectionately, and the four women began to chat among themselves.

Emma craned her neck a few times to see if Nancy had arrived, but it was early. She did see other personalities. Of course, she recognized the first man she spied. One of the best hires she had ever made was to lure Gabe Pressman back to

NBC News. She rose and chatted briefly with him before returning to her pew.

Emma also spied Chuck Scarborough seated near Gabe. She'd been only too glad to extend Chuck's latest contract. Not only because he was the best at what he did. It was deeper than that. All those years ago, when Nancy whispered to Chuck, she'd asked that he look after Emma once Nancy was back in D.C. Chuck had, and under his watch Emma rose steadily through the reporting ranks. Eventually she cracked into management, where she was able to repay Chuck's kindness.

A number of other dignitaries were there, among them newspeople, politicians, entertainers and philanthropists. Three caught Emma's eye and she dwelled on each for a second, thinking about how far he had come.

The first one she spotted should have been the hardest to see because of his tiny stature, more pronounced now because he was stooped with age. Mayor Abraham D. Beame. After the Lindsay loss, true to his word, Beame did return. In the next mayoral cycle, he ran and won back his old job as comptroller. Then another four years, and he again tried for the mayoralty. This time, Beame was successful. Successful at elective politics, that is, not the mayoralty.

Beame had the misfortune to assume office at a time the city was on the brink of default. Years of spending like a drunken sailor topped by a deteriorating revenue base made for a frightful four years for the Beame administration. The voters were harsh in their verdict, and Mayor Beame could not even win the 1973 reelection primary. Given his fiscal background, they had expected much more from him. To be fair, Houdini would have had a difficult time in the 1970s to single-handedly save New York. Worse, the economy was sliding into stagflation everywhere due to a recession coupled with high inflation, so the Ford administration in Washington was loathe to bail out the city. Beame had long counted on a federal handout. When it failed to materialize, he was sunk. A consortium of fiscal patriots, state Tax Commissioner Jim Tully, Governor Hugh Carey, Treasury Secretary William Simon and financiers Richard Ravitch and Felix Rohatyn, rode to the rescue. They put together the Big Mac, a nickname for the Municipal Assistance Corporation. Big Mac, composed of the delegates of the above-named gentlemen, effectively ran the city until the ship was righted financially. Harsh budget cuts, federal and state guarantees, no tax reductions, an end to accounting gimmickry and forcing the unions to play ball and rein in their wage and pension demands eventually purged the poison from the system.

There were still gimmicks, to be sure, but they were not as widespread as before Big Mac. One example of lingering shenanigans dealt with the stock transfer tax. When Wall Street howled, to placate this source of New York's fiscal stability, the tax was repealed. However, under the Big Mac covenants, no tax could be reduced until the ship was able to stay afloat. Hence, they devised the stratagem of a 100 percent rebate. So a taxpayer went to one window at City Hall and paid the full stock transfer tax, then walked to the next window, where he received his check back as part of the full rebate. Silly, but it worked and, as noted, the shenanigans stopped there. By the time the next strong fiscally minded mayor arrived, another Republican named Giuliani, the city was in better shape. Giuliani took firm control and brought New York all the way back.

With age comes forgiveness, and recognizing the situation he inherited as well as the fact that the city did not go into bankruptcy after all, Beame now was regarded as a kindly old man who tried to do his best to give back to the city he loved.

The person who also ultimately suffered at the hands of the voters was the man who had handed this mess off to Beame. Still tall, though a little stooped, John Lindsay sat with his wife Mary in the same pew as Beame and the current mayor, Giuliani. Emma saw that while Mayor Lindsay had aged, he still displayed his striking good looks.

Lindsay had the misfortune to rule in troubled times. The nation, not just the city, was convulsed, seemed ready to implode. Vietnam, civil rights unrest, the counterculture, the youth movement all fueled chaos. To the mix was added the fact that the financial mess Lindsay bequeathed to Beame was not of Lindsay's doing. It was a part of what Wagner had handed off in the first place. Moreover, in assuming power, Lindsay acquired powerful enemies. Mike Quill was good to his word and got even with "Linds-lee." On Day One of the Lindsay administration, the transit workers mounted a crippling strike. Thus, unlike any other mayor in the history of New York, Lindsay was denied a honeymoon period during which he might get acclimated to his new job.

Because of the social unrest and the economic blight that hit home shortly after he left office, Mayor Lindsay was blamed by voters for these new troubles. There had been other pratfalls. One winter, the city snowplows were exceedingly slow to clear the streets in Queens after a snowstorm. Lindsay could not be expected to personally drive the trucks, but the buck stopped with him.

As his popularity dipped, Lindsay was denied renomination in 1969, losing the Republican primary to the lackluster state senator John Marchi. Only Alex Rose remained loyal, and the Liberal Party endorsed the mayor for another term. Thus, like Buckley in 1965, Lindsay in 1969 would be a minor party candidate. Last time, the three-way race had hurt Lindsay as Buckley ate him up. This time, there was again a three way race, and it helped Lindsay. The third candidate was the Democratic nominee, Beame's 1965 running mate for comptroller, Mario Procaccino. Procaccino had won the primary and thus was the party's standard bearer for mayor. This was the election where the ticket was reversed, Beame now running for his old comptroller position as Procaccino's running mate.

Unlike the retail campaign Price had engineered in '65, this time David Garth took greater command. Inspired by Alex Rose, Garth engineered a television blitz that counted on two themes. One was to have Lindsay admit his mistakes, especially regarding the snow removal (or lack thereof) and pledge that he had learned from it. It was incredibly effective. In retrospect, Emma could see why. At first blush, a politician acknowledging serious lapses in judgment would hardly seem to augur well for election (or reelection), but the public's capacity for forgiveness is indeed great. Emma lived this herself. Once she screwed up big time. When called on the carpet, rather than make excuses or defenses, she made abject and profuse apologies. Once Emma said "I'm sorry," that took the sting out of the hearer's intent to administer a tongue lashing.

The second part of the Rose-Garth strategy was to show Lindsay late at night in his office, sleeves rolled up, tie askew amid the slogan "Re-Elect Mayor Lindsay: It's the Second Toughest Job in America."

Years and years ago, Emma had done a great piece of investigative reporting that ballyhooed Rose's contributions. Garth originally had hoped to capitalize on Lindsay's outreach to the underclass by suggesting as a slogan "Building Bridges."

While sympathetic, Rose believed that would fire up racial backlash, add to the unrest and beat Lindsay. Hence the "second toughest" slogan.

Lindsay's luck also held as the erstwhile doormat Mets sprang to the World Championship, and Lindsay was in the locker room for the champagne baths as the city was drawn together by television in celebration. For now, the Mets owned the town, and Lindsay benefitted from the halo effect.

With all that, and poor campaigning by Marchi and Procaccino, Lindsay eked out a second term. Yet, although he had grown in office, the social and economic woes of the city had deepened. Blame was attached to the mayor, who suddenly did not seem so fresh. In two subsequent bids at redemption (after he had switched to the Democratic Party), a run for president and one for senator, Lindsay was soundly rejected by the electorate.

He spent his post-mayoral years with a white shoe law firm. Then full retirement and, with his health declining, he and Mary moved to the warmer climate of South Carolina, largely forgotten figures.

Emma and Nancy had talked about Lindsay much in the intervening years. Both felt that he got a bad rap. On balance, Lindsay was a much better mayor than he was given credit for. He pioneered many initiatives in areas such as consumer affairs, environmental protection, civil rights and women's rights, many of which were ahead of their time. And his revamping of the city's antiquated tax code remained in place.

But Lindsay's biggest contribution by far was his retention of his ties to the black (no longer Negro) community that allowed him to keep New York calm when rioting struck other major cities such as Los Angeles, Detroit, Washington and Newark. At great personal peril when many inner cities burned, Lindsay walked the streets of New York's black neighborhoods and helped keep the peace by sheer force of personal effort.

That achievement could not be overstated, Nancy once told Emma. Emma had to agree. As a young correspondent, she had been sent to Los Angeles to cover a story. Her flight was delayed so it was late when she checked into her hotel. The hotel restaurant was closed and she was starving. So she walked out in search of a fast food spot. In the far distance was a McDonald's. A middle-aged black woman was the only person in the vicinity.

"Excuse me, Ma'am. Do you know if that McDonald's is still open?" Emma asked.

The woman seemed preoccupied and failed to answer.

Emma repeated the question.

The woman glanced up, a look of feral anger in her eyes. "Don't you be talkin' to me. An' don't you know there are color rules. We not spos'd to be talkin' wit' one another!"

Emma was taken aback. This was the 1980s, after all! "I'm...I'm sorry," Emma stammered. "I didn't mean to disturb you. It's just that I never heard of such rules in this day and age."

The woman spat (on the sidewalk, fortunately) and uttered "White c—-."

That's when it struck Emma that although racial tensions existed, the damage they had exacted in LA and other cities had not visited New York with such brute force. This was thanks in great part to the efforts of John Lindsay. Considering the dreadful cost of rebuilding the infrastructure mass rioting would have caused, such riots in a city on the financial precipice could have been enough to topple the house of cards.

So Nancy's and Emma's assessments of Mayor Lindsay were more balanced than most. If anything, Lindsay suffered from two things. While the fiscal crisis was not of his making, he certainly did not solve it and unwittingly contributed to it, especially by his sympathetic accession to municipal union demands.

Second and more significantly in Nancy's and Emma's views, Lindsay suffered from the expectations game. He had been hailed as a young Lochinvar, promising great things for the city, thus setting the bar quite high. Unfortunately, it was not a limbo bar. Perhaps no one's performance could have met the promise, but the indisputable fact is that Lindsay suffered for it.

The third man Emma focused on at Saint Pat's was the one she and Nancy had also chatted about often. He was the one who never won elective office, yet had the most estimable career of the three mayoral candidates. Still puckish in his advanced age, William F. Buckley lived to see the conservative tide he had bolstered become the dominant force in contemporary American politics. One commentator wrote the authoritative treatise on the transformative 1968 presidential election. Entitled "The Emerging Republican Majority," it could more aptly have been named "The Emerging *Conservative* Majority." It was this swing to the right that tossed the Democrats out of office. By 1980, conservatism was ascendant as Ronald Reagan was elected in a landslide. The former actor then imposed his conservative vision on the government that has lasted to this day.

Aside from his contribution to the movement (brother Jim was in fact elected to the senate in 1970), Buckley was a prolific best-selling author and hosted a long-running talk show called *Firing Line* that was devoted to substantive discussion of matters of public interest. All while maintaining control of the *National Review* tiller. Nancy and Emma had little doubt as to which of the three candidates from the 1965 New York City mayoralty election had emerged triumphant in the campaign of life.

It was at this point that Emma cast an impatient glance at her watch, for the one person she most expected to be here was still absent. Fortunately, as soon as she saw the time, she heard a woman in the pew behind her remark to a friend, "Isn't that Christopher Reeve? I thought he was paralyzed." Reeve was the actor who had played Superman in the popular movies and then been confined to a wheelchair after a horrific equestrian accident.

The lady's comment reassured Emma, for in the next instant Clark leaned into the pew and pecked her on the lips. It was a chaste kiss. They were in God's House, after all. He bade greetings to Peggy, Lesley and Barbara to Emma's left and then sat next to his wife.

Emma asked if the kids were all right. Wedding plans for one of their children were underway, so there was a crisis a day. Since Emma's workdays began earlier, Clark shouldered the morning's daily dilemmas. All was well. "That's not what held me up," he said. "I had an impromptu meeting with Roger." Roger Ailes was Clark's boss at Fox News, where the young Clark had gone after forsaking the newspaper business. Clark was one of the new network's top draws, along with a bevy of blondes. He whispered to Emma that he was excited about the network's prospects. "We just hired a new guy. He could be huge. Former CBS man named Bill O'Reilly."

Lesley leaned over when she heard the name and made a face. There was no time to pursue the conversation, however, for the organist had started and the choir began to sing. The congregation rose.

Emma turned to see Nancy and felt a pang when she spotted the casket. The bishop led the way, followed by the pallbearers bearing Nancy's remains, then the family. Emma took especial note of Nancy's son John. He had "gone into the family business," as Nancy used to say. John Dickerson was a political reporter for *Slate* magazine and CBS News. Emma vowed to latch onto him at some point for NBC. She had tried once, but "JD" turned her down. Despite the close personal connection, John yearned for a prime political spot, such as hosting one of the prestigious Sunday morning programs. But NBC's *Meet the Press* had Tim Russert well ensconced, and it did not look like he was going anywhere soon. Bob Schieffer hosted CBS's version, *Face the Nation,* and since Schieffer was approaching senior citizen status, John felt there was better chance for career advancement at the Columbia Broadcasting System. Still, Emma kept her eye on the young man. She was pleased for Nancy's sake; how proud the mother had been of her son. All the Dickerson children had turned out quite well.

As happens in so many career marriages, not to mention ones with the added pressure of the trail-blazer's burdens that Nancy bore, her marriage to Dick broke up. In the late '80s, she met and married another financial wizard, John Whitehead, so the obituaries reported this as the funeral of Nancy Dickerson Whitehead. She had succumbed to a debilitating stroke followed by months of a steady downhill progression.

The cleric began the Mass of the Resurrection. Clark squeezed Emma's hand. She was glad for that, and for this service. If the Catholic Church was good for anything, it was that it knows how to handle the death business. Apropos of the upbeat nature of a Mass of the Resurrection (better than reading from the Book of the Dead), the bishop-celebrant told the crowd they were here to celebrate the life of Nancy Dickerson Whitehead.

Emma paused, as countless others were doing, to reflect on Nancy. Emma, of course, knew about the early years. She had just been re-living them up to the time of the Lindsay-Beame-Buckley campaign.

After that election, Nancy returned to Washington and continued to cover the national political scene, and do it well. More women were cracking into the business. ABC News hired Lisa Howard and Marlene Sanders, as Nancy had noted long ago. And more were on the way. Yet it was too great a leap for the stodgy businessmen who ran the corporate offices to allow women into the boardrooms, except to clean up discarded drinks and cigarette butts.

By the early '70s, it was clear there was no opportunity for Nancy to move ahead, and she had already excelled at her current tasks. There was little challenge. So she moved on to the new PBS network. One of her main achievements there was being included, along with the top reporters from each of the three main networks, for a rare one-on-one (actually four-on-one) interview with the then newly elected president, Richard Nixon.

About as quickly as you could say "Richard Nixon," he was gone, forced into resignation in 1974 by the sordid Watergate scandal. By then, Nancy had gone on to form her own news production company, which went on to produce documentaries such as one on the 784 days of the lingering Watergate episode. Nancy won the prestigious Peabody Award for the Watergate broadcast.

After a while, she tired of the grind of producing, reporting, and marketing on her own and quietly retired from journalism. She did write her memoirs, then moved to New York, where she busied herself with an array of charities and an active social life. Which is where she met John Whitehead.

She was 70 when the stroke hit. She was a strong 70, but the stroke proved stronger.

The Mass moved along. After communion, Peggy sidled past Emma and Clark as she headed to the altar to deliver the first eulogy.

"She had a good life. For all that, she was a complicated little pirate," Peggy spoke clearly as many smiled at her fond characterization. "She had some struggles along the way, deciding what things she really wanted, really needed. She was worldly, navigated well in the world, knew the ropes. And yet she said her rosary every day. She was a secret sayer of rosaries, a sneaker into churches in the middle of the day, a friend to ministers and Jesuits and do-gooders of all sorts."

Soon Nancy's son John rose for the second eulogy. "This is the toughest assignment Mom has ever given me," he said. "Where do you begin talking about a woman both tender and brave, both willful and soft...? She had a big and messy Irish heart. The right song or line of poetry could make her cry. But she could also hold wounds in that heart and never show it. She was a tough lady in a brutal business, and it was very cruel to her at times."

A few days later, another memorial service was held for Nancy in Washington, her truly formative city where she was so well known even now, decades after her most prominent public role there. At a brief ceremony at Saint Matthew's, the First Lady spoke of how Nancy talked up the city when she and the new president first arrived.

From there, it was on to Arlington National Cemetery. John Whitehead, a veteran, already had chosen a plot. Under the national cemetery's rules, spouses of service men (and women) could be buried alongside their mates.

And so, with a few final prayers, they laid Nancy to rest. The mourners stepped up one at a time to lay a flower on the casket before it was covered by the earth. After each mourner fulfilled this last tribute, he or she left for the ride home. Except for two.

Emma and Clark hung back at the edge of a small grove. Emma's eyes glistened as she watched Nancy's family pay their final respects. Then they, too, departed. As he walked off, John noticed the hangers on and walked over. "You meant so incredibly much to Mom," he told Emma. "Both your friendship and your success. Mom took such great pride in nurturing both."

Emma dabbed at her eyes. When she spoke, her voice broke. "And she…she was so very proud of you and your siblings, John. It meant so much to her that you in particular followed in her footsteps, on her trail, so to speak. And that you kept your sense of balance for your family."

John promised to keep in touch as Emma hugged him and Clark shook his hand. And with that, he was off.

Clark gently led the love of his life away as well. With a sniffle Emma paused and turned back, casting a last long look at her friend's grave.

Clark ran his hand along Emma's back. "Are you all right?" he asked in his tender, solicitous voice.

Emma tightened her grip around her husband. Sniffling a final time and still looking back at Nancy, she said, "All the better, for having known her."

AUTHOR'S NOTE

We are losing our sense of history.

The technological explosion in communications, from personal computers to smart phones has counterintuitively rendered us stupider. The sheer volume of messages, spam, tweets and snapchats is unrelenting. So much so that every waking hour is consumed with running in place on the information treadmill. With no time to reflect on the past, let alone carve out quiet time to plot the way ahead, the best foot forward is likely to be a stumble.

Hoping to buck the trend, I set out to write a story about the world I grew up in a half century ago, albeit in novel form, since apparently no one reads history anymore either. Being a political junkie, my setting became what still is the most thrilling campaign in my experience, the 1965 Beame-Buckley-Lindsay race for mayor of New York City.

While the winner, John Lindsay, became a much underappreciated mayor, at the time he was a thrilling presence. The real hero however was the one who started out as an asterisk fringe party candidate and ultimately moved the nation. After the 1964 Goldwater debacle, many pundits heralded the demise of the Republican Party unless it embraced liberalism in the form of candidates like Lindsay. Yes, there was a time when mainstream Republicanism did not drink of conservative nectar. William F. Buckley held to a contrarian view, and his relative success in the '65 campaign demonstrated that if conservatism could resonate in a liberal enclave like New York, it could be a fashionable alternative theory of government. Buckley's success spawned other right-of-center candidacies, notably Nixon's Southern Strategy and Reagan's Age of Conservatism. To this day, the GOP remains a bedrock conservative party, the roots of which hearken back to Buckley's wild electoral ride. While this is a fictionalized account, the basic story line and outcome follow actual events closely. So too do the words attributed to Bill Buckley. They are priceless.

In addition to marking an electoral milestone, 1965 also represents a quieter, more innocent time. Yet past grasslands are not unremittingly greener. While the country may have gone too far toward politically correct-speak, 50 years ago we were decidedly less tolerant. Racial, sexual and gender attitudes were less civilized, as reflected throughout The Nation's Hope. One noticeable difference is the role of women. The marketplace, and certainly the political world, were largely bereft of professional women. Hence for my frame of reference, I chose one of two women who pioneered television journalism, and to whom every female reporter on the tube and in business today owe a considerable debt.

Pauline Frederick covered diplomacy, chiefly the UN, and thus did not fit into the context of the 1965 political campaign. Nancy Dickerson did however, inasmuch as politics and government was her beat. Moreover, at an early age I fell in love with Nancy. Oh, it was nothing romantic or sexual. I was still in my "Girls! Yuck!" stage. My affinity for Nancy stemmed from the flimsiest of reasons (though as Prince Charles might rationalize, "Who knows what love is?")

Nancy broadcast a 5-minute news summary every afternoon when I got home from school. Watching that as I raced to change into play clothes and hasten to Geshmann's field where the neighborhood kids played ball every afternoon (there were no video games), I gave Nancy credit for allowing me to complete my social studies current events class in five minutes. It struck me that if every teacher could do the same, the school day would last but 35 minutes. It was not until much later that I became a political junkie, appreciated how good a reporter Nancy was, and realized how attractive she was.

In any event, while Nancy covered politics, she was Washington-based and it is only my fictionalized Nancy who was assigned for the duration of the Beame-Buckley-Lindsay campaign. I have tried to keep her character as true to life as possible. For sure, Emma is a purely fictionalized construct. She symbolizes all the women in media today who owe much to Nancy Dickerson. Of course as noted above, all of us, regardless of political persuasion, owe much to Bill Buckley for enriching the fabric of public discourse. It is a lesson the current crop of "leaders" would do well to absorb.

Anyone interested in learning more about the 1965 election should read *The Ungovernable City* by Vincent Cannato. It is the preeminent history of the Lindsay years and the early chapter on the 1965 election is an invaluable resource. The other major source is William F. Buckley's own memoir of the campaign, *The Unmaking of a Mayor*. As for Nancy Dickerson, the two accounts I highly recommend are Nancy's own memoir, *Among Those Present*, and her son (and current *Face the Nation* host) John's biography, *On Her Trail*.

In addition to the characters in the book I am indebted to the following: all those who read and reviewed my first novel, *Knight to King 4* and helped it land on one of the Amazon best seller lists; my editor, Karen DeGroot Carter whose own novel *One Sister's Song* is a must read for anyone who loves history and/or good literature; Amy Siders and Rob Siders of 52 Novels who again amazingly handled the production side of the publishing business; the nonpareil Gracie Anthony for another truly inspired cover; photographer Marvin Lichtner for the wonderful cover photograph of Nancy Dickerson and for being a true mensch; and the people at Amazon who are the only ones in the publishing world open to new voices.

From my EY family, Bill Katz and Larry Abowitz have been steadfast supporters, as has Marty Flashner, who inspired me with his modern brand of enlightened conservatism. My AndersenTax family did much to boost Knight to King 4 and I am indebted to all, especially Raymond Freda, Mark Vorsatz, Dan Depaoli, Peter Coscia, Lance Lamprecht, Eric Anderson and Sonny Ankrah. My parents, Catherine and Peter and my brother Brian encouraged my early interest in political history, and my uncle John Wallack was the original "Mr. Conservative" and with Aunt Anne got me hooked early on to the brilliance of Bill Buckley. The other person who enthusiastically shared first-hand knowledge of the campaign and makes politics come alive is Commissioner Louis M. "Jake" Jacobson. To all these, I am indebted though any errors rest with me alone. Nothing hones a writer's skill as much as reading. A shout-out is in order to the unsung heroes staffing our libraries, in particular for me the wonderful people who work at the Nanuet Public Library. My musical tastes, like my literary, are eclectic and while writing The Nation's Hope I was saddened by the loss of country music giant Little Jimmie Dickens. I have borrowed one of Little Jimmie's riffs in the intimate discussion between Emma's parents. To show that things do come full circle, Nancy began her career with CBS. In the latter stages of this book I had the good fortune to spend time with a CBS executive, Anton Guitano, who like my brother succumbed way too soon to the same cancer. Anton's gentle soul and decency as a leader are seriously missed.

Finally, my most loyal fan base to whom all my efforts are dedicated, my wife Grace and children Richard, Marisa, Christine and Caroline.

I am always interested in hearing from readers, so for news and views, please go to kennethtzemsky.com

COMING SOON FROM KENNETH T. ZEMSKY

TO THE CLOSE OF THE AGE

Spring 2033...A husband and wife team of scientists working in a top-secret government installation on anti-terrorism weaponry, makes a discovery far-reaching in its ramifications. So much so they cannot trust it to the bureaucracy. Accordingly they leave Homeland Security and privately refine the world's first time machine. For their initial run, they travel to the seminal event in human history: Jerusalem, 33 A.D., the first Easter. Did Jesus actually rise from the dead?